WORSE THAN MURDER

Stephen Wechselblatt

This is a work of fiction. All characters, organizations, and events portrayed in this novel are either products of the author's imagination or are used fictitiously.

For information regarding permission, please write to:
info@barringerpublishing.com
Barringer Publishing, Naples, Florida
www.barringerpublishing.com

Design and layout by Linda S. Duider
Cape Coral, Florida

Original cover photograph: *Still Waters* by Jonna Hakala

ISBN: 978-1-954396-15-9
Library of Congress Cataloging-in-Publication Data
Worse Than Murder / Wechselblatt

Printed in U.S.A.

To Michael, In Memory
It was too short.

SEEK NOT TO UNDERSTAND THAT THOU MAYST BELIEVE BUT BELIEVE THAT THOU MAYST UNDERSTAND.

—*AURELIUS AUGUSTINUS*

NO MATTER HOW THIN YOU SLICE IT, THERE WILL ALWAYS BE TWO SIDES.

—*BARUCH SPINOZA*

CHAPTER ONE

Alicia

My name is Alicia Flores, and I'm clairvoyant. The first time I had a vision of Betsy Lamb was after a particularly grueling day spent searching for a missing boy in what I already knew was a pointless effort; he was nothing but bones. Later, at home, as I sipped from a glass of chamomile tea to unwind, my hand started to shake. The glass slipped from my fingers. It fell with a dull thud. Tea sprayed across my Persian carpet, darkening its pattern.

The air took on a weighty stillness. Time stopped for a moment and then lurched ahead. It was night, too dark to see anything more than the hulking high-rise. I swooped through a window and down a narrow, dimly lit hall. When I saw a dark figure ahead, I drew up short. It was a man, hunched over, face partly hidden by the shadows of the hall. He walked backward, looking over his shoulder, dragging a young woman by the feet across the cheap carpet.

Her eyes didn't even flicker and for a moment I wondered if she was still alive. I couldn't look away. Where was he taking her?

My focus narrowed to her eyes. Wide and emerald-green. They drew me closer and closer. I passed into the blond girl's body and felt her fear, pain, and uncertainty. My legs ached from being yanked. My head bumped along the carpet. A rug burn seared my scalp. I inhaled the reek of urine, sharp and acrid.

At the elevator, the man stopped. He fumbled behind him for the elevator button and dropped the girl's legs. She moaned, a weak sound, almost a whisper. But then panic locked her throat—and mine—choking off the air.

A ding, and the doors slid open. He pulled her into the elevator. Her head barely cleared the threshold before he stepped back, turned, stopped and stared back at the girl—and somehow, I was sure he was staring at me. His eyes were razor sharp, cunning and cold.

Trembling, I struggled out of the girl.

He vanished.

On the dingy-carpeted floor of the elevator, the girl stirred.

I hovered above her. This was the price I paid for my gift, watching tragedy unfold.

She blinked twice. Wide eyes took in the open door, the empty hall.

I watched her realize the doors were going to close.

She bent her knees and pushed herself onto her elbow. Then one hand at a time until she sat. With her hand on the floor, she pivoted toward the side of the elevator, using it to brace herself as she pushed to her feet. The wood wainscoting slid down her spine, rubbing over each vertebra.

Her legs shook. Her breath came in shallow, fast gulps. I closed my eyes. Willed her to feel me breathe with her. Just when I thought she was going to pass out, her gasps eased, and her breathing slowed, and matched mine.

The doors remained open, stalled. She stepped out and peered down the dim hallway.

She froze. My mouth went dry.

I zoomed forward, away from the elevator, up a flight of metal stairs to the building's roof and into the darkness then down, down, into icy water.

Minutes passed, maybe hours. She floated face up in water, her flesh gray, drained of life. Her parted lips were caught on a word she would never speak. Green eyes stared at the vacant sky. Moonlight in the water gently cupped her head.

The flapping of leathery wings sent ripples through the water. Whatever it was—or whoever—passed overhead.

My heart thrashed beneath my ribs. I tried to scream but couldn't make a sound. Abruptly, I was in front of the elevator again. The elevator door closed.

Opened. Closed. Opened.

Then closed again.

CHAPTER TWO

Alicia

The next morning, children's voices and the green honey-smell of an unkempt hedge floated into my study. I lay on my upholstered sofa feeling practically weightless, with no density, no bone, nothing to hold me in place, ice cold.

A wet nose nudged my arm, and I opened my eyes. "Nemesis." I breathed in her warmth but still didn't feel warm. I sank my fingers into her soft-gray fur and glided them over the two ridges behind her ears.

She nuzzled her cheek against my palm.

"Can you make yourself useful, you lazy cat?" I rolled onto my back and picked her up. "Tell me what to do." I stood her on my belly and stared into her dark, knowing eyes. "Should I go to the police? Tell them a girl I've never met has been murdered?"

Nemesis purred.

"You're right." My fingertips played across the delicate, bony ridges of her back. "They'd laugh at me. Even if they listened and believed, they'd want more information. They'd ask for details about the victim—who killed her and where."

The vertical slits of Nemesis's eyes showed no sympathy, only hard truth. I alone bore the awful gift of knowledge. I alone carried the burden of being too late—unable to protect the innocent.

She jumped off my lap, a blur of motion. I had to move, too. Keys and purse in hand, I climbed into my car. I headed north for the Santa Monica Mountains. As the psalmist said, "The mountains shall bring peace, and the hills, righteousness." It's a reminder that a refuge always exists where love stands supreme.

No more than an hour later, I steered along the twisty curves of Mulholland Drive, ignoring both the stately mansions and the cliffs that plunged just past the flimsy guardrails.

The clouds were low and thick when I stopped at a trail in Point Mugu State Park. In spring, its wildflowers soothed and enchanted. But it was not spring. I got out of the car, and a shiver rippled through me. Just now, only chaparral currants bloomed. I bent down and studied their small, pinkish blooms and puffy, mallow-like leaves, inhaling their fragrant air and asking for guidance—or the strength to do what I should.

Three miles in, I stepped off the trail and sat cross-legged in the grass. I heard the wind in the trees, a blackbird's high-pitched squeak, and the faint crick-crick of bugs scurrying.

I opened my palms to the sky and turned my attention inward. I breathed, waited, urged my body to calm, but my fingers twitched. My muscles cramped. My brain would not shut off. The phantom killer knew I was there. He'd stared at me. That never happened in any other visions.

We are all human. We try very hard to connect with each other. But what linked me to the figure dragging the girl? And stranger still, what threads tethered that figure to the thing with leathery wings?

Four hours and an ache in my backside later, I returned home without any answers, without any clarity or peace of mind. I felt guilty canceling my afternoon clients, but I couldn't possibly help them.

I lit tiny candles to banish the darkness. Each flame fluttered bravely in the breeze of my open window. Each created its own small glow and flickering shadows. *Las candelas* represent more to me than wax and wick. Their flames gave permission to take a deep breath and relax, become part of ceremonies, add warmth and renew spiritual energy.

It didn't help. I continued to feel unsteady, as if my feet no longer rested on solid ground. I'd always thought no danger could befall me where I lived in Silver Lake—its narrow, winding streets, snaking stairways and green hills. Its black walnut trees, macadamias, and avocados are just five miles north of downtown Los Angeles, but a world away from the gritty streets of the city. From here, you can see all the way to the Pacific.

I sat down with a warm cup of coffee at my new, granite tabletop to skim *The Los Angeles Times,* folding my feet lightly at the ankles to get comfortable Suddenly, the hairs on my arm rose. There it was. An article about the girl I'd seen. The one I'd watched die.

I felt as if the air had been forced from my lungs. *That poor girl!* The newspaper report seemed more concerned with contaminated water than the bright spirit whose life had been so cruelly taken.

I tapped the floor. Nemesis padded over on hairy cat paws and nuzzled my hand. "What do we do now?" I asked her. "We know the girl's name, Betsy Lamb. Who was the wolf that caught her in its grip?"

I thought of the memories she would never have. It seemed so sad and senseless. I brushed away a tear while Nemesis cleaned herself. The fan overhead blew cool air.

Something else in the article made me shiver. A serial killer named Richard Ramirez had stayed in the hotel years before.

I did an online search and learned he'd committed horrific, stomach-turning crimes in the 1980s. It wasn't enough for him to kill people. He'd rape and sodomize his victims. Slit their throats or mutilate them in some way, as if to deny the dead any possible integrity or dignity. One woman's eyes were gouged out. On another, he drew a pentagram in lipstick. Eventually, he'd been caught and died in prison.

Could there be a link between the dead serial killer and the teenager? It seemed tenuous. They'd stayed at the same hotel almost thirty years apart. But he was a devil worshipper, and she was a lamb.

A sacrifice?

The thought came in a sick, stomach-churning wave and I couldn't keep my bearings. I was on a road I couldn't get off. I was in a car that swerved and veered and plunged into the ocean. Water covered my head. I was about to drown, and I had to angle, kick, and fight to reach the surface.

The things that normally calmed me, such as nature or prayer, hadn't helped at all. If I were to stay sane, I had to talk to someone. Phyllis. I thought of her bright- paisley scarfs, and the book-lined study with its framed diplomas and photos of her deceased husband. She'd been my therapist when Mami died. Now she was my friend, and I appreciated her willingness to make an exception after I ended my therapy. At the time, she told me that not every therapist would make that decision. Some would worry they were crossing a line, being overly invested. But she made it very clear that I could never return to her professionally.

I dialed her number. The phone rang four times before she answered with a yawn. Water was running in the background.

After exchanging pleasantries, I asked, "Can I come over?"

"John and Bethany are in town with Lucy," Phyllis said. "They'd love to see you."

"Are you sure I won't be imposing?"

"Don't be silly."

"I'll be there as soon as I can."

"Is anything wrong?"

"Maybe. There's something I want to discuss."

"Something personal?" Phyllis's voice changed, taking on the enigmatic calm of a therapist. "Do I need to come up with an excuse so we can talk in private?"

"Maybe. I think so."

After driving to Brentwood, I said a quick hello to Phyllis's family before we settled in the cozy kitchen. I must not have seemed myself as I dropped my purse and sat down without another word. Phyllis eyed me with concern. With John off picking up pizza, the tension of what-do-I-want all but crackled. Even Phyllis's granddaughter, Lucy, seemed to feel it. Unusually quiet, she snuggled into her grandmother's side. I didn't know where to start. My childhood had been a solitary one, and this family's closeness, the love and well-being that radiated from the faces in the photos covering the walls, felt more uncomfortable than the Naugahyde wing chair my mother had salvaged from the sidewalk.

"So?" Phyllis reached across the table and took my hand. Her nails were manicured, her smile inviting. "What's this about? I've seen you sad and upset. But I've never you seen you flummoxed before."

I put my hand over my mouth. Flummoxed. Yes, that was exactly how I felt. But how was I going to explain it when I didn't understand myself?

Phyllis filled in the silence. "Before I met you, I spent three decades arming myself with all kinds of knowledge." She let go of my hands and turned me so she could stare into my eyes. "But then I met you. Saw how you used past-life regression to cure people. You had a way to access that place within that's connected to The Source, or God, and has unlimited knowledge and healing ability." Phyllis shook her head at me. "You have nothing to be afraid of. You have more power than you know."

Phyllis was my friend. I shook off her compliments, and my mind lurched about trying to find a way to begin. "Do you know anything about Richard Ramirez? His name came up in an article I read earlier in the day."

Phyllis cleared her throat. "Lucy, why don't you go into the living room and draw some pictures for Alicia."

Lucy didn't move, so Bethany took her hand. "Let's go, sweetheart. We can draw together."

Phyllis waited until they were out of sight and lowered her voice. "I remember it like it was yesterday. Just thinking about it still gives me the shivers." She bit her lip. "Everyone, *and I mean everyone*, was terrified. We made sure our windows were locked at all times. People used to walk to their cars with guns. The papers called him the Night Stalker."

"But they finally captured him, didn't they?"

"Yes, but that didn't end it. Before they put him on trial, he inked a pentagram on the palm of his hand and flashed it in court."

"He must have been totally insane." My hands shook, so I dropped them to my waist. Under the table, they couldn't be seen.

"He was so dangerous they put him into a maximum-security prison. I suppose he rotted there. They say he never repented. And he insisted that the statements he'd made at the end of his trial were literally true—that he'd return from the dead to take his revenge."

But the dead don't necessarily stay dead, I thought.

She paused.

I waited.

Phyllis leaned forward. "But you weren't even born when all this happened. Why are you asking about it *now*?"

"Phyllis, something strange is happening."

She tilted her head, and her tongue stuck out for a moment. "For you, my dear, something strange is *always* happening. That's your M.O."

I didn't smile back. "This is different."

Phyllis' brow knitted. "Different how?"

"I had a vision of this frightened girl in an elevator. She came to me just before she died." I leaned forward and gripped the table. "And today I pick up a paper, and there's a story about her. Years ago, Ramirez stayed in the same hotel."

"So?"

"So, I think there's a connection. You said he wouldn't completely die. That he'd be back."

Phyllis rolled her eyes. "Are you saying he returned for a girl he'd never even seen? That sounds pretty farfetched, to say the least."

"Yeah, you're right. The trouble is, the more I think about it, the more certain I am that it's *not* a coincidence."

Phyllis walked over to the refrigerator and took out a pitcher of lemonade. "Your intuition never led you wrong, as far as I know. Maybe you ought to go to the police. Suggest to them that they find the connection. If there *is* a connection. That's *their* job, not yours." She poured glasses for both of us.

"You don't think they'll send me to the psych ward?" I ran my fingers around the rim of the glass.

She snorted. Lemonade squirted from her nose. "They might kick you out of the office, but nothing in your manner screams 'watch out for the crazy lady!'"

I wiped it up with a napkin. "That's a comfort, I guess."

"So, you'll go to the police?"

"I suppose I should. But I don't have much to tell them. I hate dealing with skeptics—and police are the worst."

"When you decide, let me know what happens. If they

lock you up, my professional opinion that you're as sane as anyone else might come in handy." Phyllis laughed lightly. "Of course, I'll have to charge you."

"Thanks for the vote of confidence."

"Any time. What are friends for?"

I heard the front door open. John had returned with the pizza. He handed the pie to Phyllis as Lucy ran up for a hug. There was a catch in my throat. I thought of my father who left—and never came back. Lucy clung to John. The energy of love that tethered them, one to the other, felt like my cue to leave. Phyllis urged me to stay, but truth be told, she hadn't made me feel any better.

I was alone with my problem and afraid; not anxious or scared, but afraid for my life, though I didn't know why. Nor why I felt frail and insubstantial in my very bones and beyond, as if the ancient cells of my body knew more than my mind could accept.

CHAPTER THREE

Carver, the detective

There was nothing at all like working a murder.

I stepped around a tangle of devil's weed, dodged an overgrown hedge, a dying bed of marigolds, and a rhododendron that nearly dwarfed a crumbling statue of St. Peter. And there she was.

I stared down at the small body. Jet-black curls of hair festooned with small, yellow flowers. A harsh contrast of light brown skin amid dark green leaves.

The child could have been asleep, caught in a late-morning nap in the garden. Except for the vicious, angry slash where her severed larynx formed a white circle centered in the bloody gash. A bright red book bag lay next to the girl.

I used my phone's camera to capture what I saw. The team would do high-res photos, but these were for me, to jog my memory and give me a place to start. A twisted foot turned to the right. A short, blue skirt smudged with dirt; a white blouse as pristine as it had been when the girl's mother last saw her—when the girl was alive.

Back at the road, a crowd of gawkers shouted and hollered. Janice zigzagged her way through the crowd and ducked under the yellow police tape.

"What do we know, Carver?" She tugged on a pair of latex gloves.

I flipped through my notes. "The stepfather reported the girl missing two days ago." I kept my voice low so eager spectators or vulture reporters wouldn't catch the details. I didn't want another damn case ruined. "Said she was last seen leaving the school library at four thirty by Olivia Cruz, her teacher."

Janice moved a step closer. The blue strobe of the emergency lights glanced off her pale, cherubic face. Her looks hid a knack for nailing down the truth. She was a fine partner and a kickass cop.

"Did she often stay at school after the other kids left?" Janice asked. She stood next to me, not more than three feet from the dead child.

"Don't know yet."

A light wind blew. In the distance, the crowd had quieted somewhat, but a few people still pushed up against the police tape.

"The parents organized a search but came up empty.

Then an hour ago, a woman named . . ." I scanned the papers for that detail, "Sofia Salguero showed up. She'd been walking her dog right there on Mercy Street, same route she takes every day."

"She walks her dog through these weeds?" Janice always picked up on every detail, every movement, every single step of every suspect.

I rubbed the back of my neck. "The dog must've caught the scent. He pulled on the leash, yanking her into this thicket. She finds the child, screams, and grabs someone nearby to call 911. Body temp and rigor mortis put the time of death between nine and midnight last night."

I held up the bookbag. "Assuming it belongs to the victim, she's Maria Cordero, a fifth grader at Saint Columbkille Elementary School. She lived in an apartment on San Pedro Street, not far from here."

"I hope you catch the cocksucker who did this," a homeboy with a split lip shouted. Janice smiled faintly. She and I knew the local dealers and dopers might try to help, but whatever information they had, some of it would be incoherent, most of it would be useless, and all of it a waste of time.

"Cordero's Spanish for lamb," Janice said.

When the photo experts moved in, Janice and I moved off. We fanned through the garden and into the adjacent yard and trash-filled alley, eyes fixed on the ground, looking for footprints, a blood trail, or a sharpened tool, maybe a knife. Any hints the killer might have left behind. We found nothing.

"It's time to tell the parents." Her voice hitched, but she didn't move. She didn't turn, wade through the weeds, or go to the car. She stood still, very still. She had two small boys of her own.

I fished the keys out of my pocket. "Come on." I kept my voice business-like. Janice wouldn't want me to notice how she felt. "I'll drive."

The Cavalier I'd grabbed from the lot smelled of sweat, and my stomach knotted. I hated how some of the others kept their cars. Hated how I never had my own car with its hint of expensive cologne. Hated the way the Cavalier's carburetor rattled announcing our presence to anyone in earshot. Still, I scanned the neighborhood as we drove to the victim's house.

A couple of blocks later, I parked at the curb. The Greenview Heights high-rise was the kind of place residents trashed and landlords didn't make repairs. A place where families without hope lived. And now a family had lost a child. I took a deep breath.

Janice hauled in a deeper one. "Should get this over with." She pushed herself out of the car.

The gray and white lobby was well-lit, but the elevator smelled of beer and vomit. The stench was overwhelming. I pulled Janice away from the suspicious brown stain in the far corner and was pretty sure she held her breath until the elevator doors opened on the fourth floor.

Down the hall, the sounds of a couple arguing in Spanish coupled with the smell of fried beef and fresh tortilla assailed us. Give me catfish battered in seasoned cornmeal, collard greens and my dad leaning over my mom's shoulder with his arms around her waist.

At 4B, I knocked. From inside, a dog barked, but no one answered. I knocked again and finally the sound of a chain rattled and a bolt flipped.

"Hold yourself." The voice was male, gruff and sounded half asleep. The door opened a crack.

"Police." I flashed my badge.

"It's about time," he said. The guy pulled open the door. He was short, plump, in his mid-forties, and wearing nothing but underwear—a white cotton tank top and boxers.

Lips firmly pressed together, I walked past him and entered the room. Why wasn't he out looking for his daughter? But here he was, sitting around half-dressed. He noticed my glance and two vertical lines appeared between his brows. They were gone in an instant.

"I'm Detective Carver. This is Detective Silver."

"Did you . . . find her?" His voice trembled, caught between hope and fear.

"Let's sit down." Janice was solemn. She had a way of getting a man moving without asking more.

He led us into a living room that didn't look lived in. No pictures hung on the walls. On the far side of the room, a woman lay on a black sofa with her head on an orange pillow. She faced the wall, her legs pulled up toward her chest.

The man picked up a chair and brought it over to the sofa. "My wife has been out of her mind with worry since Maria disappeared." He reached over and touched his wife's shoulder.

She didn't uncurl.

He sighed. "I called the doc and went to the *pharmacia* for meds to calm her. I put up posters in the neighborhood. It's a terrible thing, not to know." He looked up through a dirty window, as if it were an escape hatch.

I'd seen that look before on the face of a suspect. When we had had him dead to rights and there was no way out. But hell, maybe I was too cynical, too quick to point the finger of blame. The man had lost his child. Of course, he'd want to escape the truth.

"We are so sorry to have to tell you this," Janice said. "Your daughter was found in an abandoned park near her school."

The mother shot up. "Is she all right?" Her body convulsed, and my heart constricted. Parents always fear the worst. I knew. I had a teenage girl of my own, Dani. And I worried about her all the time.

We hadn't come out and said the girl was dead. But the mother knew and so did her husband. He put his hand on her shoulder, more firmly this time.

"Tell me." She shook him off. "Is my daughter all right?" She looked past us to the door as if any second she expected her child to bound through, throw her bookbag on the floor, and yell "I'm home."

"I'm sorry." Janice sagged into the only other chair in the room. "It looks as if Maria was murdered."

"We'll do our best to find the person responsible," I told the woman. The same thing I've told countless other mothers.

She looked at me blankly, as if all her energy and emotions were being held inside. Because we were there, watching, assessing her every move. I hated this. Repetition and familiarity kept me from being unsettled. It kept me professional and distant. Alert. The way I had to be. But this situation called for something else. Something I couldn't allow them to do.

Grieve in peace.

"Can we see Maria's room?" I asked.

"Only got the two rooms. The man rubbed his whiskers. "Maria sleeps back there."

I nodded, led the way down the dark hall, and stopped at a small, foul-smelling cot. Janice flipped the mattress. A yellow stain covered most of the fabric.

"She's still wetting the bed," I whispered. "Something's not right."

"Doesn't prove anything. Some kids are just bedwetters," Janice whispered in response.

I looked back toward the living room. Maria's mother had fallen into her husband's embrace. She turned toward me and tried to speak, but her words were lost in a hard swallow. Her husband looked dazed. I hoped they understood we needed and expected their cooperation.

"One of you will have to go the medical examiner's office for a positive identification. And then, if it's at all possible, we'd like you both to come to the precinct," I said.

I walked back down the hall and headed into the kitchen. The refrigerator held a single photo. Maria, a couple of years younger, wearing a pink bathing suit and holding a bottle of bubbles. The picture had caught her in mid-bubble, with a half-smile on her face that spoke of mischief and spirit just like Dani at that age. My daughter thought the sun rose and set on her daddy, and she would climb onto my lap at the end of the day to show me a picture she had drawn or a rock she had found. Back when the world had been filled with wonder and joy for her. Maybe even for me.

My cell phone rang. I answered, listened to the dispatcher say, "10-7 at 457 Greene Street. Now."

My heart raced. "Please excuse us."

Maria's father looked as if he wanted to ask a question. Thankfully, he didn't. Relief surged through me. What could I have said? That we might be pulled from the case. When I nodded Janice to the door, I didn't wait to see if she would follow.

"What are the brass thinking?" Janice complained,

closing the door a tad too firmly. "We've just started another case!"

"Bet this time it's someone," I made air quotes, "important."

"More important than a dead child?"

"Than a dead *Latina* child." Without making eye contact, I slipped my hand into my pocket. Felt for the car key and gripped it hard enough to etch its shape into my finger. A new thought took hold, and my anger lost its bite.

"It's the Greene Street Hotel," I said as if to convince myself. Strange things happened in the grimy hotel with faded, red shutters and gold lettering. It had been a haunt of two serial killers and numerous acts of mayhem and lunacy.

CHAPTER FOUR

Carver

Greene Street wasn't the kind of place anyone wanted to end up. Shards of glass sparkled amid the colorful tarps of the homeless. Sitting in a rickety chair outside the Union Rescue Mission, a man with a bandaged ear passed a penny-sized baggie with crystal meth to a kid with dark, red sores on his face. The seller smirked as the Cavalier rolled past. Our presence must've provided unexpected entertainment, far superior to the gang tags and genitalia spray-painted on the metal garage door of the auto shop next door.

On Sixth Street, a mural of a young Hispanic woman with long, flowing curls and a red banner with yellow lettering said, "I am a survivor of sex trafficking." A thin, young woman in hot pants emerged from a sidewalk port-a-john, followed by a middle-aged ass-wipe, pulling up his fly.

No other cars passed. All signs read "One Way" or "No

Right Turn." Perfect for a place where people who have taken wrong turns regularly end up.

Outside the Greene Hotel, I cut the engine. Once, it epitomized the glamor and possibility of the Roaring Twenties, with its opulent Art Deco architecture, marble lobby, stained glass windows, and alabaster statues. In its prime, it must have seemed the most daring flapper of all. The girl that smoked and drank and partied the hardest—exotic and thrilling in her beaded, fringed skirt.

These days, it was damn near impossible to glimpse the Greene Hotel and imagine that dream before the rot set in. She was like a daring flapper that spent her life doing meth and hooking.

Inside the once opulent now run-down lobby, Janice took in the decorations. A grimy, white buffalo head stared with glassy eyes; a black porcelain minstrel with a red-checked shirt and yellow pants held a banjo; a life-sized cloth ballerina sat on a swing. "This place gives me the creeps."

I gave her a wicked smile. "Whoever decorated it had serious problems."

A short, slender Indian male in a wrinkled white shirt and a wisp of a mustache stood behind a well-worn front desk. It held an old-fashioned cash register, the kind that dinged when the drawer opened. A tiny bell with an elegant hand-lettered sign said, "Ring for Service."

I couldn't imagine who in the name of hell would bother to ring or what kind of service they could possibly want.

"Can I help you?" the man asked.

"I'm Detective Carver." I showed him my badge. "This is my partner, Detective Silver. And you are?"

"Sulman Sahai, the hotel manager." He licked his lips. "As I told the officer on the phone, we have a cistern on the roof. It provides water for washing and drinking to all the rooms. A few of the guests said the water smelled funny, so I told our handyman Juan Ortiz to take up a ladder and look around. That's where he found her . . . the young girl."

I leaned on the counter. "On the roof?" I asked but didn't need to know. I'd heard him, but damn if he didn't sound like he was giving a prepared speech. Too quick, too prepared. And I wanted more.

"In the cistern." He blinked twice, took a step back and dropped his chin. If he had more to tell, he wasn't going to give it up yet.

"We'll want to talk with you later." My hand thudded on the counter. "But first we want to examine the crime scene."

"Do we need a key, or does forensics have it?" Janice asked. She tried to stifle a cough and failed.

"It's with them. I suppose they're still securing the area and taking pictures. Some of them left. They told me they needed special equipment to remove the girl from the tank." He started filing receipts. "Get off on the top floor. Turn right. You'll see the stairwell. It's normally padlocked." He shook his head. "How she got up there . . ."

He was still talking as we walked away.

On the roof, the wind carried a slight scent of sulfur. The muscles in my lower back tightened. I took off my glasses and wiped my forehead with the back of my hand. Detectives were hard at work; grim faces setting up the tripod and flash unit or bent down to place the remote cable release to trip the shutter. I waved a general hello and walked over to Lieutenant Simpson, who was holding a thermos of coffee. Janice stopped to talk with the photographer, stepping in front of a sketch artist measuring the distance between the water tank and the girl's clothes.

"Look, Janice and I just started a case. Don't you got anything better to do than interfere with us?"

Simpson's eyes narrowed. He looked down at his shoes and then back up in my face. His voice was only a little bit better than whisper. "I'll reassign the other case. You take this one. We've got a body, a name, and not much more. And you're like a dog with a bone. If you get a case and there's anything there at all, you won't let go of it."

My jaw tightened.

Compliments were all very well. But why should a white teen take precedence? Was her blood any redder than Maria's? That's what my *zayde*, Grandpa Mordechai, would have asked.

He wouldn't have thought so. And neither did I.

"What do we know so far?" I asked him.

"The victim's named Betsy Lamb." He took a sip of coffee. "A high school senior at a private school in Peoria.

Lives with her mother, Bree Lamb. The mother's a big-shot corporate lawyer at Caterpillar with connections in the mayor's office."

I glanced at Janice and mouthed the word "politics."

"Why would the girl stay in a dump like this?" Janice pulled out her cell and punched on "record." She was like me in that way. She wanted to rehear the details while I needed the photos. Basically, we made a perfect team.

Simpson shrugged. "The mother doesn't know. Said she gave the girl a credit card and lots of cash. And said the girl sounded fine last time they spoke."

"Did you ask why she came here?" I said.

"Mom thought she was visiting a friend at UC Santa Cruz."

"So why was she in L.A.?" Janice asked. She looked pale, covered her mouth, and coughed again.

"The mother doesn't know." Simpson sniffed. "She doesn't seem to know much." He shook his head, as if he'd never understand parents. "According to the hotel manager, the girl checked in on June twenty-ninth. Couple days later, a member of the maintenance crew saw her. But she didn't check out on July second as expected. On July fifth, the mother called the precinct, frantic, and we issued a missing person report." Simpson took another swig from the thermos. "A handyman found her in the water tank. No one knows how she got up here."

I put on a pair of gloves and walked toward the cistern.

Rusted and slightly dented, it rested on a high platform. If you wanted to drown yourself, you'd have to bring a tall ladder. Whatever happened was no accident.

An aluminum ladder lay on the cement. A plainclothesman picked it up and brought it over to me. I climbed up and looked inside. The girl still floated, her skin greenish bronze in the water. It had started to come away as the tender fat deposits beneath it liquefied.

I moved the flashlight and saw straight blond hair, large white teeth, and pink lips. Her eyes appeared opaque.

I didn't expect her to look so young.

I headed down. Bent over to examine her clothes, which lay piled roughly thirty feet from the tank. Sand-like particulate adhered to them, so I guided the light along the ground, looking for more sand on the cement floor, but the twilight shadows gave me nothing.

The girl wouldn't have been strong enough to lift the lid on that tank by herself. It was hard to see how she could've ended up on the roof. Or why she'd *want* to. But if she didn't go up voluntarily, how did the killer get her body through a locked door and up a narrow stairwell? Okay, maybe he somehow managed to lure her to the roof, but why drown her in a tank people use for drinking water? And why of all places, did he choose the city's most notorious hotel? It was like some sort of sick joke.

CHAPTER FIVE

Carver

Janice and I made our way down to the victim's fourteenth floor hotel room. When the elevator doors closed, she told me what she'd heard from the photographer.

"The medical examiner's team is on its way. They'll supervise the body's removal. It'll be a hell of a job. Engineers have to cut out a small piece of the tank and collect the water before it contaminates the crime scene." Janice shook her head. "As if last night's downpour didn't fuck it up enough."

The first responders had already cordoned off the room, along with much of the surrounding hallway. A short, fat man handed me a room sketch. Janice and I stood outside the door to make sure it was consistent with everything we saw, then slipped on booties and latex gloves.

The room was featureless. Faded-gray wallpaper, a double

bed with a bright green, red, and white patterned bedspread, and a laminated headboard with two large globes that shone like fake pearls. It would have been a miserable place to die. But there were no signs of struggle, only the faint floral scent of perfume.

Janice stood on tiptoes and peered over my shoulder. "She unpacked her bag, so she must have planned on staying for a while. I wonder why."

"A good question." I pointed to a letter that lay on the white shag carpet "Maybe this will help." When I knelt over to pick it up, my right knee creaked—a reminder of the day my leg splayed out an awkward angle on the ten-yard line. I'd been sure to score when my knee gave way. Life turned on a dime. Catastrophe doesn't announce itself. It comes when least expected.

And I was sure the girl in the water tank never expected this.

"It's a letter from the California School of the Arts," I said. "According to Amanda Wright, the Director of Admissions, Betsy had to present two contrasting monologues, one from Shakespeare, the other of her choosing. And she had to bring a headshot. If she went, the audition was last Tuesday."

Janice stood by my side. "Parents are always the last to know. The girl must've had a reason for staying here. But it could be hard to figure out. I don't see a cell phone or laptop anywhere."

"At least we have this." I waved a glossy photo. In life,

the girl had looked like a model, with blond hair, a slightly long but finely featured nose, and a rosy pout. She had an aura of sophistication, a clever gaze and finely curled lashes. If I were her father, this was how I'd want to remember her. Not as a bag of sodden flesh floating face up in a cistern.

I walked into the bathroom and dumped out the trash. Janice followed me in. She logged each item, including several used condoms, which would be tested for DNA.

When she finished, we dropped it all into a black garbage bag. Everything the girl touched, every piece of her clothing, her makeup, the glass of water on her night table, and even her tissues would be checked for trace evidence.

We walked back into the room, looking for anything out of place. I glanced around. No phone or laptop. Janice picked up a lumpy pillow and a purse fell out. She gingerly opened it and looked inside. "It's stuffed with cash. She was not robbed."

I swallowed hard and wrestled with raw doubt. "The girl had a credit card. Why did she need so much cash?"

Janice stood in the center of the room, considering. "Drugs?"

I nodded in agreement. "If so, I can almost see the killer: tall and well-built. Young enough to attract the girl and strong enough to carry her unconscious body or overcome her physically. Maybe he's a dealer. In this neighborhood, he's likely a Hispanic male."

The pattern would form. Conjecture would lead to fact.

"You've always had a hard-on for this place." Janice wore a Cheshire grin. She'd seen me get lost in thought before and understood too well. "The crimes committed here that never got solved. But yours will be different. The Greeks used to say the gods punish a man most by answering his prayers. And here it is, you've got your wish."

"My wish? Yeah, right. Thanks to the good people of Los Angeles, the corpses keep coming. They stack up like firewood."

Janice grimaced. We waited for the elevator.

"You okay?"

"Not really. I must be coming down with something." She'd been pale, but now her forehead was beaded with sweat.

"Go home. See you back at the precinct when you're up to it," I said in a calm voice.

I'm not normally superstitious, but then an unexpected gut-punch of sheer anxiety struck me hard.

CHAPTER SIX

Carver

In the lobby, the damp smell of mildew rushed to meet me. Behind the desk, Sahai shifted his feet. I approached the counter. His aftershave didn't quite mask his scent.

"Did you know the identity of the victim?" I got out my iPhone to take notes.

"Me? Not for sure. I assumed it was Miss Lamb, at least that was the name she gave us." He glanced at me with sad brown eyes. "A beautiful, wealthy girl alone like that, she didn't belong here."

"Why do you think she stayed here?"

Sahai's face showed mild confusion and a half-subdued disquiet. "I didn't ask. I never pay attention to our guests unless they have a problem."

I grabbed his forearm. Held it. "But you paid attention to her, didn't you?"

Sahai pulled his arm away gently. "She paid in cash. Took out a thick wad of bills and gave me enough for a week. With that kind of money, she could've stayed in Beverly Hills."

I shook my head, incredulous. "You thought it was strange? But you checked her in anyway?"

He looked down. "What was I supposed to do?" His fists were clenched. Did he regret that he hadn't asked her why she was here, or was he hiding something?

"You said she came alone. Did you see her with anyone later?"

"Not that I know of." Sahai smiled, lips quivering. It didn't mean anything. When people are caught up in the shitstorm of a homicide, they try to ingratiate themselves.

"Okay. Let's move on." I gave Sahai my good-hearted cop look. The look that said he and I had no problems with each other. We were just having a friendly conversation. "How do you think she got onto the roof and into the cistern?"

The manager stroked his pencil-thin mustache. "No idea. The door to the roof's always supposed to be locked. It never occurred to me we needed a camera there."

"Was it? Locked?

"Yes," he said. His voice cracked. He took a deep breath. "When the guests, complained, I thought maybe it was a dead squirrel. But Juan saw the girl lying face-up in the water."

"How many keys to the roof are there?"

"Sahai's face paled. "Just two," he whispered. "One of them is with Juan. The other one I gave to the police."

He wiped his face. Poor guy was sweating like a chicken roasting on a spit. I felt for him. But after twelve years in homicide, where every day brings more violence, I don't get all worked up.

"I didn't do it," he wailed. "I swear. And Juan Ortiz is completely trustworthy." He clasped his hands and seemed to shrink into himself. "How could this have happened? It doesn't make sense!"

I brushed a piece of lint off my pants. "You think someone could've taken a key. Made a copy?"

He bit his lip, thinking. "I suppose there *could* be an old key. The lock hasn't been changed for years."

A bead of water brushed his cheek. Sahai wiped his face and flicked his gaze to the ceiling. A round, transparent drop of water clung to the lobby's curved and peeling dome, hanging above his head like a threat.

My thoughts bounced back and forth between Sahai and the damp ceiling. "Who'd know if an old key exists?" But in my mind, I was telling him to fix the leak before it got worse.

"Juan. He's been here the longest."

"We'll have to interview staff, starting with Ortiz. Then the guests on the fourteenth floor. Maybe one of them saw or heard something."

"Surely they didn't," Sahai said.

"Why do you assume that?"

His eyes widened, and he raised his hands. "I don't want to bother the guests," he stuttered. "But I understand. And I want to help." He retreated behind the reception desk, opened a drawer and removed a green file. He thumbed through a few sheets of paper. "Here it is," he muttered, handing me a list with the names of the hotel staff. I scanned the list.

"Which maid cleans the fourteenth-floor rooms?"

"It varies. Usually Tricia."

"Thanks. That'll be all. You've been a great help." I smiled at him insincerely and watched his body relax.

He turned over a green ledger. Opened to a blank page. "Do I need to . . . say anything to the guests?"

"You might want to tell them not to drink the water. But I assume they know that already."

I sat across from the desiccated handyman in a faded purple chair. Surely in his mid-fifties, he could've passed for the husband in Grant Wood's painting, American Gothic. Same stolid face, wire-rim glasses, and dirty overalls. Staring down at him was the morose, white buffalo's head.

"You and the manager have the only keys, right?"

Ortiz nodded. He appeared unafraid as he picked unobtrusively at a mole.

"According to your manager, you found the body."

Ortiz crossed himself. "Never saw such a thing."

"I certainly hope not." I leaned forward in the chair. "You didn't happen to touch it or move anything around?"

Ortiz had looked at me while speaking, but now his shoulders hunched, and he seemed to move away. "Touch the body? Are you kidding?"

"When you went to the roof, where was the ladder?"

He rubbed his hands together. "Where you found it."

"So, the ladder wasn't by the tank when you found her?"

He shook his head. "No."

I passed my hand along my cheek, feeling stubble. Vexation might've crossed my face. Of course, Ortiz didn't move the ladder. After finding the body, why would he? So, it had to be the unsub. But why not leave it propped up against the water tank? Or if he didn't use the ladder, how did he get her into the water?

"And the clothes?" I asked.

Ortiz shut his eyes as he tried to remember. "I bent down to look at them, but I'm pretty sure I didn't touch anything." He opened his eyes, blinked, and stared at me. "I came straight down to tell Mr. Sahai what I'd seen."

My mind drifts free for a moment and I see Maria Cordero. Her twisted foot, her blue skirt, and her face, as if asleep. Simpson took me off the case, but I'm not about to forget.

"Detective?" Ortiz said. "That all I got. Can I go?"

I waved him away. "Sure. Wouldn't want you to get bored," I said to his retreating back and headed over to the front desk where Sahai was filling out some papers, giving them little or no attention. He looked up as I approached.

"I need to see the maid."

"Tricia. I'll get her."

A few minutes passed and a thin, hollow-cheeked woman in her late thirties came toward me. She fidgeted with her wedding band and sank into the plush chair as if trying to hide.

"Hello, Tricia. I know you must be very busy, so I won't take more than a few minutes. Did you notice anything unusual in the dead girl's room?"

She wrinkled her nose.

"Well, what is it?"

"Not unusual exactly." She stopped. "The two nights she slept here, the sheets had stains—under the blanket, from a man."

I turned toward her. "Nobody's touched her room since except for the officers on call, right?"

The maid nodded emphatically.

"Did you ever see the man?" I asked.

"No, señor," She smoothed the armrests of the chair, as if she didn't know what to do with her hands when they weren't emptying trash or changing linen.

"Have you heard anything about a key to the roof?"

Her hands stopped moving. She looked up at me and

shook her head. "No." Her brow furrowed. "We've never been asked to clean there."

"Thank you. That'll be all."

The next interview finally proved helpful. Jeff Decker, a retired cop, worked security part-time. He showed me into a small, dark room off the lobby that had four monitors mounted against a wall. They cast a bluish light that accentuated his jowls and the vast shadow of his bulk.

"The minute I heard about the body I came here. Searched through the last few days' footage from the elevator and found something."

"Here it is." He picked up a digital surveillance disk. "I don't know what to make of it."

I peered over his shoulder. On screen, someone dragged Betsy into the elevator. I could see nothing but his back. When he turned to leave, a cloak hid his face. The way he dressed—that strange cape—and his slow, deliberate manner suggested he was no drug dealer. He was something else entirely; a shadowy figure that had emerged from the darkness, taken this girl, and dumped her into a water tank like a sack of garbage. God, I wanted to catch this bastard. A few minutes later, the girl eased herself up. She stood and peered out of the elevator. Her legs shook. Her eyes darted to the left, and she poked blindly at the elevator buttons. But the door didn't shut; the elevator didn't move.

This girl, alive and afraid on the screen, wasn't much older than my daughter. There was a lump in my throat. We always think our kids are too smart to get into too much trouble. Betsy Lamb's parents thought that, too.

I swallowed. "Something bad is about to go down. Look at her eyes, the enlarged pupils. Could be cocaine."

When the tape ended, Decker turned to me. "I hope this helps."

Just as I was about to thank him, I stopped short. There was something about Decker, something connecting with his name or girth. Then I got it. "You used to work for the Ninety-Third Precinct, right?"

Decker's eyes narrowed. "So?"

"So, I heard you didn't leave on the best of terms."

Decker wheezed. He removed an inhaler from the pocket of his pants, shook it, and took a puff. He turned away, walked over to a chair, and plopped himself down. "I don't give a shit what you heard."

"No? You don't remember that guy. What was his name? Oh yes, Betts. He fell asleep at a McDonald's drive-through. You gave him a sobriety test, right? And then he grabbed your Taser and ran off, so you planted five bullets in his back."

Decker's face reddened. He took a deep breath and sprang to his feet. He got into my face, at least as close as his stomach would let him. "I don't have time to listen to this crap."

A kernel of rage tightened in my gut. "And I don't like people yelling at me. And by the way, did you see the girl around much?"

"No," he muttered. "She kept to herself."

"Smart girl," I said on the way out. I usually don't go out of my way to hassle witnesses. But I didn't want to breathe the same air as a brutal, ex-cop.

CHAPTER SEVEN

Carver

Strapped to my government-issue metal desk, I spent the morning compiling Betsy Lamb's murder book, including the evidence lists, crime scene photographs and diagrams, our notes, and statements from forensics, logging every single scrap of information we'd found.

We didn't have shit. It was the skimpiest murder book I'd ever seen. The body had little maceration. No signs of struggle. No obvious defense wounds and nothing under the nails. The cistern cover and the ladder had been moved, but not by the victim.

As for the scene itself, there were no fingerprints, no footprints, and no drag marks. Sand on the victim's clothes but no sand on the roof. And none in her room.

I'd been in homicide for years. But I still believed that if I did my job, the truth was always knowable. I poured a cup of coffee and read through Betsy Lamb's posts on her social media accounts trying to find out about her.

Lieutenant Simpson sauntered over and leaned his butt cheek on the edge of my desk. "Janice won't be back for a while. She's checked herself into the hospital."

I jerked my chin up. "What? I don't believe it."

Simpson's lip curled into a half smile. "Believe it."

I felt like throttling the smug bastard "But I talked to her just yesterday. She sounded tired, but insisted she felt strong enough to trace Betsy's movements. She'd followed up with a wealth of information."

Simpson stood up. "Well, you won't be getting anything else from her for a while. The doctors aren't sure what's wrong." He sounded almost gleeful that I was on my own as he returned to his office.

"Ass." I wondered for the umpteenth time what his problem was. Envy? He knew I was the better cop. I'd closed more cases for him than anyone else in the precinct. And he was nothing but a glorified paper pusher.

I was about to call the hospital to see how Janice was doing, but then my phone rang.

"The victim's mother insists on speaking with you personally," the desk sergeant said, and I sighed. Betsy's mom was a career woman who'd lived her entire life in safety and security. Now, suddenly because of a violent crime, she found herself dragged into a police station to meet a detective—the kind of man she never met before and hoped never to meet again. I felt for her, but I also hoped I'd get some answers.

"Show her up."

A few minutes later, a tall, elaborately coiffed blonde in her mid-to-late forties wearing an expensive business suit strode over to my desk. The other detectives in the room busied themselves in routine paperwork.

"Detective Carver? I'm Bree Lamb." Her face was pale, almost without expression, except for her eyes, which held a look of apprehension. She took a deep breath. "I'm here to see her."

I took her hand. "Thank you for coming in."

Her look wasn't uncommon. I'd seen it before, the fear of identifying a loved one. A look that already carries the trauma of being led up an empty hall into a cold stark morgue. The fear of seeing a sheet dramatically whipped off or a body bag hastily unzipped. Reality is nothing like that. Everything we do is designed to make the process as humane as possible. Some would say it's too clinical but in the end, it's the best we can do.

Mrs. Lamb swallowed. "It's a parent's worst nightmare." Her mouth turned down. "It's even harder to bear because what I've heard doesn't make sense. How could Betsy have access to the rooftop and climb up the water tank? If the hotel had secured the tank properly, Betsy would still be alive." Her eyes bore into me, as if expecting that I'd admit the hotel had been negligent.

You never know what to expect—grief, anger, or numb

indifference. Talking to a victim's parents is the hardest part of the job. One minute they have a child ready to discover the world. Then she's gone, and so is her bright future. What if it were Dani?

"I'm so sorry to meet you in such trying conditions." I led her into an adjacent room and pulled out a chair for her. She sat down, crossed her legs demurely, and waited for me to continue.

I brought over a bag with Betsy's clothes and personal effects and lifted out a red and blue scarf. "Perhaps we should begin by confirming if these belonged to your daughter."

Her mother lifted her eyes and looked at me. She nodded. "This was one of her favorites." Her voice choked up.

"Would you like to see a grief counselor?" I asked.

"I suppose I have to see the body." She was resigned and ready for the worst.

"No need. We've pulled two photos for identification." I took out a small clipboard with two pictures. "One is her driver's license. The other was taken after we found her. I must tell you that she was in the water tank for a couple of days, and her features are . . . altered, particularly the texture and coloration of her skin."

I didn't go into detail because death stinks—literally.

Mrs. Lamb shifted in the chair. She took a cigarette from her purse but changed her mind and pulled out a crumpled tissue.

"Please take as long as you need to turn the photos over

and view the images," I kept my tone gentle. I was relieved she didn't ask to see the body. Bodies that have been in water for an extended amount of time smell worse than anything. If you view a drowned body even a few seconds, you will carry the memory of the smell away with you for the rest of your life.

Mrs. Lamb picked up the photos. Her hand was steady, her expression unreadable. "Yes. This is my daughter." She turned the pictures face down and put her hand over them. Women usually wept. Many men did, too. Some closed their eyes as if that could obliterate the truth of death. A few gazed into the distance, as if trying desperately to feel nothing. All of them appear to shrink under the weight of their loss. Bree Lamb did none of these things.

She stared at me, her eyes hard as flint. "I intend to find out why this happened. Am I making myself clear?"

"Sure, as long as you remember only one of us is a homicide detective," I said quietly. "She lived with you, not your husband, right?"

"Yes. He's coming in on a later flight." She folded her arms defensively.

"How was your relationship?"

Mrs. Lamb looked confused. "With my ex?"

"No, your daughter."

She tensed up. "Why do you ask? Betsy was a great kid. Ready to take on the world. A little like me when I was her age." She moved her head to the side. In profile, she looked sick at heart, even guilty. But then her expression changed so entirely I couldn't be sure. "Betsy was very focused. If she wanted something, she went for it. We didn't always agree. I thought she spent too much time acting in plays. But I always went to see her, no matter how busy I was at work."

"What can you tell me about Betsy's friends?"

"I only knew a few, Alice, Beverly, and Cathy. I used to call them the ABC girls," she smiled reminiscently.

"Any boys hanging around?"

"Sure. But no one in particular." She dug into her purse again for a cigarette. This time she also took out a gold lighter. Her hands shook, and I decided not to bother telling her she couldn't smoke in the building. When she took a drag, she seemed to calm down.

"Would she have told you if there was someone special?" I asked.

"Probably." She didn't look at me and her voice wavered. "Do you have an ashtray?" I brought over a plastic garbage container. She took one more puff and stubbed it out. "I'm trying to stop."

I waited.

She took a deep breath. "Oh, what's the use? Betsy was still coming to terms with being a girl who looked, well, beautiful." She spread her hands. "Who can tell what she might've done?"

"But she never complained to you about a particular boy?"

"No." She paused for effect. "Absolutely not."

I started to shake my head and stopped, hoping Mrs. Lamb wouldn't notice. Girls who look like Betsy attracted all sorts of attention. Much of it was unwanted.

"She ever mention meeting anyone in LA?"

"Never." Emphatic now. Either she really didn't know or she was hiding something.

"So, what was she doing here?"

She took a deep breath and let it out again slowly. "I don't know. Betsy was *supposed* to be visiting her friend, Cathy Waters, at UC Santa Cruz. Cathy graduated a year earlier. Betsy was thinking of using Santa Cruz as a safety school. There's no way she would have ended up anywhere but an Ivy. She'd already taken an online genetics class from Harvard."

"What can you tell me about Cathy Waters?"

"She's a sweet girl. Interested in the environment. Not in Betsy's league intellectually, but they've been friends since kindergarten."

"Did she have any trouble with kids at school?" Something seemed off. Betsy sounded too good to be true.

Mrs. Lamb glared at me. "Absolutely not. She was very popular. She was active in theatre and sports. A wonderful girl. Somewhat reserved, but very bright, with a wide-open future ahead of her." She paused, "Do you think she made an enemy at the hotel?"

"I'm not at liberty to discuss ongoing cases." I adjusted

my glasses and decided to move in a different direction. "Do you think your daughter's death might have had anything to do with one of your cases in LA?"

"As a corporate litigator? I doubt it." Her voice caught for a second. "The man at the front desk said she was found in a Skid Row hotel. Why would she stay in such a place?"

"I don't know." I gave in just a little. The woman was hurt and confused. I could imagine myself sitting in her place. Hell, I couldn't have told anyone what my daughter was doing right now. "We do know she kept to herself. As if she tried to be smart and safe. But then she let must've her guard down."

We were both silent.

Blood drained from her face, and she started crying.

I stood up and went to her side. Until this moment, she'd managed to maintain her cool rather impressively and chillingly. But now I bent over her and gently placed my hand on her shoulder as it convulsed.

"You think she killed herself, don't you?" she cried out. "And I drove her to it. That I pushed her too hard. Oh my God, is it possible? Could I have?" The poor woman was caught in a web of grief that would be hers forever. But I could provide her with a shred of consolation.

"You have no reason to feel guilty. Betsy couldn't possibly have done this herself."

Mrs. Lamb looked up at me. Her eyes swam with tears, but also with something else. Gratitude. I hadn't earned it.

But I could. If I retraced the girl's steps and found her killer, I could get her justice.

And that would have to be enough.

CHAPTER EIGHT

Carver

Dealing with the victim's families exhausted me. I knew that feeling sounded mean, but all I wanted to do was find them peace.

I rubbed my forehead.

I wasn't the type to offer a great deal of emotional support. Hey, what can I say? Sometimes I think I'm better with the dead. The living? Unless they have something important to say about the case, they're more likely than not to complicate things.

Better to focus on the facts.

I pulled up Janice's notes on my computer. Betsy arrived at San Jose International Airport at 5:53 p.m. on June twenty-sixth and checked into the Paradox Hotel in Santa Cruz two hours later. She asked for a room by the pool, indicating that she would go for a swim.

Good thing she'd typed it out. Her handwriting was shit, and my head hurt.

At 11 a.m., on June twenty-seventh, she met her friend, Cathy, and spent the rest of the day and the evening with her. That night, she took a train to Los Angeles and checked into the Greene Hotel.

On my note pad on my desk, I circled the phrases: *She came to L.A. for the interview. But of all places to stay, why the Greene?* I grabbed the extra strength pain reliever from my desk and dry swallowed a couple. No matter how many times I went through this file, I couldn't figure out how or why she ended up floating in the water tank of a cheap hotel. All I seemed to come up with were questions. I took a swig of cold coffee. Where the fuck would I get answers?

The following day, Betsy went to CalArts for an audition, then returned to the hotel, where she apparently had sex with an unidentified male.

I sat back in my chair and glanced out the window. It was dark. The kind of dark that should keep people locked behind doors. Wouldn't mind if they all put me out of a job.

"Detective Carver."

I jerked upright. Bree Lamb stood in the door with a tall, gangly man in a cheap-looking suit. She led him over to me. "This is my husband. My ex-husband."

"Edward Lamb." He stuck out his hand His eyes were red and puffy, the wisps of light brown hair lay across his head like a badly fitting wig.

"Sorry for your loss," I said.

His shake was soft and weak. I couldn't picture him married to someone like Bree Lamb. She was brisk and self-assured. He seemed unutterably sad and alone.

I clapped him on the back. Hell is that special pain that dwells in the loss that you yourself have caused. I recognized it because I felt it myself. "Excuse us for a few minutes, Mrs. Lamb." I led her ex-husband to a small interrogation room.

He took a seat at the other side of the generic steel table and I settled across from him. I pulled out my cell phone. "Do you mind if I record?" The logical question would've been why'd you separate, but because of his wistful tone, I went for a throwaway question. "How'd you meet Betsy's mother?" Sometimes you just have to let people ramble before you work up to the relevant issue.

"We met at a college party." He relaxed into the chair and managed to look as gray and featureless as the table. "It's the only way a boy from St. Joe's gets to meet a girl from Bryn Mawr." He learned forward. "I wanted her from the moment I saw her. At the time, she wanted me, too." He swayed a little in the seat as if he were a little bit drunk. "We were young and foolish. I was a poor boy from Port Richmond, Philadelphia. I lived with my parents in a brick building with square windows and a coal heater. Bree grew up in Gladwyne. Old money. But you can't deny chemistry." He shrugged. "Even when you should."

"You lasted how long?"

"Fourteen years."

"A long time."

"Yep."

"What tore you apart?"

He ran his hand through his thinning, light-brown hair. "She was always ambitious. I was just along for the ride. She got a job at Caterpillar and moved up the ladder."

"It must've been hard. Just following on her coattails." I watched him closely for a reaction, any reaction, but he just nodded.

"I spent a lot of time with Betsy." He laughed. "You could call me Mr. Mom."

I smiled with what I hoped was a sympathetic bartender vibe. "Again, I am so sorry for your loss."

He nodded. His eyes looked sad.

"And I'll do everything I can to find out what happened. But I need your help."

"Me? I wasn't even here." He rubbed a bony wrist.

"Just details. Did Betsy know anyone in Los Angeles?"

He lifted his glasses over the bridge of his nose and rubbed his eyes. "I doubt it. She'd never been. You should ask Bree, though."

"You didn't know why she was here?"

"Not until Bree called to tell me what happened. I didn't know she was looking at any schools here."

"You and your ex didn't talk much. Have you been separated long?"

"Uh huh. Betsy was almost six. The most beautiful little girl in the world. I stayed in Peoria. Made sure to see her every week. I got a job doing PR for the Rivermen."

"What's that?"

"Our local ice hockey team."

Someone must've been doing him a favor. He seemed altogether too quiet to have anything to do with contact sports.

"How was your relationship with Betsy?"

"Like I said, I saw her as often as I could. We got along fine."

"Your ex says you don't see much of each other of them anymore."

Lamb's face was flushed. "I would've liked to see more of her. But that was the way Bree wanted it." The words suggested resentment, but his tone of voice, acceptance.

He didn't resent his ex-wife enough to harm the girl. So, who might have?

"Betsy was a beautiful girl with a vibrant personality. Did she ever complain that a boy was hanging around too much or giving her trouble?"

"Not that she ever said. But who knows? She could have turned all the boys' heads. Betsy was a sensible girl. But she might not have known how to handle the situation if a kid went ballistic."

I was frustrated when we finished up. After spending time with the parents, I was no further along than I had been prior to their arrival.

As Lamb and I emerged from the room, his wife grabbed my jacket. "I've heard the coroner wants to label it an accidental death by drowning," she said.

"Who told you that?" I asked.

She stared at her ex-husband, then at the ground, and at the wall behind me. "Just heard." Her voice lost some of its firmness, and I saw her questioning for what it was—too many cop shows watched.

"Of course not. The investigation's continuing."

She followed me as I walked her and her ex-husband past a line of photos of grim-faced past police commissioners. A row of white men whose tenure stretched back almost a half century.

As we came up to the elevator bank, she put a hand on my shoulder. "Listen. What if I offer a fifty thousand-dollar reward?"

"You'll have all kinds of lowlifes crawling out of the sewers spewing bullshit and wasting valuable time. It's been tried. A lot. It doesn't work."

She pursed her lips. "I've got to be sure we've done whatever we can."

"Okay. How about this? There's an elevator tape from the hotel. Your daughter's on it. If I can get permission from the brass, maybe we can release it to the public and see if anyone knows what happened." I raised my voice for emphasis. "No reward, though."

Her eyes went wide. "A tape? No one said anything about a tape. Can we see it?"

I felt an odd mix of sympathy and irritation.

Mrs. Lamb pulled her cell phone out of her purse, punched in a number, and walked back past the framed commissioners.

"Bree, don't . . . ," Mr. Lamb said.

She looked at him. Her eyes were narrowed, rigid, hard. He went silent.

"Helen, it's Bree. Put the mayor on. Of course, I'll hold." But she wouldn't, or couldn't, whisper. She wanted to make sure I could hear every word she said.

She turned away. After a long pause, she spoke again. "I'm here in L.A. to pick up my daughter's body. I've found out there's a tape from the hotel of the last time my daughter was alive. If it's released to the public, maybe someone will know something. Could you speak to the commissioner about it?" She listened. "I appreciate it. And one other thing. Ed and I are with the detective in charge of the case. We'd like to see the video before we fly home."

She walked back. "Your mayor wants a word with you."

Anger flashed through me, but I took the phone. The mayor made my position quite clear. I was to do everything in my power to facilitate Mrs. Lamb, which meant she was in. In the same country club, in the same charmed circle of friends. I thought of the Cordero family. Might not seem fair, but a girl with Betsy's political connections has a solve rate of seventy-five percent. Maria's killer might never be found. All because of the color of skin and the size of a bank account.

I handed the phone back to Mrs. Lamb and without a word led them to the viewing room.

As they watched their daughter's jittery movement and inexplicable actions, I could only imagine the horror they must've felt. Mercifully, the tape ended in less than two minutes.

Bree Lamb turned to her ex-husband. "She looked so scared. You've got to find the bastard." Her voice shook.

Her husband took her arm and they left. Grief can bring couples together, if only for a short time. Those petty resentments that rob couples of their ability to appreciate a loved one crumble away. They remember a time before tragedy struck, when there was nothing worth crying about, when their fears and concerns had been petty and unwarranted.

Privileged? Maybe, but still, human.

If I didn't know how deeply they were grieving, I would have envied their closeness, however temporary it might be.

The days' work ended. I picked up the phone to check on Janice. The hospital switchboard connected me to her room, but after a few rings, it went to voice mail. I couldn't even remember the last time Janice had taken a sick day.

CHAPTER NINE

Carver

I finally made it home after twenty-four hours of nonstop and was just pulling into my parking space when my cell rang. Eve's name flashed in the window. The minute I hit accept, she started in on me. "You have to pick Dani up for the weekend."

"I'm on a case."

Silence. The distance between us had grown immense in the five years since the divorce.

"Just take her tonight, okay? Drop her off in the morning." It wasn't a question but a demand with enough urgency to spark jealousy.

"Date night with Freddy?" I hated to give in to her, and I hated how cramped my tiny apartment was. I dropped my keys on the small kitchen counter.

"You're not my husband anymore. *He* is." Irritation rode

her tone. "So, unless you show me a warrant, you've got no right to invade my privacy."

"Touchy, touchy." I kept my voice neutral and yanked open the refrigerator. "Remember you're the one asking *me* for a favor."

"You should see your daughter while you can."

My shoulders sagged. Eve was right, as usual. Dani would be going off to college soon, and I'd just seen a couple of parents suffering from the anything that could happen. "Tell her I'll be there by seven."

It's a hell of lot easier to nail a killer than it is to parent a seventeen-year-old girl. Especially hard when you see her only every other weekend as part of a custody settlement.

I made my way out of downtown Los Angeles, my Toyota wheezed and grumbled at every stoplight, every left turn. The tires probably needed a rotation, and the engine certainly needed a tune-up. The cramped city gave way to the manicured lawns of Beverly Hills—Grecian-style homes with pools, cabanas, and statues; expansive Spanish-style haciendas; stark modernistic boxes with swiveling electronic eyes. Any extravagance the rich could waste their money on.

I turned onto Loma Vista Drive and gripped the wheel tighter. Eve lived with her husband, a pudgy, gray-haired lawyer, behind secure gates in one of the most prestigious cul-de-sacs in Trousdale. They had a spectacular view of Catalina Island.

The black gate opened silently. I drove up her long

driveway and rang the doorbell, Eve answered wearing a stunning camel-colored silk jacket, a white shell, and black linen pants as if ready for an outing on Rodeo Drive.

I couldn't help staring. Lack of attraction had never been an issue in our marriage.

She didn't look at me. She didn't even greet me, just waved me in as if I'd come to clean the house or fix an appliance. As if we'd never shared a bed or a life.

I stepped onto her white terrazzo floors, past her book-matched Calicatta marble walls, and pivoting walls of glass that opened to an infinity-edge pool and spa. Boxy gray chairs with black cushions looked coldly comfortable. A glass coffee table rested on four artfully battered blocks of wood.

It was an oddly cheerless place to live.

"So, how's Freddy?" I asked.

Eve arched her eyebrows. Her mouth turned down as if she'd tasted something sour. "Do you really care?"

"Sure." I plastered a smile on my face. "He's a nice guy."

"That's so like you." Eve ran, or should I say, tried to run her fingers through her spiky hair. . . . "To damn with faint praise."

I opted for a blank stare, but I was really thinking about her hair. It used to cascade down to her waist. My fingers would caress it, ever so gently, as if reading braille, feeling my way to meaning in its silky softness. Since she met Freddy, she'd turned sleek and shiny, like the sharp edges of her ultra-modern furniture.

"That new?" A brown and orange abstract painting hung on the opposite wall.

"Oh that?" Her eyes sparkled. "Don't you just love it? Freddy picked it up. He has such great taste."

"Daddy." Dani burst into the room like a breath of fresh air. Dani had Eve's figure and height. Both were tall and willowy with snub noses and pouting lips. But while Eve was blond and glamorous, exuding an inevitable air of success and privilege, our biracial daughter reflected my African and Jewish roots.

"Hey, baby girl." She was seventeen and nearly a woman, but I grabbed her into a bear hug I knew she'd hate. Not because I felt comfort in expressing emotions, but because I'd just seen a dead girl, a grieving father, and I wanted to feel my own daughter alive. "What's new?"

As expected, she wriggled out of my grip. "I'm trying out watercolor." She grabbed a sketchbook off the dining table. "Wait till you see how this paper shows textures and shadings. It's amazing!" She opened the book and showed me her spectacular sketch of Avalon Harbor at twilight, when the lights blink on the shore just behind a line of tiny boats.

"That's just perfect, Dani."

Eve clattered over in her too high, too expensive heels. "Have her back early. She has schoolwork to finish."

"I know." Dani shut her sketchbook. "You don't have to remind me. I get it, Mom. Art is for fun. School is for life."

Her tone was unmistakably derisive, and I thought about calling her on it, but I figured I wasn't Eve's husband, her partner, nor any part of her real life.

With her streaming low music on her iPhone, the ride back to town was peaceful, though her tight tank top and tight jeans reminded me that she no longer a little girl but a woman, not much younger than Betsy. I wished she dressed a little more conservatively, but hard experience had taught me that keeping my mouth closed and my eyes on the road made for a safe, pleasant trip. I never had enough time with her.

Dani leaned against the passenger side door, and I couldn't help myself. I hit the locked door button

"Can you buy me some paints? Eve won't get me any until I raise my chemistry grade to a B+."

I cut her a glance. The hard one I used with smartass kids in lock-up. "Eve is my ex-wife, and she is *mom* to you." My tone was just as hard, and I caught the flit of hurt across her face. "Already did that and you can have them. But I want the grade up, too. It's important, and so is dinner. What would you like?"

"Rascal's." She gave me a slow, heartfelt smile. "We haven't been there in ages."

Half an hour later we pulled into Rascal's. Millie, a large, motherly woman, rubbed away barbeque and coffee stains. I'd been coming here for so long, still it always shocked me how gray-flecked her nappy hair was.

Hey, Carve." She tossed the cloth, "Look at you, Dani! She wiped her hands on her apron. "You're all grown." She waggled her fingers for the hug she always expected. "You two find someone who serves better chicken?"

"No way," Dani and I said as one.

"Not in this city." Back when my mom first brought me here. I'd sat up on the high counter stool. Now, I stood at the cash register. But the food hadn't changed. It was still delicious.

"What can I get you, sugar?"

"Start with the usual. The world's best fried chicken an' waffles. Ribs, collard greens. And one of those delicious pecan pies you make. Two dinners worth for Dani and me. To go."

"How about some sweet tea while you're waiting, Dani?"

"Sure. Thanks." Dani pulled out her sketchbook and started making quick charcoal lines. Of what, I couldn't see, but whatever she captured I was glad she did. When Millie and her husband packed it in, the city would lose a landmark most of them never even guessed we had.

Mille poured our drinks. She headed for the kitchen, favoring her right leg.

"Are you okay? What's with the limp?" I asked.

"Nothin." Millie didn't meet my eyes. "My hip's been acting up lately. I keep meaning to go to the doctor." She swung open the door and called to her husband. "Jimmy, come out here and say hello to Detective Carver and his beautiful daughter."

A large, heavy-lidded man bathed in sweat lumbered around the counter. "Hi Dani. Hey, Carve," He gave me a hug. "Good to see you, man."

"That bald spot on your head looks like it's grown some."

"Yeah, like the Sahara." Jimmy touched his forehead chuckling. "A little more every year."

When Millie peppered her favorite customer with how's school, art, boys, Dani nudged me with her elbow. "Tell her, Dad."

"Ouch!" I rubbed my arm. "One of her paintings won first prize at that fancy private school Eve put her in. Two weeks from now. it'll be exhibited in the Parkhurst Gallery in the San Pedro Art District." I wrapped my arm around Dani's shoulder. "Certainly, didn't get her amazing talent from me."

"Look at you!" Millie shook my hand. "That's one proud papa," She hugged Dani. "You got to tell us when it opens. We wouldn't miss it for the world. Would we, Jimmy?"

"Of course not," Jimmy said, "I never knew a real artist very well before." He winked. "Of course, there was the time Leonardo Da Vinci stopped in for chicken wings."

"Quit your talk and fill their order," Millie slapped Jimmy's shoulder. Looking at us, she added, "You'll be here all night, if you let him ramble on."

Fifteen minutes, two full bags, and a thirty-minute slog

through evening traffic, Dani and I made it home to my nondescript apartment.

"I'm starving." She dropped her backpack on the floor. "I bet this tacky carpet is older than me."

I watched my girl—no, my young woman—unload the food at the kitchen counter. Everything felt better when she was around. "It doesn't bother me. I guess I'm used to it." I set the table with two plates, two forks, two knives. It felt so good to be sharing a real meal instead of standing at the counter scarfing a bowl of cornflakes, and for the millionth time, I thought about asking her to live here with me.

For the millionth time, I swallowed what was good for me so she could get what was best for her.

We sat across from each other and dove into the best fried chicken this side of paradise. "When are you leaving for school?" I tried for casual and must have succeeded; she didn't even look up

"On September 4. Mom and I are going to spend a few days in New York before orientation seeing museums."

"Anything I'd be interested in?"

"The Brooklyn Museum has an exhibition *Soul of a Nation: Art in the Age of Black Power.*"

"You going?"

"I'm not like you, Dad." Dani shrugged. "Everything isn't black and white."

"Unfortunately, the things that matter *are* black and white."

"Come on." Dani leaned back in the chair. "Not that again."

"You probably don't remember that when you were a little girl, you liked to crayon your bedroom walls. I suppose you could call them your first canvases. One time you drew a family portrait. You were in the middle. Your mother held one hand. I held the other. We were smiling ear to ear. Your mother's face was white as the wall."

Dani stiffened and put down her fork.

"You didn't color her in, but you colored the two of us brown." I spoke slowly and quietly. "Your mother was furious. She wanted the wall repainted immediately." I picked up a rib but didn't take a bite. "I don't know what bothered her more, the defaced wall or the drawing of our family that exaggerated our skin tones." I dropped the rib back onto the plate. "Your mother wanted the world to be color-blind. But wanting something doesn't make it so."

"Are you done with the lecture?" she blurted angrily.

I put up my hands. "Okay."

When I talk to Dani, it's easier to relive memories than discuss what's *really* on my mind. Soon Dani would be in Providence, attending the Rhode Island School of Design, one of the world's top art schools. She really was gifted. But she would be in a competitive hot house, with other talented kids. What if she decided she wasn't good enough?

"I love you too, Dad. But I have to find my own way." She went back to eating, and I went back to trying to eat, but the food had lost all taste. Assaults were all too common on campuses. A boy could slip a drug into her drink. Or some bastard might sneak up on her while she walked by herself in the dark. I insisted she carry mace and a whistle with her when she went out a night. Anything could happen to a girl on her own.

Look at Betsy Lamb.

Dani stared at her plate, moving some collard greens around. Maybe she worried, too.

"What's wrong? You haven't changed your mind, have you?" My throat tightened with hope. There were fine art schools here in California. She didn't have to move across the country. If she stayed close to home, I could protect her.

"No. it's just—"

"What?"

"I worry about you, Dad." She looked anywhere but at me. "About what'll you do when I'm gone."

I was touched, but pride kicked in. "Maybe I'll join a dating service."

She sighed. "I wish you would."

But we both knew better.

She took a few bites of food and went into the living room, stepping over several neat piles of chess magazines and books, to turn on the television.

Sirens blaring. A police car shot across my too-small screen and turned into a narrow alley. A ski-masked burglar knocked over garbage cans in an effort to impede their progress.

"Turn that thing off, would you? I'd rather just talk."

"Fine. This show is seriously uncool." She returned to the kitchen. "So, what do you want to know?"

"Now that school's almost out, what've you been doing?" I took the dishes to the sink and scraped the leftovers into the garbage.

"Besides art class?" She squirted dish soap. "Most days, my friends and I hit the beach. Or go dancing at the Santa Monica Pier. Thursday nights, they bring in some very cool bands. Or we shop at Melrose Avenue. There's a boutique where you can buy and exchange stuff. You can find all sorts of vintage items."

"That's all well and good. But you've got to keep your grades up. Rhode Island School of Design can rescind its admission if your grades keep slipping."

"Why are you so pressed, Dad? It's a frigging B- we're talking about."

I picked up a dish towel. Hanging out with friends was one thing. But like the Lambs, I had no idea what was really going on. Boys, parties, drugs—it could be anything.

When we finally finished cleaning up, Dani rushed off to her bedroom. At seventeen, a father's pretty much taken for granted like the comfortable old sofa a child curls up on to watch her favorite TV show. Of course, Dani was happy to see me, but she was much happier to see the paint tubes waiting to take her from the anonymity of childhood to a place where the spotlight would shine on her. She was starting another life; one she'd begun to imagine for herself. She was going to become Dani Carver, *the famous artist.*

I leaned against her partly open door. "You know, I love to watch you paint." She dipped her brush into one color and then another, until she found just the right tint. She pursed her lips, took a breath, and drew her brush along the side of the canvas.

Someday soon, the door would shut. I just hoped it wouldn't be in the sudden and terrible way it had shut on Betsy Lamb's parents.

I went back to the chess match laid out on my old, wooden desk. I keep a classic chess game on hand at all times and make one move in the morning and one each night. I moved the black queen to QB2—the final coup in Capablanca's 1914 match against Osip Bernstein. It looks like a sacrifice, but it isn't. If Bernstein takes the queen, he'll be checkmated, but his position is hopeless if he doesn't.

With black and white chess pieces, no blood is shed, no families are left to grieve, and there are no messy emotions.

CHAPTER TEN

Alicia

After I left Phyllis's house, a memory flickered to life. Opening my mouth so Carlos could drop a caramel onto my tongue. I hadn't seen him for over a year, but somewhere downtown, my once handsome and muscular brother wasted away, popping pills for recreation and smoking crack for life support. All my joints burned, as if nerves from a phantom limb were stabbing me with feelings of guilt.

Danger was all around. Carlos was my only living relative. I needed to find him for support—and to feel less alone.

As I searched downtown's derelict streets for Carlos, I almost tripped over an emaciated, middle-aged woman in a faded, pink muumuu and taupe knee-highs splayed out on the sidewalk. Except for her vacant expression she could have been my mother.

I knelt. "Can I help you up?"

Her mouth gaped open, but no sound came out.

"I can call someone?"

She turned her face away.

I knelt by her side. No, she wasn't like Mami. Mami had been indomitable. Unyielding. When she'd caught Carlos stealing her jewelry and slapped him viciously across the face. I'd lain curled up in bed, cowering, a skinny eleven-year-old. When we were little, Mami spanked our bottoms but nothing like this. I could hear the smack from my room.

"How much lower can you sink?" Mami screamed. "Get out. And don't come back. I don't ever want to see you again!"

I thrust aside the awful memory.

A few minutes later, I spotted Carlos on San Pedro Street, a block away from the Madison Hotel sign. I recognized his grimy white shirt with its frayed collar. Carlos always wore a black stocking cap, but now his greasy hair blew in the wind. For the first time, I noticed his gray strands. I went to hug him, but he put up his hand.

"Stay away." He was hunched over a garbage can as if I were a thief coming to steal his possessions.

"It's me." Was his brain so drug-addled? Why? What is it?

"I know it's you." He coughed up blood. It splattered on his shirt and handkerchief. "Just fucking stay away."

My heart was beating wildly. "You have to go the hospital. Right now."

"No, little sis." Carlos smirked "I can deal with this myself."

My hands balled up at my hips. No point screaming at him, I knew, though every bone in my body wanted to let loose. "I adore you, Carlos. I always have. But right now, I hate you. I want to throw you off a cliff and then rush back down to catch you. Let me take you to a doctor." I stepped toward him. "There's a walk-in clinic not far from here."

Carlos shook his head. He sagged back into a chain-link fence topped with razor wire.

"Why is it so hard for you to accept help?" But I knew the answer. His addiction broke up our family, and he was punishing himself.

A strangled sound came from Carlos's throat. "I can't."

"Remember how you used to tell me my skin looked bright as a new penny?"

"Yeah." The memory smoothed away the lines on his face. "Hey, you want to hear a poem I made up?"

"Sure." I rubbed my upper arm. The skin felt cold.

Carlos's voice deepened, changed.

The shadows of my sins are following you.
When they suck you in, they swallow you.
King of the mountain, that's what I am.
Everybody's someone's sacrificial lamb.

I gasped. The dead girl's name on my brother's lips. This couldn't be happening. My pulse quickened. I put my hands on either side of my throat, willing it to slow. What could my brother and the dead girl possibly have in common? Could he have been involved? I prayed not.

Carlos wore a smile, baring his teeth like a wolf about to pounce on a wounded doe. Then it struck me. Maybe Ramirez was speaking to me through Carlos!

"Repeat the poem," I said, putting my palms together. "Please. Line by line."

I stepped away from the fence when I saw a rat slither out. It crossed San Pedro Street in the direction of a wet, cardboard box that some drunk mistook for a urinal. And I thought about the poem. Was it a warning for everyone or specifically me?

The shadows of my sins are following you.

The voice, stronger and even deeper with a hint of a rasp, didn't belong to Carlos. It lengthened each phrase, as if seeking to coax fear and dismay. Could someone's sins actually follow us? What did he mean when he said they would swallow us up? And what would everybody be sacrificed to?

I put my hands over my ears, but it didn't block out a single word.

"Lamb," Carlos shivered on the last syllable. He coughed and spit more blood. He moved away from the fence and sat heavily on a stoop in front of a padlocked metal garage door. Something had rushed through him, drained him. A shadow. I jerked back as it crossed the street and skirted a load of gray trash piled high against a gray wall that was blackened with graffiti.

"Sis?" It was a question filled with love and fear. The voice belonged to my brother again. I wanted to sit next to him and wrap my arms around his shoulders. But I just stood there. Tears ran from my eyes.

"Don't worry so much." He fingered a thin chain necklace. "The pity on your face depresses me more than the blood." He waved me away.

My heart ached. Tears burned behind my eyes. "Why can't you find your way back to me?" I stood there, waiting for the smallest sign from him that he wanted something, anything from me, but he hunkered down into himself, and I walked away, past cramped diners, neon signs, and tattered displays. But the neighborhood was gentrifying. Just two blocks away a new restaurant with fancy canopies took up the right side of the road. All these diners laughing, eating, living when my brother was so sick.

"He will die," a deep voice said.

I turned around, expecting to see a large man instead of the thin, anxious-looking mother who stood behind me.

She held the hand of a plump, tow-headed toddler.

"What did you say?"

The little boy's hand slid from his mother's and his face shifted, becoming the face that matched the picture of Ramirez.

I stumbled back, colliding with a storefront window. The wolfish expression I'd seen on Carlos was on the little boy's face.

The boy wriggled in its mother's arms, inching slowly in my direction like a white worm smelling its way toward me. I slid against the glass, then turned and ran. Everywhere I looked, I saw two faces on each person that passed by—the person's and Ramirez's. Emptied of all but terror, I stumbled past faces that morphed insidiously from one to the other as if made of quicksilver. Sometimes, the Ramirez face dominated, with its long, curling hair, piercing eyes, and smirking lips and I swore he must still be standing right in front of me. At other times, I could barely make out the ghostly features.

But now he was here, communicating without words. You can't avoid us. There is no place to run, and no shelter at night or by day. I will add your brother to my collection of souls.

I ran down San Pedro Street, past a blue-and-red sign that read "Golden Doll USA" and around the corner past the Midnight Mission. I didn't stop. I couldn't stop. I had to escape the Ramirez faces—blurring, leering, following.

Somehow, I made it home, locked the door, ran upstairs to my bedroom and threw myself onto my bed.

Nemesis curled up beside me, and I petted her with a hand that could not stop trembling. Oh, to be a curled nautilus spiraling into a deeper tranquility, and having no fears of the evil around me!

CHAPTER ELEVEN

Alicia

I tossed and turned. My bed felt lumpy. I couldn't get comfortable. Couldn't shut off my mind. The image of the girl in the water. Carlos coughing up blood on his shirt. The leering face of Ramirez. I gave up trying to sleep.

I stared into the dark and lonely hours just after midnight.

"Aishe," I whispered to the empty room. "I need your help." I slipped into the living room and curled up on my sofa. "Aishe."

My wise spirit had guided me since childhood, taught me to focus and create a silence in the soul.

Now she was silent.

Stupid! I put myself—and others—in danger. The dead girl's final thoughts rushed through me in anguished bursts. *And I don't even know why. All I know is when I saw him, nothing mattered, just him. The things I always cared about—mostly gone.*

Shivering as if slivers of ice inched down my body, I folded my arms against my chest to press the chill from my heart.

They'll be here soon. And then I'll be gone, too.

They? I stared into empty night. Who were they?

Mom. Dad. I am so sorry.

I blinked and blinked, but the words kept running through my head. "Why am I hearing this?"

I pushed from the sofa and stormed into the kitchen, as if my pounding feet could still my hammering pulse. This wasn't for me to hear. I rummaged through the fridge. I wasn't her mother. I pulled out some leftover chicken, decided I wasn't hungry, and left it sitting on the countertop. She wasn't my daughter. I have no daughter. And no mother. She wasn't reachable in life or in death.

The last time I'd felt so uncertain, I'd been just a child and Uncle Roberto had taken me by the hand and pulled me into the dark garage.

I knew something bad would happen.

He unzipped his jeans. "Just a little squeeze." He put my hand on his clammy stiff skin, and I cried and sobbed and felt sick, but he told me to hush and not make a fuss. "I'll buy you an ice cream cone later."

When he was done, he said, "No one will believe you."

My breath felt sour in my mouth. Sour as the memory. I wanted to pretend it didn't happen. That I was okay. But things weren't. And neither was I.

Because then, I'd tiptoed around my mother and avoided my uncle. I was a victim then. Now, I wasn't sure what I was. I'd spent most of my life fortifying myself with knowledge of the occult, so I would never be helpless again.

I left the kitchen, slipped into bed, and turned onto my back. "Aishe, please."

The ceiling fan whirred.

"I need you." I forced myself to breathe evenly. I tried to sleep.

Something scraped the window. Hollow voices muttered indistinct curses. A brief clatter like a rusty electric fan gave way to blue sparks of light.

A hush fell.

I held my breath and listened for whatever might come next.

Footsteps, soft, quiet. An evil crept into my room and that evil sat in a chair next to my window, next to my bed, next to me.

That evil's eyes bored through my head and waited in silence.

"Sitri?" I spoke the name aloud. I didn't know how I recognized him. I knew little more than his name. I'd found it only in the Picatrix and the Clavicle of Solomon, obscure medieval Grimoires. Sitri was said to be a prince among demons with a man's body, a leopard head, a griffin's wings, and an ability to move fluidly, possessing one person after another.

I let myself take a small breath. I expected the rancid odor of feathers or fur to fill my nostrils, as he stretched out his sharp claws. Instead, the dark-haired spirit smelled of cinnamon. It glanced down at me with eyes that peered into the abyss for eons.

I hugged my pillow tight to my chest, shaking as if the foul thing held a knife to my throat and very gently scraped at my flesh, not enough to draw blood, but to remind me that I could bleed to death in minutes.

"Can you see me as I am?" A man—no, more than a man—he leaned across the small space between us. His human face hovered just beyond my reach. "I assume all you can see is Richard Ramirez as a young man. His body looks good on me, doesn't it?" His voice held a terrible, empty blankness that could ripen at any moment into an immense and oceanic rage.

Shivers ran down my spine. "Why are you here?"

"Why are you here?" The dark spirit imitated the quiver in my voice. "You must know why." His voice turned menacing. "You see connections other people miss. Rather clever, for a human. But dangerous." Tendrils of sulfurous smoke shaped themselves into beckoning fingers.

"What do you want?"

"From you? Nothing." His eyes were locked on mine. "You're a minor distraction, slightly more interesting than other members of so-called civilized society. Not one of you in a million can see yourselves for what you are—liars, haters, crooks, killers, and cowards."

My hands stiffened at my side. Under the smell of cinnamon, I caught the scent of decomposing flesh.

Sitri rested a hand on his thigh. "Alicia . . ." His voice dripped with pretend pity, "Why do you hate your caramel skin? Your long curly hair? You couldn't wait to leave the barrio. Change the person you are. Turn yourself into an Anglo."

I felt a prickle of horrified laughter trying to escape. I was on the border between life and death, and the thing standing above me quoted my mother.

His tongue snaked out. Licked his lips. "Why on earth would you change the person you are?"

I forced my eyes closed, but I couldn't block out his next words.

"That is my job. Death's job. The knife that slides smoothly between your ribs. A firm dividing line between your present and a future which will never be."

Tremors ran through me, and I tried to moisten my throat, willing myself to swallow, to breathe, to speak. "Wh-what are you?"

"Call me anything you want. Sitri, Ramirez, Rojas, or any other name you might come up with. We're all at your service." The dark spirit bowed.

I put my hand to my mouth.

"You look confused. I believe you were raised Catholic. Perhaps this analogy will help your primitive human mind understand better. Think of us as an unholy trinity: Ramirez, the father, Rojas, the son, and Sitri, the demon spirit."

"Ramirez kept his promise." I shuddered. The one he made at the trial. I could barely move. It took a lot more energy than I'd ever drawn into myself, but I forced myself to sit up. I faced the monster. "Why have you come to me?"

Sitri disappeared into a blue flame.

My heart hammered. A marigold, the traditional spirit-offering, sat on my night table. It was a forget-me-not from a demon, already wilted and brown. I climbed out of bed to snatch the flower and throw it away. I wanted no part of his offering. I stepped in a puddle of water, and my insides turned to liquid. Betsy died in water. In the hotel where Ramirez planned his crimes using the body that Sitri now inhabited.

I left the flower and fled my room, which should have been a sanctuary, but now the whole house felt tainted. In the kitchen, I filled my kettle, grabbed a cup.

Water is Neptune's element active within us. Within our aquatic nature is hidden our deepest fears and secrets—and an as yet undiscovered potential. Our aquatic nature is the most mysterious part of us—the most tumultuous and dangerous.

The kettle's scream near jerked me out of my skin. I had to calm down, to slow my pulse. I could not think. I poured the water over a bag of chamomile tea. "What defense do I have against such a powerful spirit?" I cradled the warm cup. Dispel the fear. I took a healthy swig, then another and a breath.

I crumbled dried sage leaves into a brown, porcelain bowl and set them alight. The leaves smoldered, and I fanned the smoke over my head, down my body. "Great Goddess," I said, "purify my soul. Grant me clarity of mind." I gradually brushed the cloud along the floor, allowing the earth below to absorb the spirit's dark energy.

And from the back of my mind, the itch I'd wanted to scratch all day came forward. For whatever reason, Aishe was MIA. Someone killed the girl. It wasn't Ramirez. He was dead. Sitri could possess bodies. He must have used a different pawn, maybe another criminal.

I no longer had a choice. I'd have to go to the police. Tell them what I knew. Make them believe.

Unbidden, a phrase ran through my mind. *Walk softly in your way, and your foot will not stumble.*

CHAPTER TWELVE

Alicia

I approached the police station, squared my shoulders, and headed for the double doors, dressed in black jeans, a pair of tan-brushed suede boots, and a white shirt with black horizontal stripes. I wanted to appear sophisticated, well-put-together, like my client who played Claire on Netflix's hit show about vampires. But putting on make-up and tying the little blue and tan scarf only made me more like a small child playing dress-up.

Someone coughed and the cough wasn't the kind of cough that should be ignored.

I detoured around the side of the building.

A heavy, middle-aged woman lay sprawled by the side of the building like a puppet whose strings had been cut. A line of blood stained the front of her wrinkled blouse.

"Do you need help?"

"No. Go away." She coughed again, and blood frothed her lips. "Need to rest."

My insides twisted with pity and fear. First Carlos, now this. Something was going on. I turned away, stopped a policeman, and pointed to the woman. "She needs a doctor."

He nodded and pulled out a phone.

With a final look back and a hope that I'd done all I could, I entered the police station.

A tall officer behind the high desk looked up. "Can I help you?"

"I would like to speak with the detective in charge of the Lamb investigation."

While I fidgeted like a convict waiting for cuffs, he ran me through all the usual questions: name, age, purpose of visit, etc. When I told him that I had information about the murder, he pointed to a row of hard plastic chairs. "Wait there."

And I waited. Police came and went, and men and women in handcuffs were led in. I nearly memorized the Most Wanted notice board and stared at my feet for more than half an hour.

"Ms. Flores." A uniformed police officer called my name. "Please, come with me." He took me to another room and asked me to sit down. "The detective will be here shortly."

This time the wait felt worse. No people watching, no posters to read, just four cold, yellow walls, a buzzing florescent light, and shiver raking up my spine until I couldn't sit. I paced.

After an hour, two, or maybe only fifteen minutes, the door opened. A light-skinned African American entered the room. I looked up and thought, *I know you. You're every skeptic I've ever dealt with. A man who looks around to see only darkness and corruption, whose words have tiny barbs that would lodge in the flesh.*

"Ms. Flores." He held a file, a phone and notepad. "I'm Detective Carver." He took the seat across from me. "Thank you for coming in." He was clean-shaven, with sharp cheekbones that made his face seem triangular until you noticed his squared-off, dimpled chin. Not handsome, but very masculine. "You have information about the murder of Elizabeth Marie Lamb?"

"Yes." I cringed at how high-pitched my voice sounded. I couldn't help it. It's how I talk when I'm nervous. Not the best first impression to make with a homicide detective.

He settled back in his chair. Even across the width of the metal table, I felt his aggravation, bordering on something I couldn't identify. I leaned closer. Frustration? Annoyance? Exhaustion? No, it was anxiety, but not about the case. There was something or someone else on his mind.

I straightened up. I was not here as a professional advising a client. "I saw Elizabeth Lamb in the elevator before she died."

"Tell me." He sat up. "Everything."

"I saw her there four days before she was found." I

leaned in. "She told me how scared she was."

He pulled out his iPhone. "So, you knew her?" He punched the record app. "Did she tell you what was scaring her?"

"Ah." Okay, so I started wrong, and didn't really know how to backtrack. "I didn't actually know her, and she didn't actually tell me why she was frightened." The room was hot and stuffy, but my skin felt cold and clammy. "I felt her fear." I bit my lip and added, "I am a clairvoyant."

He stopped taking notes, "Great." He leaned back in the chair. "You have visions." For a moment, I thought he was going to laugh. Instead, he sighed. "Wait here," he said. A couple of minutes later he came back out with another man, tall, sandy-haired and good looking.

"I'm Lieutenant Simpson," the good-looking man said. "Did the spirits tell you who committed the crime?"

"Wait, stop." My voice pitched to a fever. I needed them to hear me, listen, believe. "This isn't a joke. I'm one of the most sought-after mediums in the entire city. I can charge up to one thousand dollars for a single reading. Why? Because spirits *do* talk to me. And. I wouldn't be here if I didn't see a connection to your case."

The lieutenant studied my face. He turned to Carver. "I've got a feeling this won't be a homicide you can handle in the usual way. It will call for something more . . . probing. Janice is on medical leave." He gave Carver a sideways glance. "I didn't tell you?" He winked at Carver. "You don't have a partner. Maybe Ms . . . "

"Flores," I said.

". . . can assist you." The lieutenant rubbed his chin, "Of course, there are liability issues." He pivoted toward me. "You'll have to sign a waiver. You don't have any experience with police work, right?"

I nodded, too stunned to speak. Things were happening all too quickly. The lieutenant had taken my arm and was leading me into his office. I glanced back at Carver, who followed, lips tight, eyes burning. We passed a desk with a picture of a pretty teenager who looked like Carver. When we entered the lieutenant's office, Carver shut the door.

"What the fuck is this about, Loo? I work my cases harder than anyone. And close more cases than anyone. But you've had it in for me since you got here."

"Because you're a troublemaker." Lieutenant Simpson's face purpled. "Nobody but Janice would work with you. You and your fancy law degree." He spat, really spat on the floor. "You look down on everybody."

"Not everybody, Loo." Carver put his hands on the lieutenant's desk and leaned in. "Just you."

Lieutenant Simpson stuck a finger in Detective Carver's face. "You will work with her. Or you're gone."

Carver's jaw tightened. He took me by the arm, led me back to the small interview room, and sat down at a table opposite me.

"Okay." His voice was clipped. "Tell me about this

vision." The derision in his voice made me bristle, but if what I saw and what Sitri said was true, I needed his help to find the person Sitri used to kill his chosen victims.

"Let's start with a bit of history." I sat to my highest height. "You know that Richard Ramirez stayed in the same hotel as the girl, right?"

"Yeah. So?"

"I'm telling you." I gripped the edge of the table. "He came to me last night and warned me something terrible was about to happen. And somehow, I knew that he or his alter ego, Roberto Rojas, must have had something to do with her death."

"Look. I like my job and I'm humoring the lieutenant, but are you seriously trying to tell me a dead serial killer is involved in a kid's murder?" Detective Carver laughed, a harsh, grating sound. "That's about the stupidest thing I ever heard."

Blood rushed to my face.

He shot me a long, hard look. "Okay, I'll bite. What do you know about this Rojas?"

I gripped the bottom of the chair. "I only know Ramirez said he *was* Rojas. The same evil spirit possesses both of them."

"An evil spirit?" His lip curled dismissively. "I'm sorry, Ms. Flores. I don't have time to listen to this."

I was about to leave in a huff when a policeman walked in, bent down, and whispered to Carver. His eyes went wide.

"Get them to the hospital ASAP." He stood up and looked down at me. "It's been a pleasure chatting with you, Ms. Flores, but I've got to go."

There was a tiny voice inside of me that I wanted to silence at all costs, but I couldn't. Spirits spoke to me, and the responsibility was too great to ignore. "The sickness in the Greene Hotel is just the beginning. It will spread quickly. Ramirez is filled with rage. We have to stop him."

Carver looked at me with eyes that looked like a child's when it wakes up in an unfamiliar room and seeks reassurance, a semblance of order, and I fell into a vision. Carver the child stands in a small hall. He clutches a hand-made dog covered in soft brown and white fur to his chest.

I blinked and came back. Before me, Carver the man wore no mask. He was just a harassed homicide detective who didn't know what he was up against. Perhaps he suspected, if only for an instant, that the case was beyond anything he'd ever encountered. If so, he recovered quickly. "What the hell are you talking about? You think what you're saying helps me?"

"You need all the help you can get." A formidable adversary had swept into our lives and set us on a path where trouble and distress lay in wait.

"Thanks anyway, but unlike Simpson, I'm not impressed by New Age bullshit. I prefer obvious things, like hard evidence. Actual killers." He walked to the door, and I thought he would just leave me, but his shoulders slumped.

"Come on, Flores, I'll show you how it's done."

I hustled after him. "Where are we going?"

"We'll start with the college she visited." He was half a foot taller than me, and he didn't bother to slow down. "We follow the victim's movements until they lead us to the unsub."

"Unsub?"

"Haven't you ever watched a TV cop show?" He shook his head. "You don't know shit. And you're supposed to *help* me?"

CHAPTER THIRTEEN

Carver

I drove up Interstate 5 North for about forty-five minutes with the ridiculous psychic riding shotgun. We exited at McBean Parkway and turned right into CalArts's parking lot.

Tight with anger, I uncorked my words. "You're not going to like what I'm about to say."

She held the sides of the seat. "If you're going to lecture me, I've already heard it."

"Tough. If you don't want to listen, I swear I'll just leave you here." She didn't speak. She didn't even look at me.

"I've put away lots of killers and know that people don't need a reason to act like a monster. People can act like monsters without any help."

She bit her lip. "Have you ever considered the problem of evil?" Her voice was even, but her knuckles whitened.

"Why do some people who grow up in an atmosphere of comfort and love commit horrendous things? Or why do others who were brutalized overcome all their," she made air quotes, "challenges?"

I leaned forward. "So, you're saying what?"

"Maybe some people are open to receiving influences. Anger opens a portal, so does hope." She glanced at me. "I don't expect you to believe me." The pencil lined brows over her beautiful eyes arched "At least not yet."

"Good."

I didn't say another word until we walked over to a white, modernist building with a long tier of windows overlooking a large outdoor deck. "Follow me. And don't say anything." I spoke to her like I would a disagreeable child, but damn I didn't need her going all crystal guru shit on me or anyone else. "You can tell me what you think after we're finished."

She crossed her arms. Her mouth puckered as if she'd eaten a lemon.

I ignored her and pulled open the door and asked for the chief admissions officer.

"I'm Amanda Wright." A brunette in her mid-thirties turned from a bank of file cabinets. She wore a blue, long-sleeved knit dress tailored to enhance her hourglass figure. "How can I help you?"

Once I dispatched the formalities of being a police officer, without bothering to introduce Flores, Ms. Wright took us into her private office. She sat behind a streamlined wooden desk with a sleek tempered-glass tabletop, bent down, opened a drawer and took out a file. "I pulled Betsy's file this morning." She dropped it on the desk unopened. "I expected someone would come. What a tragedy."

Flores took the only other seat in the room and smiled up at me as sweet as Millie's cornbread lathered in syrup, and it took about all I had not to glare back at her. "Did anyone accompany Ms. Lamb to the audition?" I kept my gaze on Ms. Wright.

"That kind of information wouldn't be in the file." She leaned back in her chair. "But I can ask Byron."

I cocked my head.

"He's the grad student who was in charge of the registration on the day Betsy auditioned."

"But you interviewed her, right?"

"Yes. She seemed like a lovely girl." Ms. Wright licked her index finger and rubbed away a smudge on the glass. "She wasn't at all nervous unlike so many of our applicants."

"What did you discuss with her?"

Ms. Wright thumbed through the file. "We discussed her acting experience and went over our admission requirements. She interviewed very well; and I heard her audition was spectacular."

"When we're through, I'll need to speak to the judges."

"Usually we have two, but George was out sick. Pauline West saw her." She picked up her phone. "I'll let her know you're on the way up."

"Do you know if Betsy spoke to anyone else while she was here? Another student auditioning that day?"

Ms. Wright shrugged. "Not that I know of. We'd canceled the other appointments. All locals. But made the exception for Ms. Lamb. She'd flown in."

"Thanks for your help." I gave her my card. "Call me if you remember anything else."

On the way out, we caught up with Byron. He confirmed Betsy came alone and walked us to the elevator.

I didn't look at Flores as we went up. Yeah, seeing Mrs. Wright was a waste of time. She didn't have any new information. I was no wiser than I'd been when I arrived.

But psychic chick needed to know that answers didn't just appear out of thin air.

Pauline West's office was much smaller and more chaotic, crammed with books and pictures of a much younger Pauline with a couple of well-known actors.

At her laptop, she was lost in her own mutters.

"Ms. West."

"Oh." She looked up as if she hadn't even remembered we were on our way. "Call me Pauline." She was a frizzy-haired, middle-aged woman with dyed-red hair and turquoise jewelry. "Everybody does." She picked up a glass of water, her hand shaking slightly, and took a sip. "Amanda says you want to hear about Betsy Lamb's audition."

"I do." I moved a couple books off a chair. "I want to

know what she was like as a person."

"I saw her act." She put down her glass. "That's all. I didn't actually know her."

"Right." I pulled the chair close to her and leaned my arms on her desk. Interviewing is all about reading people, and this gal was a people person. She liked contact. I used what I could.

"What scene did she choose? Anything unusual?" Flores asked.

I glared at her to shut up."

"That's an interesting question." She leaned back in her chair and Flores shot me a smirk from the doorway. "I try to suspend judgment about an applicant, but that can be challenging." She spoke with a quiet authority that suggested intelligence and empathy. "The girl looked like a typical pampered teenager, so I expected something obvious—Juliet's soliloquy from *Romeo and Juliet* Act II, Scene. II. You know, 'Romeo, Romeo wherefore art thou Romeo.' Or Portia from *The Merchant of Venice*, Act IV, 'The quality of mercy is not strained.' Lots of girls do them."

"And Betsy?" I pushed record on my cell.

"She chose to do Puck from *A Midsummer Night's Dream*." Her gaze flicked from Alicia to me. "You know the one where he comes upon Titania doting on the ass, 'My mistress with a monster is in love.'" She shook her head, wrinkled her brow. "We don't get that as much. It calls for a combination of delicacy and bawdy humor. Teenagers can't usually pull it off." She picked through the files on her desk. "Here it is. Betsy's." She read a comment aloud. "Her Puck was beautifully androgynous and slightly inhuman."

"So, Cupid was armed and dangerous." I kept my tone light, but inside I wondered what the girl was really like.

Pauline West took another sip of water and put down the glass. Her hand steadied. "But the real eye-opener was her performance as Mother Courage in Brecht's play."

Alicia interrupted again. "What do you mean?"

It was a reasonable question. But I should've been the one asking. Flores wasn't a cop. She was a pain in the ass Simpson thrust on me.

While I fumed, Pauline stood and moved away from her desk. "Let me set the scene." She spread her arms wide, as if opening a curtain onto a bare stage. "Imagine this young girl. She'd just played a fairy. Ten minutes later she comes back in a grimy soldier's jacket with a bullet hole, and a ragged, shapeless skirt. Dirt and grease mucked over her forehead and cheeks. She's aged thirty years. Then she starts to speak."

Pauline West growled, spitting out the words of the play. Guttural consonants. Ferocious vowels. Fired with the force of a semiautomatic. She moved around like a boxer about to deliver a blow. All to make one simple point: virtue is weakness, vice strength.

As abruptly as the performance started, it ended. She looked drained. "Wish I had half that girl's talent."

"Seemed like a risk-taker and a shape changer." Flores said.

Pauline jerked her head up. "Yes." She covered her mouth with her hand. "Exactly." Her voice hitched and I worried that she might break down. I glanced at Flores, but, damn her, she just settled back against the door and crossed her arms.

I cleared my throat and eyed Alicia. "We need facts, not opinions."

"That *is* a fact," she answered.

Yeah, right.

I turned to Pauline. "Did you have any further contact with her?"

"As a matter of fact, I did."

"Can you describe it for me?"

"Sure." Ms. West tilted her head ever so slightly "She was sitting in the student lounge talking to a tall, muscular young man with long hair. He was saying something to her that made her laugh and nod."

"Was he a student?" Alicia, said, and I shot her a warning look.

"I've never seen him before and . . ." Ms. West stopped.

"And?" I prompted.

"He was young and very handsome. Sculpted cheekbones, and hair down to here." She put her hand to the middle of her pudgy neck.

"Color?" Alicia asked.

"Jet black. He had a day or two's growth of beard."

"Picture the scene." Alicia just couldn't stop talking.

"What else do you see?" I was determined to keep the interview in my control.

Pauline closed her eyes. "He wore one of those wife beater shirts. I could see his muscles. He was strong. He used his hands when he spoke. He had surprisingly delicate fingers."

"Rojas," Flores whispered.

This time I ignored her. "What was your impression of him?"

Ms. West opened her eyes, and they were blue and expressive. Maybe in an era where actresses didn't have to be rail thin, she could have been a star. I'd bet anything she had more talent than she let on.

"He looked a lot like Timothee Chalamet but not as pale. And he seemed old somehow. Maybe, it was his expression. As if he'd seen too much in his life. He seemed too knowing, not in a good way. I wanted to walk over and tell him to leave her alone." Her hands moved erratically. "But that seemed, well, stupid. Now I wish I had."

"We don't know if this is important, so don't start blaming yourself. You gave us a fine description. Enough for a forensic artist to work up a sketch." I shifted the chair slightly toward Pauline and patted her arm lightly. "Did you see them leave together?"

"No. I had student DVDs to watch."

“Thank you for your time,” I said. Ms. West sat back in her maroon chair. As we left, I noticed a vague expression of guilt remained on her face.

CHAPTER FOURTEEN

Carver

Driving away from the college, I felt pissed at Flores for interrupting. I was not impressed by her "insights" but glad we'd gotten a lead. And with Janice out, it might be useful to have someone to bounce ideas off of. I glanced over at her. Even if she was a novice. Even if she claimed to see beyond the fucking veil, which in my experience consisted of worms and maggots and a smell that could make a grown man vomit.

"This doesn't make sense." I grumbled more than spoke. "According to her mother, the victim was a studious girl with big dreams and strong focus. According to her father, she was a golden girl, just perfect."

"How well do you think they knew their daughter?"

"How well does any parent know their teenager?" I was sure Dani would never do something stupid and impulsive with a stranger. But maybe she would.

I shook her out of my head. This wasn't about Dani. "Would Betsy just walk off with a stranger like that?"

"I can't see it." Flores stared out the window, but I couldn't help wondering if she wasn't talking like it was a vision.

"But maybe she did. Maybe she'd checked into a flophouse so they could screw."

"Or maybe she'd known the man before. Friends with benefits."

I ground my teeth hard enough to crack a walnut. Dani better not be having these ideas. She was still a child. But the boys wouldn't think so.

"Perhaps the girl didn't have a choice." Flores' gaze peered into me. "Perhaps, her will was taken from her."

"By a rogue spirit?" I slapped the steering wheel to keep from laughing. I so didn't need to deal with a psychic all hot and bothered and weepy because the big bad cop didn't believe her. "Sorry, I'm not buying it." I grabbed my cell, called Lieutenant Simpson and put it on speaker. "Flores and I are driving down to Santa Cruz. I'm going to speak with the Waters girl." I expected him to say no, get her up here right now, you should have called the local police first, because he liked to give orders and he didn't like me. "I'm thinking there was something going on with Betsy Lamb, and her friend might know a lot more than she's told the mother."

"Right. Play nice with the locals, Carver. We don't have jurisdiction."

"Ten-four that, Loo."

When the call ended, Alicia spoke up. "Would you like to hear a story?"

I jerked to look at her. "I'm not five."

"Yes, but you have a lot to learn."

"And you're going to teach me?"

Women, all women, it doesn't matter if they are twenty, forty-five, or a hundred and two. They have a look they wear when they know they're right. She kicked off a shoe, tucked a foot under her leg and settled back. "When I was twelve, I ran to my mother and grabbed at her skirt. I screamed that Uncle Roberto's leg's been torn off. That his blood was leaking all over the street. My mother looked shocked. She said, 'You shouldn't say such things.' She slapped me."

I listened without making eye contact. "She was frightened." Her mother was superstitious. I, on the other hand—

Alicia leaned toward me. "Less than an hour later . . ." She pinched her thumb and index finger together and pointed them at me. ". . . someone called to tell us Uncle Roberto had been in a severe motorcycle crash. He'd need his leg amputated. Mami turned to me with a horrified expression, as if she believed my prediction *caused* the accident."

"That's ridiculous. You set her straight, I hope."

"I tried, but she didn't want to hear it." Alicia's face

darkened. "Discussions about spirits made her uncomfortable, and even frightened." Alicia's eyes brightened mischievously. "A very common response, wouldn't you say?"

"Wouldn't know," I growled. My foot pressed the accelerator. "What did she do?"

"She retreated to her bedroom. Proceeded to light candles to all her saints, to la Divina Providencia, and especially to a small statute of la Virgen de Guadalupe she kept on her dresser. She knelt down, hands clasped and lips moving silently. She prayed for my visions to stop."

Alicia touched her necklace as if to calm herself. "Even as a little girl, I understood what she meant. I suffered from a disease too awful to name." Alicia stopped talking and looked out the window. Maybe hoping I'd be impressed. That I'd come around.

Not likely.

I turned onto the Pacific Coast Highway. It was the most beautiful road I'd ever driven, with its hairpin turns and rugged, coastal rocks and beaches, its clear sun-dappled water. If it took a little longer to arrive at my destination, it'd be worth it. It would clear my head, banish thoughts of urine and death on Skid Row, and the image of the brilliant, drowned girl that loved the stage the way my Dani loved her art.

I kept driving, and below the water swirled. One wrong curve, and my car would be flying. I peeked through the side window. What was it like to drown? If it were Dani?

No, don't go there. Stick to the case. Someone had wanted to hurt Betsy. Someone had held her down.

"And the cover of the cistern was heavy." I hadn't realized I'd spoken out loud until Alicia chimed in. "How could he hold it up while he drowned her?"

"Don't know. She would've been scared, terrified, thrashing about." I'm not psychic, but it's easy to imagine what happened next. Betsy exhaled and white bubbles surfaced. Her agitation ceased, her eyes and mouth opened, and her pupils dilated. Losing oxygen fast, she made her terminal gasps. When it ended, she floated face-up. From submersion to death took roughly four minutes.

Alicia went back to staring out the window, up at the sandstone cliffs above us. For the briefest moment, I wondered how she saw the world. Did she perceive everyone and everything together in some strange mystical scheme? And if so, would that constitute a mild form of insanity?

I steered the car around a looping curve. What about the time of death? A slender girl, no clothes in cold water, that'd make the body grow colder faster, wouldn't it?

"Could Betsy have been drunk?" Alicia pried into my thoughts as if she'd read my mind.

"Maybe so. Drowning under the influence of alcohol is common." I felt a grudging respect for her. "I worked a case once of an elderly man. He got intoxicated, fell in a river. Alcohol causes a rise in skin temperature. The victim undergoes very rapid skin cooling, which may cause sudden cardio-vascular collapse. "But liquor or drugs wouldn't explain why Betsy ended up in the water tank.

We arrived in Santa Cruz after ten p.m. and checked into separate rooms at a mid-scale hotel less than two miles from the university. I arranged for us to meet Betsy's friend at eight a.m. the following day.

Cathy Waters attended a college located in the middle of a redwood forest. Alicia and I took an early morning run through campus, and she kept talking about admiring the unobtrusive, wooden buildings nestled among the trees. Me, I admired something altogether different but kept those thoughts to myself.

After a quick shower, change, and a stale cup of coffee, we arrived at the student union on time for our meeting.

"Sorry." Cathy showed up twenty minutes late, wearing a T-shirt and jeans, no makeup. She had a thick body, a boyish haircut, and a silver tongue stud. "My alarm didn't go off."

"Happens all the time." Alicia was already to go full force again, but I caught her elbow and gave a squeeze until she nodded.

The food court was packed with students laughing, talking, grabbing food or just hanging out. I pointed to a round table by a tree. "Let's sit over there," the hanging branches made it a quiet place to talk.

"How can I help you?" Cathy sat.

"Tell us about Betsy?" I eased down next to her.

"She's awesome." She stopped short. "I mean *was*. I still can't believe she's gone." She rubbed her upper arm to her shoulder. "You know there are just those people. The amazing ones. The beautiful ones. Talented and totally sane, although I don't know how she did it."

"Why?" I leaned forward.

"Her mother is a bitch on wheels." She spoke urgently, as if trying to convince me. "She divorced Betsy's dad because he wasn't ambitious enough. But Betsy stayed close to her dad. They used to go watch hockey together at the Candler Center. Sometimes he took me along."

"Betsy's mother said otherwise."

"She was so controlling. Betsy's dad would've kept it quiet all that time, so Betsy didn't get into trouble."

About twenty feet away, a boy sat down and dropped his backpack on a table. He pulled out a book and started reading.

"What else did she like to do?" Alicia said, and I rolled my eyes. Sure, it would've been my question, but couldn't this woman just stay quiet for two minutes?

"She was good at everything. School, sports, you name it. But except for acting, she didn't seem really *interested*. Not even boys, so much. She dated, but she told me she'd never gone all the way because she didn't like any of them well enough."

Cathy's last comment struck me. The sheets at the motel were stained, so she did go all the way.

"Was there anybody in particular?"

Cathy blushed.

"You loved her." It wasn't a question, and her blush turned into a full-on blaze.

"We'd fooled around a little, and I was stupid enough to hope she'd come here for me." Cathy looked at the ground and kicked a pebble away. "What a drag to find out I was an excuse for her to apply to CalArts."

"When did you know that was why she was visiting?"

"The day she left Peoria. She texted me about it. Said she'd be here overnight to say hi and head back to LA for the week."

"But you didn't tell her mother."

"Why would I?"

"Maybe because Betsy lied to her and used you as an excuse?"

"It wasn't a big deal." Cathy shifted in her seat.

"Did you follow her to L.A.?

"You think I . . . No!" She recoiled as if I'd slapped her. "My marine biology class went to La Jolla to observe the sea lions there. We're studying pinnipeds."

"What?"

"Marine mammals that have both front and rear flippers. We went to observe their behavior. Stayed for two nights. When I came back, I had to write a paper about it."

"And someone can corroborate your whereabouts?" I didn't figure she was lying but I did figure that if I made her nervous, she might give up even more.

She tilted her head and gave me a "duh" look. "Only my professor and the whole class."

"Did you talk to her again when she was in L.A?"

"She said she met a guy." Cathy swallowed. "Didn't tell me much, but I kept after her. She sent me an email. I kept it because it proved once and for all that I had no chance with her."

"Do you have it with you?"

Cathy turned on her laptop, found the email. "Here." She shoved her screen around so I could see.

. . . Listen, Cath. It was really great to see you. You were incredibly romantic and heroic when you shared your feelings. No doubt about it. And that's great. But I've thought about it, and my thing is this. I met this guy, Roberto Rojas. He's really hot. And don't get me wrong, you're cute too, but Roberto is like, cut. From marble. He's gorgeous. He has this beautiful face and this incredible body, and I genuinely don't care that he's weird. Course, I like you more than I like him, but Cath, I'm seventeen. Maybe it'll be a different story someday, but right now, I can't help myself. I never felt this way about a boy. He's a sex magnet. I just want to grab him and fuck his brains out. So that's where my priorities are right now. Sex, specifically with Roberto and not with you.

Alicia gave me the I-was-right look.

I rolled my eyes at her and turned to look across the table at Cathy. I felt bad for her. "Unrequited love is a bitch."

Cathy shrugged.

"That was the last time you heard from her?"

"Uh-huh."

"Thank you for sharing this with us. You're a brave young woman. I hope things improve for you."

"Me too."

Alicia looked thoughtful. "Did the note surprise you?"

Cathy tilted her head. "Yeah. Betsy never talked like that. Not about sex. It doesn't make sense."

Sure, it did. High school and hormones. Chemistry. You didn't need a science teacher to explain it.

When we'd finished talking, I watched Cathy walk away, feeling an unmistakable rush of excitement. I was getting somewhere. I felt ready to shift gears and find the man she'd met at CalArts. Roberto Rojas. He had a name now.

CHAPTER FIFTEEN

Alicia

Back at the precinct Carver and I climbed out of his car.

"I've got to write up a report." The stretch he took raised the front of his shirt and I caught a glimpse of his abs. "If I need you, I'll call."

I forced my eyes off his caramel skin. I knew his kind of man. He thinks he's smarter than everyone else. "I'll be back tomorrow."

I didn't wait for a response but took off down the road, hailed a cab, told the driver to take me to Greene Hotel, and settled back.

On Sixth Street, I jerked upright. An African American man leaned against the Star Apartments. Tall, slender, gorgeous, he reminded me so much of Carlos.

Four blocks away, I asked the driver to stop. I wanted to feel my approach.

Out on the sidewalk, I unwrapped my scarf, pulled off my sunglasses, tried to look like I didn't stand out, but with each step my heels screamed *I'm here*. Did I really think going to the crime scene would reveal anything? I raked my hand over my sweaty brow. Intuition told me something monumental was at stake, a shift in the life force of the city. If I kept going, I would hurl myself off the solid ground of my safe, private world, but could I stop? The girl's death had unleashed something I could practically taste. And I knew it had something to do with my brother's illness.

God, I wished for the tiniest ghost of a breeze.

A square brick building, the hotel seemed to sag in on itself. I expected chaos and destruction, but the closer I got, I saw and sensed neither. Just two relaxed-looking police officers talking to each other in front of the entrance. The tall one was blond with a buzz cut and sunglasses. The other was short and heavyset with basset-hound eyes framed by wire-rim glasses.

I dug around in my purse and hauled out a newspaper clipping about the crime. It was wrinkled but legible. "I work with Cindy Wyatt." I held out the article to them. "It's about the girl in the water tank." Neither of the police officers made a move to take it. "I'm doing a follow-up."

"So it's your story now?" The short cop's voice rose with the barely concealed irritation of a policeman who dealt with reporters and didn't much like them. "Have a press ID?"

"I'm freelance."

The short cop's mouth turned down. "A killing, and you snoops show up like flies on shit."

"Just let me in for a few minutes. I won't touch anything." I took a risk and leaned in, batting my eyes like the ingénue in a movie.

"No can do." He leered at me. "But when I get off, how about I buy you a drink?"

Not much of a flirt, I took a step back. "I don't drink."

The tall blond cop snickered

I shot him a don't-be-a jerk look. "I can help." I turned back to the short cop. Examined his face for a softening but found none. "I know I can."

"Uh-huh." He checked his phone, not bothering to look at me. "Move along, miss. We're not here for your entertainment."

I couldn't fool them. I couldn't charm them. It was time to come clean. "Maybe this will help." I held out my business card.

"Alicia Flores, Clairvoyant Intuitive and Medium," read the short cop. "Making Divine Spirits Accessible." He laughed and tapped his colleague lightly on the shoulder. "Hey, Pete, guess what we got here. A psychic. She's come to solve the case. What do you think? Should we let her in?"

"Sure, why not? This case is way too complicated for us dumb cops." He looked at me. "We may live in La-La Land, but we don't believe in supernatural bullshit."

My chin jerked up, and I gave Pete my best you-ass glare.

I had been frustrated, laughed at, and ignored before. Most recently by Carver. A couple of L.A.'s finest weren't going to intimidate me.

Pete's jaw tightened, and an air of anger exploded around me, hot and urgent.

I sensed it had nothing to do with me. I pushed myself deeper into his aura. He genuinely loved his job—the pursuit of the guilty, the click of handcuffs, the gun, the authority. Deeper, in the back of thoughts, a blackness formed around his home life.

"It's tough when you can't have the child you want. But adoption is a viable option." I touched his hand. "You should consider it." I felt myself nod. "You would make a good father, and she will leave you if you don't at least think about it."

He jerked from my touch and yanked his sunglasses off so hard I thought they might break. "What?"

I shrugged. "It's how my mind works."

"Why are you here?" He glared. "You know one of Marybeth's big-mouth friends?"

"Marybeth?" I saw her then. A pretty woman in a yellow sundress. She cried in a baby-less nursery. My heart ached for her and for him.

A car screeched around the corner and veered toward the sidewalk. I stumbled against Pete.

He instinctively shoved me to the side. Serve and protect. But he couldn't protect his wife from all her pain. He couldn't protect the women on these streets from the murder awaiting them.

"Pete," I looked up at him. "Just tell your wife you love her. It'll help."

"Right."

I walked away, and the hairs rose on my arms. The old building now hummed with dangerous potential, as if its spiritual energy tuned to an unknown spectrum of particles or waves that could communicate images of the past and the future.

Again, I saw the young woman in the tank. I saw her die. Coldness spread through me. I felt fear, anger, surprise, and an explosion of pain. Over the years, death had come to the hotel in many forms before. More would come.

I flashed on a young bride all alone in a room; I couldn't see what floor but saw her open a window. I watched her stare at the lights all across the city. Then she flicked her gaze to the street below. The warmth of the woman's breath carried the scent of anguish.

An ache filled my heart. Behind her, on the night table, sat a piece of crumbled wedding cake.

"You're wrong," I said, but my words couldn't reach the past, and she couldn't see that two blocks away her husband was headed to the hotel with a brown bag filled with boxes of Chinese food.

A band of sweat ran down my temple.

She pulled a chair over to the window. She stepped up.

I suppressed a scream.

Her body fell forward, plummeted for long seconds and landed on a parked car with a sickening thud.

I gripped my elbows and felt myself shaking.

The scene shifted to another room, larger, nicer, filled with men in dark suits and women in colorful taffeta dresses, mingling, laughing, and flirting.

A handsome man in a white suit and silk tie stood in the center of the room. His eyes sparkled, his arms waved, laugh lines crinkled around his eyes as he regaled a handful of entranced listeners. He finished his story, and everyone threw back their heads and laughed along with him.

A waitress wove through the crowd with a tray with crystal champagne flutes.

"My dear." He stopped her with a glance. "Do keep these coming." He winked. "One can never have too much champagne."

A wash of dizziness hit me. I almost dropped to my knees. The white-suited man repelled and horrified me.

After the party, a prostitute shimmied down the Greene Hotel's fire escape to meet him. As he pulled her over the railing, she stumbled and laughed.

He removed her clothes and assaulted her, and then wrapped her bra around her neck. He pulled the ends, strangled her.

Her body tensed. She tried to push him away. Her mouth opened. She tried to scream. Too late.

I closed my eyes to the sense of intoxication that ran through his hands, his power over life and death.

"But he seemed so charming," a woman from earlier might've said. And the mouths of his friends and acquaintances would gape and widen in disbelief.

Prostitute and bride had died many years before. It was too late to cry, but still I felt the sting of tears. Their suffering still permeated the air.

Even now, the suffering of the past attracted evil.

CHAPTER SIXTEEN

Carver

I sat down at my desk to write the report. I hated the paperwork. But I hated Simpson even more for foisting Alicia Flores on me. A few of my colleagues huddled in front of a television. Simpson sat in his office; blinds closed. For all I knew, he might've been absorbing gynecological mysteries from a porn site.

I picked up the phone to call Janice. Turned out she'd checked herself into her local hospital, Cedar Sinai. I called the hospital but couldn't get through to her.

I tapped my pen on my desk. Not good at all. I pictured Janice's round, alert face with its restless eyes and infectious grin.

The office felt cold, emptier without her.

I checked phone messages. The precinct EMT liaison left a voice mail that the Health Department told him there'd been an outbreak of disease at the Greene Hotel, and I'd need special equipment to return to the crime scene or interview suspects on site. Knowing this was a priority case with the brass, he'd worked to get me an appointment for 4:30 that afternoon with the city's medical officer.

I slapped my palm against my desk. I hadn't seen any signs of illness. Would I have to drag the psychic along? And what was the deal with her? Was she trying for headlines? Business? It didn't matter. Right now, I needed to find out how the sudden outbreak of sickness at the crime scene would affect the ongoing investigation. Then I'd see Janice.

As soon as I stepped into the L.A. Department of Health Services building, a harried-looking secretary directed me to the medical officer's suite.

Three floors later, I knocked on Dr. Jeffrey Cohen's office door.

"Come in." He didn't sound eager to be interrupted, but when I stepped in the air was toxic with the smell of disinfectant. "May I help you?" His tone changed from surly to obliging.

"I'm Police Detective John Carver. Your people called us in." I didn't wait for an offer but took the chair across from him. It was important to be assertive. Behind a sleek, metal bookcase, filled with shiny books about evidence-based healthcare and change management, was a wall decorated with degrees from Stanford Medical School and the Fielding School of Public Health (UCLA). He had the ability to influence the brass and determine how quickly my case would move ahead. I wanted to keep him off-balance.

He sat back, squirmed in his seat, and shuffled his papers. "Looks like we have an epidemic on our hands."

"Of what?" I leaned forward. "A water-borne disease from the dead girl?"

"No." Cohen fidgeted. "She has nothing to do with this."

"If it's not connected to the dead girl, how does it affect my case?" I pulled my chair closer and leaned my elbows on his desk. He couldn't look away even if he wanted to, and if his darting eyes were any indication, he definitely wanted to.

"We're implementing a quarantine for the Greene Hotel." He slumped back in the chair. "We've notified the courts, hospitals, and emergency medical services, and they're all ready to assist us. Our orders are based on protocols for controlling the spread of infectious diseases. As long as the outbreak is limited to the hotel, we should be safe. As we speak, my staff's testing residents for both latent TB and the full-blown disease."

I gave him a steady look. "So?"

"So, you're in an ongoing murder investigation. No doubt you'd like to continue working on it. But it's my job to make sure you, your colleagues, and the general public aren't subject to the risk of infection." He straightened. "I suggest you and your colleagues conduct interviews another way. From a monitor set up inside the hotel or by telephone."

"Not good enough!" I tented my fingers. "I need to

eyeball the witnesses." Tapped my fingers once, twice. "Gotta read their body language, and monitors don't cut it." I shifted in the chair. "I'll work with you, of course. But this is a murder investigation."

Cohen folded his arms. "I'm prepared to deny you *any* contact with hotel residents if necessary. You want to call the police commissioner and complain? I already spoke to him. Do you think he'll care more about a dead girl than a potential epidemic?"

Checkmate. I was the one leaning back, the one not wanting to make eye contact. I didn't like to lose. "Hey, your people wear protective gear. So what if I was properly equipped? You get to keep the public protected. I get to keep working the case."

Cohen nodded. "I don't see why not. But you must comply with all our instructions."

"Absolutely." I nodded twice for emphasis. "Suit me up as soon as possible."

"I'll have Dr. Khalil, contact you."

"Thanks."

He returned to the papers littering his desk. As I stood up to leave, it struck me that the Flores woman was right.

More people at the hotel were likely to die.

CHAPTER SEVENTEEN

Carver

I waited for Dr. Khalil to call. Seemed all I did was wait. Wait for suspects, wait for toxicology reports, wait for permission to run my case. Fuck all that.

I walked to the desk of our young computer tech. She'd told me she wanted to take the police entrance exam. "Melissa, pull up the Ortiz file and tell me what you see."

"Ortiz was born in Reseda in 1955 to immigrants from El Salvador."

I shook my head. "Tell me something I don't know."

She tucked a stray strand of mousy-brown hair behind her ear. "No criminal record." Her voice ran low enough that I knew she was skimming and not reading. "At least not as an adult." She looked up at me. "But he did pull juvie time. Got thrown out of high school after he pulled a knife on some white kid during an argument."

"OK, anger, resentment." I smiled. "You rarely get a jury to convict a killer unless you give them a motive." I hovered, staring over her shoulder. "What else did you find?"

"He lives with his parents. Shares a room with a nine-year-old nephew." She straightened. "That can't make a middle-aged man feel good about himself."

"How's he set financially?"

"Nada." Her forehead creased.

"Probably not. But if he owed someone a favor." I snapped my fingers. "Someone with an interest in the girl."

Melissa raised an eyebrow. Her fingers flew on her computer keyboard.

I leaned against the wall. If I could, I would've shut my eyes, but the station was too noisy with phone calls and cops. Everyone trying to do their job. Or not. A handcuffed teen shuffled past with his arresting officer. They passed a bald man with a raincoat, who shook his head.

"Wait a minute," Melissa said, "Juan didn't have a pot to piss in two weeks ago. Suddenly he's hit the jackpot."

I leaned over, looked at her computer. "How much?"

"Ten thousand dollars."

"Bingo. No way he made that money legally." A small kernel of hope grew. "And I bet he didn't inherit it, either. Did someone pay to have her killed? If so, why choose *him*? Why not Decker, the ex-cop?"

"Hey, Diggs." Diggs raised his head from where he finger-typed paperwork into the computer. Looking way too pleased at the interruption, he joined us at Melissa's desk.

"You mean Double Decker?" He snorted, a puff of air and then a cough. "The man lived on cheeseburgers and fries. Practically inhaled them. He really packed on the pounds."

"I don't care what he weighs. What kind of cop was he?"

"You've heard the rumors. We probably don't know half of it. He served with the LAPD for twenty years." Diggs gave me the look. The one cops know and understand about the things we don't say. "Never received a commendation. What does that tell you? Double D. had a reputation for being hotheaded. There were also rumors of racial prejudice after he killed an unarmed, black teen. Eventually, he was transferred to a white community."

"Any complaints of sexual harassment?"

"None that I know of." He pulled a tissue from his pocket and wiped his glasses. "But it wouldn't surprise me."

"Interesting." I grabbed my coat from my chair. "Decker knows where the video cameras are. It's not hard to imagine he could've been in the elevator with the girl. Made sure he wasn't seen. You knew him. Could he have done this?"

"Wouldn't count him out," Diggs shrugged, and I headed to the door. "Hey, where are you going?"

"Time for me to pay the man another visit. And Ortiz also. It would be interesting to hear what he has to say about the sudden cash infusion."

"Where's your girlfriend . . ." He waited a good three seconds before finishing the sentence. ". . . the psychic?"

I gave him the finger.

I got call from Dr. Khalil as I headed to the hotel. A short time later I pulled up at the entrance.

Red and white lights of a parked ambulance flashed on and off, like a Morse code. An EMT stood by as two ambulance care workers in protective white suits and goggles carried a stretcher. On it, a middle-aged man with pale skin and blank eyes had been fitted with an oxygen mask. At first, I'd been against wearing a respirator. Now my attitude changed. Sure as shit, I didn't want to catch whatever that guy had.

Dr. Khalil introduced himself, "Detective Carver?" A short man with a trim salt-and-pepper goatee put a swagger in his step and kept his hands at his sides. "I'm Dr. Habib Khalil."

I went for the standard handshake, but he waved me away.

"So, you're the guy who's going to fit me up in coveralls and masks?" I said.

"Just follow me."

We walked past the entrance to the street. I took a seat in the tent setup for the CDC. He explained the protocol for monitoring patients, then showed me how to use the mask and respirator.

Once encased in the mask, an odor of heavy plastic

and stale air assaulted me. My breathing became labored. I couldn't get enough air. It was like being underwater and experiencing a spike of terror when you aren't sure if you'll make it to the surface. I told myself to get a grip, just as if going into the hotel with a respirator was a normal part of the job.

Inside the hotel lobby, the white buffalo still stared. The ballerina still perched precariously on her swing. Medics' footsteps echoed in the large room. Exactly how many people were infected? I headed to into the once glamorous bar, and, as expected, found Decker propped on a too small stool for his explosive gut. His elephantine legs all but hid the spindly legs of the chair. "Look who's here." He turned his tiny gray eyes toward me. "Anyone with sense is trying to get out. So naturally you show up."

"Waiting for a clean bill of health must get boring." My voice came out muffled, like I was talking through a wind tunnel.

"What?" His white shirt stretched open at the collar and his slacks bulged at the seams. "Can't hear a damn thing you're saying." He shoved his sleeves up to his elbows.

I slid onto the stool next to him. "You must be bored," I tried again, turning on my iPad recorder.

"You bet." He took a long swig from the bottle of Bud. "But not so bored I want to talk to you again." He wiped his mouth on his hairy arm.

I nodded at the barman and held up one finger. "Not

even for another round?"

He belched, a long, growling sound.

"When did you last see her?"

"Three days before she was discovered. She was walking out the door. She had one of those computer backpacks. It was light blue, like her jeans."

"She didn't stop to talk?"

"No, never. There was no reason to talk to her, either. She didn't cause trouble."

I bet he didn't like it when pretty girls passed without noticing him. He sure as hell noticed them. "A lot of people cause trouble here?"

Decker snorted. "What do you think?"

"One reason you needed new video cameras in all the elevators. Who put them in?"

"I did." Decker's eyes narrowed. "A year ago. Why?"

"Just curious."

"I didn't do it any different from anyone. That's where most security cameras are. Drugs, blow jobs, you don't miss a thing." He was practically leering.

"You have access to the roof, right?" I asked.

"Never had a reason to go there."

I settled back into my chair, nodded at the bartender for another around. This motherfucker had access, so he had a key, and he was in control of the cameras. Pressing delete would take little effort. "Not even to see a nude sunbather?"

He shot me an angry look. "When I want my jollies, I go

online. Not to a fucking roof."

"She was a pretty girl."

"Yeah. So?" His face reddened.

"Maybe she didn't like fat old men coming on to her."

"Who said that? It's a fuckin' lie!" Decker pushed himself off the barstool. His agility startled me.

"You two fight? Maybe things got out of hand."

Decker's face reddened further. "Listen, dipstick, you got anything on me, pull me in. Otherwise, get off my ass. And by the way, you sound like a fucking robot."

"Remember, Decker you're not a cop anymore. You're a suspect."

Decker's flush subsided. He glanced at me slyly. "*You're* the one wearing the mask. *I've* got nothing to hide."

I turned away from Decker before I ripped off my protective gear and got in his face. I didn't do it for Dani. If I contracted TB, I'd have to stay away from her until I was cured. If I could be cured. Who knew for sure? Still, Decker irritated me almost beyond my power to control myself. I had nothing on him, not yet. But I sensed he was the type of cop who worked both sides of the street. He'd make deals with pimps to sleep with their girls. Even if they were underage. Especially, if they were underage. Every instinct I had told me the guy was a pervert.

Before I did something stupid, I left and headed off to locate Ortiz.

CHAPTER EIGHTEEN

Carver

Ortiz sat on his bed, watching TV, and I envied him the comfort, the relaxation, the ability to breathe. I was sweating buckets under this mask.

"Got a few more questions." I took a chair next to a scarred desk. Ortiz turned the idiot box off.

"Don't bother." I tossed the forensic artist's sketch on the bed. "Seen him?"

"Never seen the guy." He didn't look at me and damn. I'd hoped one guy would be helpful around here, but I dealt with liars all the time. Hell, I just dealt with Decker. "Is your name Juan Angel Ortiz?" I asked in my best polygrapher tone.

"Yes."

"You are forty-six years old?"

"Yes."

"You were born in Reseda in 1955?"

"Yes."

"Mr. Ortiz, do still you reside with your family in Reseda?"

"Yes." I could barely hear him. He answered as if admitting to a secret he wanted to keep hidden.

"And you currently work at this hotel?"

"Yes. You already know all this."

"Do you have a key to the roof?"

"Yes." He sat forward.

"Did you lend it to Elizabeth Marie Lamb or a friend of hers?"

"No." His voice rose as if trying to make me believe.

"How long have you worked here?"

"About fifteen years." He was calmer now.

"Are you saying you never, in all of this time, lent or gave the key to *anyone?*"

"No, never." He rubbed his upper legs.

"What do you think would happen if the hotel manager found out you had lent out the key?"

He looked down. His hands stopped moving. "Mr. Sahai would fire me."

"Is that why you're saying you never lent out the key?"

"No." He clasped his hands like a man praying. I swear. I'm telling the truth."

My voice rose. "Did you lend—"

"No." He straightened his back. "This job is important

to me, and I don't need you fucking it up. I did not lend the key out. Ever."

"I hear you." I turned off the iPad recorder. "I'm not trying to jam you up, but a girl's been killed." I put my palms up to appease him. "You know. Someone's daughter." My voiced hitched.

Ortiz nodded. "I know." He rubbed his hand across his face. "Got kids myself. They live with my ex-wife." There was something so desolate in his expression. I thought of Dani and guilt hit me hard. "Been awhile since I saw them." He sagged as if gut punched. Kids aren't the only ones who suffer when adults fuck up.

"All right. I see." I turned the recorder back on. "Let's continue. Have you been able to save a lot of money working steadily and living rent-free?"

"I do not live rent-free. I . . ." He raised his chin. "Contribute to my father each month."

"How much do you contribute?"

"Four hundred dollars for food and rent."

"How much do you make a month?"

"Sixteen hundred dollars. Before tax."

"Still should have a lot of savings."

"No. I play the horses." His smile was little-boy sheepish.

"Yep, damn ponies." I sat back in my chair. "You're up one day and down the next and the next and so on. You lose a lot?"

His shrug said something, but his glance at the floor said

a shitload. "So where did the ten thousand dollars recently deposited in your bank come from?"

"I win, too." His voice held a tone of defensive that didn't hide its shake.

"Good for you." I went slowly. "Must be nice to get bank every now and again." I sweltered in my protective suit. "So which horses did you bet on?" I kept my tone casual, one guy talking to another.

He shrugged. "Don't remember."

"You won ten thousand dollars, and you don't remember?" I looked at my shoes to keep from laughing. "Come on, man. I'm a cop. I could surely use some extra cash. Tell me who to bet on." Under the mask, I wore an expression of mock innocence. "If I won so much at one time, I'd be sure to remember it."

A nervous giggle leaked out of his mouth.

"This is a murder investigation." I folded my arms. "I must ask you, what did you do to earn that money?"

Ortiz glanced to the corner of the room, to the open door, then back to me. "I want a lawyer."

"That's your right. But it's too bad. I thought we were getting along so well." I stood up and went over to Ortiz. He ducked his head as if scared I'd club his bony carcass with my bare fists.

"Don't worry," I assured him. "You'll be closely monitored until you get a clean bill of health. You've been here for what, forty hours now? Another eight to ten hours and a healthcare worker will check your arm for a reaction to the skin test. Depending on the results, you might need further treatment. If not . . ." I wanted him to imagine the worst. That he'd be booked for the crime.

Ortiz's face froze. "I didn't hurt her."

"I feel bad for you. But you know, I feel a lot worse for the dead girl. I have a daughter. She's almost the same age as the murder victim. If you did this, you're going down."

I left without looking back.

CHAPTER NINETEEN

Carver

Back at the precinct, Alicia waited for me. As I drove up, she approached the car and leaned in to open the door.

I shook my head. "Don't bother, I'm just going to the hospital to see my partner."

"I'd like to go with you."

I faked a cough and covered my face so she wouldn't see I was pissed off. "Why? You don't even know her."

Alicia fiddled with her ring. "I'd like to. Besides, you're probably going to talk about the case. Maybe between the three of us—"

"There is no three of us." I raised my voice. And no, I'm *not* going because of the fucking case."

Alicia perched on the edge of the seat and bent over to tie her shoe. Then she turned to me. "She's a woman. Maybe she saw something you missed."

"Maybe, my ass. She would have said something."

"But would you have listened?"

I gave her a cop look, all steely eyes and no bullshit.

She just smiled as if I'd complimented her. She sat back. Her legs were crossed at the knees, and the top leg swung slightly, as if she were impatient.

She wouldn't leave voluntarily. I wasn't about the drag her from the car, so I took a deep breath. "Okay, Sherlock. I'm not going to argue about it."

She was still grinning when we arrived at the hospital fifteen minutes later. We walked through the glass doors and headed over to the information desk.

"I'm Detective Carver." I flashed my badge. "And this is my partner. We're here to see Janice Dean."

The clerk smiled at us with the whitest teeth I've ever seen. She looked down at the patient roster for Janice. Her jaw seemed to clench, twisting her face into an odd expression, then she yawned in my face.

"Here she is. Ms. Dean's in isolation. You'll have talk to Harry, an infectious disease nurse."

The muscles tightened in my neck and upper back. "Where do I find him?"

"Her," she said, then gestured to a set of elevator banks to our left. "Take the E Elevator to the sixth floor." She picked up a phone. "I'll let them her know you're coming. She'll meet you there."

Alicia held up her hand in a gesture to stop. "Can you

also check the name Carlos Flores?"

The clerk looked down again. "No one's here by that name."

Alicia turned and headed for the elevator. I followed her. "He a relative?" I asked.

The doors opened. "My brother. I thought he might . . ." In the suffocating silence that followed, it was obvious that she didn't want to talk about him.

The elevator came to a stop and a tall, curly haired woman stood waiting, her mousy brown hair starting to gray. "I'm Harry Grove. Short for Harriet." She shook hands with us. "You're here about Janice Dean, right?"

"Can we see her? "I asked.

She took off her glasses and held them up to a light. "I should clean these." She took out a wipe and rubbed the frames in a circular motion. Then, she said, "We do allow limited visitation. But Ms. Dean is in an isolation room, so you'll have to follow protocol." She set off briskly down the hallway, turned, and gestured for us to follow.

I hustled after her and tapped her lightly on the shoulder. We've heard it's some kind of TB. An unusual strain."

Harriet stopped. "That's right." Her phone vibrated. She looked down at the message before answering. "Doctor Mullen says we've seen strains with multidrug resistance to common TB drugs like isoniazid and rifampicin. But nothing like this before. It doesn't respond at all, not even to our newest injectables."

Alicia listened intently.

Harriet smoothed an eyebrow. "We've put her in a negative pressure isolation room. You'll go in from the anteroom where you'll put on Tyvek suits, N95 masks, and goggles."

"I've done this before," I told Alicia. "I can show you."

The nurse pursed her lips. "No, I will. People don't wear always wear the suits properly. They pull down their masks using unwashed gloves and/or contaminate themselves by removing the suit incorrectly."

I put up my hands in surrender. Dr. Khalil had shown me how to put on protective equipment but arguing with her could backfire. We were not Janice's relatives. Nurse Harriet might decide not to let us in.

Alicia gave me a strange look. While listening to the doctor, I'd been rocking back and forth without knowing it; now I stopped.

"Will she recognize Carver?" Alicia spoke in a low voice. I had to strain to hear her.

Harriet's fingers played with her stethoscope. "She's conscious but weak. You should keep it short."

"Fine. But I want to see her." My stomach felt icy. They hadn't learned anything new. And more people were getting sick. "So . . . what's going to happen?" I said to her.

"We're still waiting for guidance from the CDC."

Alicia let me take her arm, and we followed Harry until we reached a gray structure with a sign that said Proflex

Barrier Module. We entered the anteroom. I could feel air being sucked into the room under a closed door. White walls enveloped us on all sides but one, which held a row of hangers with black garment bags. Each contained a Tyvek suit.

"I'll show you how to put these on and take them off when you're done. And don't you worry," she said to Alicia "These panels are opaque. I'll get you ready first." Without looking at me, she went on. "Detective Carver, turn around and give the lady some privacy."

We entered Janice's room through a self-closing door that swung outward toward the anteroom. Janice lay in bed with her eyes closed. Above her head a fluorescent light made her face look pale. She was nothing like my partner. I'd worked with her for over a year. The Janice I knew was a bundle of energy. Alert as hell. Now she lay diminished, helpless. A plastic tube snaked out her right arm. Two pillows propped up her head.

She turned her face to us and opened her mouth as if to speak but started to cough instead—hard, gut wrenching coughs. A small, pink container that lay on her chest caught the bloody sputum. When she finished, her sheet moved with each labored breath.

"I had no idea," I said, feeling like an idiot. "Is there anything I can do?"

Janice gave me a wan smile. Her lips puckered, trembled.

"So wet and cold," she said.

From the other side of the room, I leaned forward to hear her better.

"Do you need help? I asked.

"Not me." She paused to take a breath. "The little girl. *Her* bed."

"You mean Maria Cordero? From the case?"

"Her urine, fear, they're connected." Her hand reached out to grasp a glass of water on the table next to her bed. She took a sip and put the glass back. Her head sank back into the pillows. She closed her eyes.

A whistling sound came from her throat; not a death rattle, thank God, but still. My heart began to beat like a drum.

"We should leave," Alicia said. After we removed our suits, we walked to the elevator bank. "Cordero, another lamb and another death. The two cases are related."

I waited to respond until we were alone in the elevator. "You saw my partner. She's dying, for all I know." My voice rose. "And you're here spouting bullshit. The cases are nothing alike." I pushed the elevator button harder than necessary. "Besides, we're not working the Cordero case. Diggs is the primary investigator."

"So, tell him."

"Tell him yourself if you see him."

CHAPTER TWENTY

Carver

After work, I cruised north from downtown on Interstate 5, past the graffiti-scarred cement banks of the L.A. River, swirling with water after the recent rain and flanked with cattails. I pulled off the Freeway and headed west on Los Feliz Blvd., past Griffith Park, and cut across to the 101, and headed to the Goldenberg-Zimon Center for Special Care in Reseda to visit my father. Sometimes a guy's just got to visit his dad. Even if his dad has Alzheimer's. Then the phone rang.

"Detective Carver." The familiar woman's voice ran to panic. "You have to go to your wife's house right away."

"What? Who is this?"

"Alicia. Rojas is there . . . *with Dani.*"

My hands gripped the steering wheel so hard they ached. It's not okay to be scared, but I was. But get the facts before—

Alicia gulped for air and then spoke in a rush. “Nothing happens by chance. I saw your daughter’s picture on your desk. Now I know why. So that I could recognize her in a vision. She was cleaning her paintbrushes. Rojas sat with a sketch she ‘d drawn of him. His amber eyes fixed on her. Don’t you get it? He’s there in the house. She’s in danger!”

My stomach clenched “Ms. Flores, I don’t have time to play games with you.” In the photo on my desk, Dani was wearing her school uniform and a big smile. A smile you couldn’t forget. The kind of smile that would attract even a crazy woman’s attention. “Are you stalking my daughter?”

“Of course not! But *he* is.” She raised her voice. “Please. Go!”

My pulse sped. If she was right, Betsy’s possible killer was with my daughter. Likely the woman was batshit crazy. I pressed the accelerator. I might be nuts too, but damn, I couldn’t take any chances. I texted Dani and hoped the traffic on Highway 405 wouldn’t be too bad.

“Come the fuck on.” Not sure if I was talking to Dani, my aging Toyota, or the cars ahead of me.

Minutes passed. Images of past crimes filled my vision. Dani still hadn’t responded. “Shit.”

I called again.

Again no answer. A single thought ran like a frightened rabbit. May I be spared the anguish of Betsy Lamb’s parents. I raced along, swerved past every fucking car. Crossed twenty of the longest miles I’d ever driven, then screeched to a stop in front of Eve's house.

I didn't bother turning off the car. I dove out and sprinted up the walk to where Alicia waited.

"Hurry." She grabbed my arm and hauled me to what once had been my front door. The door I once had a key to.

I knocked on the door. Pounded on it. I jimmied the lock, shoved open the door. "Dani."

No answer. I pulled my gun, stepped into the entrance. "It's Dad, baby. Answer me."

Alicia breathed. The ceiling fan whirred.

"Stay here." I inched toward the living room. I heard two voices talking. I rounded the corner, and there she was, my daughter. Safe.

Dani knelt on the carpet, folded her drop cloths, and put away her paints. A young man, standing over her, had almost finished dressing. Long hair, delicate features, and cold eyes, he was just as Pauline described.

"You son of a bitch."

I lunged at the guy just buttoning his jeans. "Coming on to a fucking teenager." Before he could blink, move, put on his shirt, I had him in a headlock and dragged him across the room. When I turned him around, the back of his head struck the marble wall.

For a moment, his eyes went entirely black, as if the pupils had swallowed the surrounding color. His knees buckled.

"Dad." Dani had looked upset when she saw me. Now

she sprang into action and grabbed my arm. "You're acting crazy." She yanked with all her strength. It wasn't enough to stop me. And it would never be enough to stop a pervert like this guy.

I let him go but gave her a stern gaze. "Maybe so," The harshness in my voice wasn't directed toward her, but still she jerked back. "You should have told me." I glanced from the half-naked Rojas to Dani. "I had to learn about this man from a virtual stranger. And you," I focused my cop glare on the predator. "Stay away from my daughter."

"You're out of control, Dad. He's not some random boy. He's a classmate. He paid me to do a sketch, so I invited him over to pose."

As if he hadn't just been attacked, the young man sat down on the pale gray sofa to lace up his boots. Then he lit a cigarette, but after two deep pulls, he left it smoldering in a spotless Hoya crystal ashtray. His scuffed black boots resting on a delicate glass-and-wicker coffee table.

I kicked his feet off the table. "This isn't your house."

He stood up again and yawned. "Why are you freaking out? I didn't touch your little girl."

I wanted to smack the shit out of him.

"What's your name?" I said, wondering if he'd cop to the truth.

He pulled another drag and blew smoke. "Roberto Rojas."

"You have a driver's license?"

"Who's asking?"

"A cop. And Dani's father."

He reached out into his back pocket and handed me his driver's license. I wrote down his number and address and flipped his ID back to him.

"Get lost," I said.

"Dad, you're embarrassing me," Dani said under her breath.

On his way out, Rojas picked up his knapsack and thanked Dani for the chance to pose.

"Sure," she said. Her manner had changed. Not annoyed or angry now, but not quite her usual self.

Rojas turned to me. "You've been such a fine host."

"I'm sure we'll see more of each other," I said.

"We might at that." His tone was as derisive as the look he gave Alicia. The kind that said I-know-you.

Whoa. Here was one of my prime suspects. He knew her. And Alicia conveniently knew he was in my house. Coincidence? Intuition? Bullshit.

"If anyone asks," he glanced at Alicia, "would you testify to police brutality?"

"I'll give you brutality." I powered my way toward him, but he ducked out and slammed the door.

"God, Dad. I can't believe you." Unlike Rojas, I could never intimidate my daughter.

"He's a first-class bastard." I went over to help her clear her art supplies before her mother returned home. I folded up her easel. It didn't belong in the living room, and Eve did not like to see anything out of place.

"I'd better go," Alicia made to follow the punk.

"Don't move." The growl in my voice was an order, and Alicia was smart enough to obey. My daughter, on the other hand, huffed and stomped over to the couch.. "I'll deal with you in a minute." I turned away from the woman who just knew too damn much about my case, following my daughter to the other side of the living room. "Damn it, Dani. You come back. Now."

Everything about the way Dani looked at me made me cringe, but better hate than grief. "Does your mother know you've set up a studio in her living room?"

Dani slumped into the sofa, scooted to the side, and stuck her bare feet against a cushion. "It's not like that. But if it *was*, I wouldn't have said anything. Mom thinks I spend too much time drawing. I have to be Little Miss Perfect."

I rubbed my eyes, suddenly tired. Time to be a dad, not a cop. Not an easy shift. A bit like Bambi slip-sliding on ice. I didn't do dad well. I lectured. I nagged. I didn't listen. After, I always thought, why didn't I give her space. But then . . .

"And you and this boy—"

"News flash, Dad. I'm not a little girl anymore." The hate invaded her tone. "You don't get to choose my friends."

"No, but I'm still your father. And I have this crazy idea that I should keep you safe."

"I thought Rob was cool." Dani bit her lower lip. She

wove her hands together in nervous circles, something she did as a little girl when she was torn between keeping a secret and blurting it out. "But when he arrived, things got whack."

My stomach tightened. I took a deep breath. "What do you mean?"

Dani glanced at Alicia. "Who's she?"

"She's . . ." I waved my hand in the air, unsure what to say about her.

"My name is Alicia Flores." She approached the sofa, knelt, and put her hand on the armrest. "I'm helping your father."

I didn't contradict her. I owed her at least that much.

"Dani." Alicia spoke in a gentle, sing-song voice almost as if coaxing an unwilling child out of her room. "I know how strange it must seem. You didn't expect to see us. But you've got to tell your dad everything that went on here. Otherwise, he won't know what he's dealing with."

Dani bit her lip. "I set up the easel in the living room. Rob laid on the sofa and faced that hideous burnt-orange-and-walnut painting. His eyes were like, calm. Empty." Dani's voice sped up. "You know how it is when I paint, Dad. My hand skims across the paper. But this was different. As if there were another hand moving mine. I could almost see it." Dani closed her eyes, as if to remember it more vividly. "Bony fingers. Skin like parchment. And the picture I drew was totally weird. I got Rob's body right, more or less, but the head . . ." She stopped and put her hands over her mouth. Her eyes were saucers. "God, it was so humiliating. He looked like a leopard. Round with a broad nose, widely spaced tan, brown eyes, and downturned mouth."

Alicia stood. She cleared her throat. "That's Sitr—"

I silenced Alicia with a glance. "You know that sounds crazy, right, Dani?"

She fiddled with her opal ring. "Yeah, I know."

I leaned forward and studied her face. She was telling the truth, precisely as she remembered it. It fit all too well with Alicia's wild story about the demon. *Okay, let's think this through. The boy Betsy Lamb met was Sitri. So was Dani's art student friend. The damned thing liked young girls and really got around.*

Except spirits didn't exist, and Alicia was nuts. Rojas was definitely involved in some unsavory business. He might even have killed Betsy, but he was never a demon. Demons don't need a driver's license.

"So what happened when Rob saw the picture?" I asked.

"For a minute, he went silent. Then asked if he really looked like that to me." Dani stared down at the floor. I said, "of course not but it was totally embarrassing."

I scratched my head. Empathy as a father outpaced expertise as a cop.

"Roberto squeezed my arm and asked if I were telling the truth. Like I would *lie* about that? I saw his face close up. He had this weird look on his face. Like something unexpected but enjoyable had occurred."

Alicia stood near the hideous, orange picture. Her arms were folded, and she stared at me. My jaw felt slack. How strange could things get? I'd heard and seen crazy things, especially in the precinct at three in morning. But this was my own kid, and it wasn't funny. I wanted to believe her, so I took a risk and abruptly asked, "Can you show me the picture?"

"He put it in his knapsack."

Alicia rubbed her forehead and looked down as if her fears had been confirmed. She stood aside, to the right of the sofa, facing me while I talked with Dani. She ran her fingers over the cold marble wall, but now she stepped to my side and stood over Dani. "What did he do next?"

Dani flushed a deep reddish-brown. "Rob muttered something. I'm not sure what, but it sounded like 'What you did here, I wouldn't have believed if I hadn't seen it myself.' Then he said, 'You want me to go, don't you?' It was like he spoke directly into my thoughts."

I didn't know whether to be furious or terrified. It was as if Dani had lobbed a grenade. I turned on Alicia. "How did you know Rojas would come for Dani?"

"The usual way," Alicia said. "I can't make you believe me, but I hope you will. Imagine that I can hear sounds beyond the range of your hearing or see colors that you've never seen and don't have a name for."

Dani shook. "You're a psychic? What's going on here?"

Alicia didn't answer. She was talking to me. "Think about it. What must have run through Sitri's mind when he saw his portrait? Amazement. He must've wondered how Dani could see him that way. And did he see or imagine a ghostly hand?"

"And whose hand did he see?" I asked.

Alicia's half-smile reminded me of the Mona Lisa. She knew but wasn't about to tell me.

Dani asked another question before I could press Alicia further. "Who's Sitri?"

Neither of us answered.

Dani looked at Alicia and then back at me. She must've sensed that the apparently inexplicable was nearly catastrophic. She went to her room without saying another word, leaving me staring at Alicia, as my world spun crazily off its axis.

CHAPTER TWENTY-ONE

Carver

Alicia left. The door clicked closed.

I needed to go to my daughter. I needed to see her and make sure she was okay. I needed to keep her safe. But I felt utterly drained as I moved sluggishly through the living room and up the stairs to Dani's bedroom. The gray staircase walls displayed artfully framed photos of various family vacations. Freddy's, not mine. At the top of the stairs, a picture window peered down at an elaborate Japanese garden.

I reached for her doorknob, then let go and knocked. I waited for her to answer and tried to calm my heart, which seemed to be beating double-time.

I opened the door. Dani lay on her bed with her legs pulled up to her chest.

I sat at on the side of her bed. "Relax. It's all right." I patted her shoulder. "You weren't in danger, and I was wrong to barge in like that." Truth doesn't matter shit all when a father's worried about his child.

"Yeah, you were." She gave a morose sigh. "But I should've told you. Or Mom. Then you wouldn't have gone ballistic."

Her head leaned against the palm of her hand as she glanced at me. "You were kind of mean to that psychic. And neither of you told me what's going on."

"Well, I'm not entirely sure myself." I rubbed my jaw. "Rojas seemed to know her. If he did, I don't know whose side she's on."

"But why would she have come unless she was trying to help?"

"I don't know." I smoothed her hair. "I'm not a psychic. Ms. Flores *says* she is. And you know what I think of that."

"I get it." She smiled, baiting me. "Suppose she could see the future. Stop crimes before they happened. You'd be out of work."

"You're sassing me." I mocked her with an angry face and pretended things were back to normal

I returned to the living room and called Diggs.

"What's up?" he asked.

"I was heading out to see my dad. But instead, I found the missing Rojas."

"Really? Where?"

"At Eve's. Dani was sketching him."

"Yeah, right." Diggs snorted. "Tell me another."

"No. I'm serious."

"Things like that don't happen by accident."

"It didn't." I picked up the dirty ashtray and brought it into the kitchen to wash. "Alicia Flores said Dani was in danger. She warned me. Told me he'd be there."

A long silence. "And was she? In danger?"

"Maybe. I've got the Rojas kid's address and license number. I'll bring in Pauline, the woman from CalArts who saw him with the victim."

"Why do you think he made a connection with Dani? Do you think the psychic's in on it?"

"I've thought about it. I'm not sure. But if we get a positive ID on Rojas, we'll be a lot closer to solving the case."

After I ended the call, I thought about Dani's sketch. There was no reason to mention it to anyone. It was nothing more than the product of her imagination. And Alicia? Maybe she *was* psychic. She'd been right about Rojas being at the house. But it didn't mean she wasn't involved. And it didn't mean right about anything else. Her suppositions about demonic possession made no sense, and Dani's confused account didn't constitute proof.

CHAPTER TWENTY-TWO

Alicia

Filled with gratitude that Aishe had helped Dani see the truth behind Rojas's handsome exterior, I lit candles, knelt before them, and said a brief but heartfelt prayer.

All praise to you, Mother Aishe.
I thank you for all you've given me.
May your wisdom
Guide me always.

Finally feeling relaxed, at least in the knowledge Dani was safe, I allowed myself a soak in the tub, a tall glass of wine before climbing out, drying off and slipping into my plum-colored Carine Gilson camisole. The perfect thing for a peaceful night's sleep. But the sheer, silky material scratched at my skin. I curled around in my bed like a cat, trying to get comfortable. Finally, I took off the camisole and dropped it on the floor.

An influx of cold air and pinpricks rose on my flesh. The bathroom faucet dripped, dripped, dripped. A smell of water and decay.

I caressed my breasts. Numb, without the slightest desire, I licked my fingers and slid them past my belly. I paused, as if teasing a lover, just before I drifted them through my pubic hair and into my wet, waiting body. My hand moved in light, effortless circles. My lips spread into a smile.

The bedroom door creaked open.

I did not stop.

"Very nice." The voice was a melodious tenor. "Don't let me interrupt."

My heart jerked, but I dug my hand deeper. "Oh God." My moan tangled with fear. My heels dug into the sheets, and I drew my legs up. I tried to stand. Get off the bed. My body wouldn't budge. My mind screamed. Standing over me was an ulcerated corpse.

"Relax and you will find more pleasure." He slid down on the edge of my bed.

My hand circled, tickled, and tugged. A war raged between my action and my wants. The lipless corpse's mouth opened. Its front tooth was missing. I wanted to howl like a madwoman, but the stench made me gag.

"I'm sure you'd prefer Rojas, but he has to take a short trip." The corpse held out its arms, so I could see the grayish-purple skin pitted by burrowing insects. "This is how Ramirez looked in the mortuary." He checked to see if I was listening, saw that I was, and smiled. "The air was still and close, the tile and Formica grubby. Dead spiders and mouse droppings littered the floor. Shrouds that should have been crisp, white, and neatly folded, lay in gray, untidy heaps. A pretty picture, don't you think?"

He stroked my hair and hummed. A bolt of static made my hair leap up at him, wrapping itself around his little finger. I shivered involuntarily as my slippery ride to the stars proceeded. My eyes closed momentarily. At the center of all this sweetness, I felt unspeakably soiled.

"Don't be upset, little one." He turned away. "And forgive yourself." He preened in the mirror over the dresser. "The body always betrays itself."

"Why do you want me to suffer?"

"I don't. I want to instruct you." His oddly musical voice trilled its r's, softening the harsh words. "No creature is so utterly and unconditionally mortal as man, no creature so pathetic in its knowledge of its own mortality. And none so abject as a woman intent on pleasure."

"Please go." My own voice sounded strange in my ears.

He bent his head and peered into my eyes.

I froze, equally attracted and repulsed.

"Why do you interfere?" he asked. "A creature like yourself, a mere human, can never escape its own inadequacy. Confront me and you will learn that the doors of Pluto's realm are always open. Your fall is inevitable. And I assure you, it is a fall from which there is no return."

Nausea gripped me, as if I were aware of a still greater horror to come.

"Do you want to know what it's like to *fall?*" Hate filled his voice, blazed up and forth, billowed from a dark, unholy place. "I came for Ramirez in the mortuary. Reached out to him with my talons and grabbed his fingers. We crashed through the floor. I combed through memory's cobwebs, digging my way through to his heart with my fingertips."

Sitri had no limits. And enough hate to descend on cities and diffuse through blood and womb and semen. "I fed on his despair."

I couldn't believe I let him see me like this, unable to fend for myself. I fumed in disgust at my vulnerability. I pulled back from my torment and let numbness blanket me, pushing away trembling that still lay beneath the surface. I stared at the Ramirez-corpse with disgust. If I must die, don't let this thing take me.

"Your resistance is admirable." He went into my bathroom and came back with a glass of water. "But now you must surrender." He cradled my head and held the glass to my lip.

I sipped the water, sat up, and vomited on the camisole by the bed.

"Despite my warning, you persist in seeking knowledge of me." He folded his arms. "I want to know why."

"I want . . ." I swallowed hard, tried to keep my voice locked behind my clenched teeth, but a power roared up from my stomach, seared my throat. "I've got to stop you from hurting people." My words burst out. "Like my brother."

"Of course, you do." He ran his rotting fingers down my neck "But that would be very foolish. If you persist, what happens to your brother will not be my fault." He stroked the space between my breasts. "What happens to you will be my pleasure." He jerked his hand away. "But not my fault."

He wrapped himself in a light mist. A rush of wings and twist of skin and flesh tore through the body. The corpse morphed, changed into Sitri.

Vanished.

I bent down and fumbled with the soiled camisole. I wanted to run out of the room, but my legs shook helplessly. I took short, desperate gulps of air. He'd invaded my home and made me pleasure myself. I felt unspeakably filthy in body and soul.

I was grateful that Dani hadn't seen or felt anything like this. And Betsy? She too must have been completely overwhelmed. The demon could pluck the strings of desire like a master violinist.

The hollow drum of my beating heart offered no consolation as I waited for the sun to rise.

CHAPTER TWENTY-THREE

Alicia

The next day LA had one of its rare thunderstorms. Rain and strong gusts of wind shook the trees, snapped the branches of small trees, and pelted the roof.

I showered. Tried to wash away the fear, only to lose myself again in the horror of what had happened. Still shaken by Sitri's presence, I wandered throughout the house as if I'd been set adrift. If only it had been a dream, and I was still safe and sound in my home. But it was not a dream, and I was not safe.

I gathered up a blue candle, a bowl of water,- a small cup of sea salt, and set them down in a circle in my room. "With the purifying power of water, with the clean breath of air, with the passionate heat of fire, with the grounding energy of earth, we cleanse this space," On the door to my house, I placed a golden hamsa—the Hand of the Goddess, its open right palm representing divine protection, the eye at its center, wisdom. Then I lit a bundle of sweetgrass, knelt, and intoned a prayer, repeating it three times.

"Eye of Aishe, watch over this house.

Palm of Aishe, strike the evildoer that seeks to enter."

Perhaps it was too late. Perhaps it was too weak to ward off Sitri. But I had to try. I couldn't bear it if he returned for my soul. I hugged my knees and rocked back and forth, back and forth. Back and forth. I wanted to quit, pack it in, and not be involved. Most of all, I wanted to feel safe. I wanted Sitri to forget about me. People were dying. Maybe even my brother, but I couldn't fool myself anymore. I couldn't possibly stop any of the awful things Sitri was doing. All I could do was antagonize him further.

I sat on my easy chair in the living room. Leaned it back and let out the legs. I closed my eyes like two tiny coffins. Above my head, the slow whooshing of the fan eddied the air. The ground seemed to open its mouth and swallow all sense of the here and now. I stood in the realm of Spirit.

I trudged through the dry reeds that came up to my thighs until I came to a small grove of palm trees.

Forty in all, I counted. Like the forty years the Jews spent in the wilderness, it's an image of radical transitions and transformations. And twelve springs, betokening Spirit's divine purpose.

By the water, I stopped and rested in that mystical space. It could have been three minutes. It could have been three days and three nights.

"You're in a pretty pickle, my dear," Aishe's wise, amused voice insinuated itself in my ears.

"Aishe." I said her name like a sigh of relief. "Why haven't you come to me sooner?"

Aishe stabbed her bony forefinger at my chest. "You were hunting Sitri. Not altogether seriously, I must say. You thought it was a game. Find the killer, and Sitri will disappear." Aishe flung out her arms. "Go poof! But now that he's hunting you, you're ready to run like a jackrabbit."

My eyes were closed. I couldn't look at her. "I'm scared. You know what's the worst thing. It wasn't anything he said. Not even that he can look like anybody he wants. It's the way he plays with you. Like being in the jaws of an animal. As if he were death itself."

Aishe nodded. "That's true enough. A human has no power against a demon." Her bright brown eyes gazed into mine, perkily, like a robin's. "But the spirit haunting you is part-human."

"So what?"

"So, I can share some of its human memories with you. Ramirez was fully human at birth. Back in 1960, he was born in East Texas swampland." Her ghostly fingers touched my temples. "His mother was prone to fits of anger."

My breathing slowed. My heartbeat stuttered. Such dizziness overwhelmed me. I lay back on the grass, looked up at the palm trees. "Tell me more."

"Better to show you." Her fingertips played across my forehead, cool, quiet, and soft.

Energy pulsed up and down my spine and swept through my limbs, and I hunkered in the corner of a house better suited for a shed than a home. Holes in the walls, the ceiling, the sink was full of dishes. My sight clouded with tears. "Mommy." Ramirez and I cried.

Mama's face closed in.

"No, Mama, no!" The teddy bear sat on its tiny, wicker chair on one side of a white Formica table. It couldn't move. We couldn't, either.

"What did I tell you, Ricky?" Mama's nicotine-stained fingers formed a fist.

Warm wet flowed down Ricky's and my legs.

Mama struck. Hard. Vicious.

A crack filled the air. Our noses broke. Our mouths filled with blood. Mama pushed us away. Our foreheads hit the linoleum floor. Blood poured down our chins. Our foreheads pounded.

"Get up." Mama pulled our hands and called 911, and we bled. We cried and when the medic came with his bandages and kind eyes, she watched him fix me.

"Silly boy." Her voice dripped with sugar. "Told you a hundred times not to climb on the dresser." She smiled at the paramedic, and he smiled back.

Time and space wobbled, lurched, and changed. I opened my eyes. Not to my room but to the grove.

Aishe sat next to me, her cool hands in her lap. Sweat coated my body. Even free of Ricky, even in the blaze of the sun, I couldn't shake the fear of an abused child. "How long was I away."

Aishe didn't look at me. She didn't answer.

"His mother . . ." I shook my head, confused. "She seemed like a different person with the medic. So calm. I could almost believe her even though I'd experienced the truth along with Ricky."

"He never had a chance." Aishe put her weightless arm on my shoulder.

My trembling ceased. "Even later?"

"No. His family was a cancer. He would have had to cut out the anger eating away at him. Not just once, every single day. Each time he saw it appear in himself he would have had to excise it." Her grip, though not there, felt unbreakable. "You'll have to dig deep to find what you need."

"And what is that?" I asked, with the sinking feeling that I didn't really want to know.

Aishe sighed. "Fortitude, if you hope to face him." She pulled away. "This time, just watch."

"No!" I jerked away from her. "I can't. I won't. I'll never escape if I fly back into that poor child's skin."

I zoomed into a mobile home. The small kitchenette, the

tacky, fold-down table, the dark-laminated wood, and rust-colored shag carpet.

Clouds of marijuana trailed through the stagnant air, and Ricky barged out of the tiny door that led to a tiny bathroom. His teenage self, no longer a child, slouched onto a beaten-up couch. Mike Ramirez took up the other end. I wasn't sure how I knew, but I know those two weren't friends and weren't brothers, but cousins.

Ricky leaned in as close as he could, and Mike told him a story about Vietnam. About how Mike was a decorated Green Beret.

"You've got the coolest souvenirs," Ricky flipped through a stack of yellowing Polaroids. Mike with a Vietnamese girl he'd raped and killed. Mike with the head of an old woman he'd pistol-whipped.

"I never knew what freedom meant until Nam." Mike's voice ran low, gruff, a whisper. "You can do anything you want. Anything. You can stick a gun against a woman's head and watch her husband's face when you pull the trigger. In a war, rules and laws count for shit."

My stomach heaved.

"Tell me more." Ricky held a picture of Mike with a Viet Cong's severed finger pointed upward, as if to say "fuck you" to the world. "Can I keep this one?

"It's mine.*" Mike took the photo back but kept on talking. His words were so evocative that I smelled blood and mud and rice patties in the rain. "My memories belong*

to me. You're old enough now to make your own."

"How do I do that?" There was a yearning to Ricky's voice. I wanted to hold him, hug him, tell him these weren't the memories he should long for, but I couldn't change the future, or the man he'd become.

Mike looked at his watch. "No time like the present. Let's go to the back of the house. We'll find one there."

"One what?"

"You'll see."

They stepped out the screen door in the back and down the steps. The lawn was covered with high grass and weeds. A huge log crossed the back fence and when Mike peered under it, he smiled. "Look at that, would ya?"

Ricky leaned closer, but I would've liked to lean back. A salamander, about five inches long with smooth, brown skin and cream-colored spots lay, eyes closed. Just a creature of the world, living a peaceful life, but there was nothing peaceful in this moment.

"You know what kind of salamander that is?" Mike asked.

"No."

"An arboreal salamander." His lips knotted a warped smile. "Common as dirt. Soon to be your first kill."

Ricky breathed faster.

I quivered by the screen door, wanting to escape.

"Here's what you do," Mike picked up a stick with two hands. "Pretend this side is the salamander's head and this

side its tail. Then you pull it, like so." He imitated stretching a tiny lizard. "You can rip it clear apart."

The salamander hadn't moved. Ricky picked it up.

Bile rose in my throat. I moved in to stop him but couldn't.

He pulled at the thin, permeable skin. The slimy coating made it look hard to hold, but then the salamander's belly split, spilling its tiny, pink organs.

"It was so easy!" Ricky smiled; his eyes were bright. His breath quickened, as if a new life was beginning. Not sensing my presence, he tossed the two pieces of the dead lizard in my direction.

My skin prickled.

"Good job." Mike laughed and clapped him on the back.

Ricky raised his right arm above his head and made a fist like a prizefighter.

When he stopped, Mike said, "Next time I'll show you how to kill a cat with a simple snap of its neck."

Even after Aishe brought me back to the quiet grove, my heart jumped from throat to bowel and back again. My intestines ached until I bent over and threw up. When I'd finished, I breathed so deep my lungs shrieked.

Aishe stood over me. "You're not done."

"No." I reached up.

She moved off. Her skin was a web of wrinkles. She rubbed tired eyes. Her eyelids drooped, and I felt a stab of fear so deep it was cathartic.

"I've seen more than enough already."

In profile, Aishe seemed taller than the palm trees. Tall enough, in fact, to block out the sun. "You can't be squeamish," she told me in a kindly voice. "You must trust your gifts."

"My gifts? That's a laugh. Look where they've got me."

Tiny muscles in Aishe's face shifted and she wore on her face a disappointment I'd never seen. "Don't whine, girl."

Before I could plead with her to stop the torture, I was thrust into an apartment.

Shut blinds let in no natural light, but in one corner of the room a lamp stood on a rickety, wooden table.

Ricky sat in a chair, a knapsack on the floor beside him. He sipped from a soda can. Spilled a little and wiped it off his upper lip. I hovered above, watching.

From somewhere in the back, Mike argued with a woman.

Ricky stood up, walked down the hall to Mike's bedroom, and spied on them.

Mike sat on the bed. "Fuck you, Jessie."

The woman swung at him. The veins in her skinny neck were distended, her face an angry red.

Mike clamped his mouth tight. He looked away from her, and then reached across the bed and picked up a pistol.

"You're lazy. You're useless. You bring your retard cousin

here, and I'm supposed to play mom," Jessie screamed.

Mike shot her in the face.

Ricky shook, breathed, and licked his lips as if he could taste the coppery tang of blood. He stepped into the room. "Jeez, look at her." He leaned over the corpse of a woman whose blood and brains soaked the carpet and my thought was run, hide, it wasn't too late, Ricky. Call the police. But he didn't He didn't throw up or run from Mike. He simply smiled at his cousin. "That's ultimate power, man."

Later, he helped Mike dig a hole in the basement. After, they wrapped the body in a sheet, dumped her in the dark, poured bleach, and paint thinner and lighter fluid on her body, filled up the hole, and cleaned up the mess,

Ricky returned home. He closed the door to his room, sat on the floor, and grabbed a pen and a piece of paper from his knapsack. He drew a black circle and placed black candles at the north, south, east and west sections.

Repulsion riveted me to the spot. He was summoning a demon; I sensed it was something Ricky wanted for a long time. Now, energized by what he'd seen, he'd found the power to go forward.

He turned to the north. "Renich Tasa Uberaca Biasa Ica." He spoke words I'd only read in books, and I wanted to clamp my hand over his mouth before he invoked Belial, the elemental demon of earth.

He reached under his bed, pulled out a knife, and pointed it blade up. Blue light sparked from tip to hilt. Ricky drew an inverted pentagram to capture the ambient energy in his circle.

The sky darkened. The bedroom window shattered with a quick boom and shards tinkling. Rain swept into the room, dripped down his neck, into his shirt, and trailed down his belly.

The walls seemed to bend inward, enclosing me in a prison.

I feared tight spaces. I feared the collapsing roof, the crumbling wall, the massive cave-in.

Ricky continued his summoning chants, invoking the demons of air, fire, and water. He rocked back and forth. Eager and impatient, he asked, "Which of you will choose me?"

A spectral body of brownish gold emerged. Its skin looked tough as the bark of an old tree. In the center of its black lidless eyes, spiders spun busy webs. Ricky's mouth gaped, slack with amazement. It wasn't what I'd expected, either. Not Lucifer in a fiery cloud, red-faced and horned, but a solemn forest creature of tangled roots and branches. But apart from books, what did I know of demons? Thank the Goddess that the thing didn't sense my presence.

"Aishe?" my voice reached back to the meadow. "Why must I see these things?"

If she heard, she remained stubbornly mute.

The thing before me opened a toothless, downturned mouth. "The demon you deserve. The one closest to your heart." It stretched out its hands, untouched by the raindrops sere leaves rustled.

"Sitri, demon of water." It cocked its head, and tiny roots in its neck entwined. "Surely you have guessed as much, Ricky." It tried to smile, but its mouth didn't curve upward toward heaven. "He can charm anyone."

The sinuous, enchanting sounds of a flute, Sitri's flute, filled my ears.

Ricky took a deep, satisfied breath. Elation transformed his expression, and I knew he thought he'd gotten all he wanted—had the power. I knew better. No mortal stood a chance against a demon.

I had to get away before Sitri sensed my presence. He would, for sure. And then God help me.

Aishe spirited me away, through the rain, and clouds, and the unchanging past. We flew by the springs where I'd sat. They'd all but dried up. The palms faded. The spirit realm rolled away. I sat on the grass. Aishe lingered by my side.

"It's good I saw all that," I said. "It helps me understand how Sitri came into our world. But not why. What does he want from us?"

"Who knows what a demon wants?" Aishe said. "Power, I suppose. The respect of his peers. Sitri didn't become a demon prince by accident. Over the centuries, he's fought hard for it. Gaining strength, gaining authority. Human pain gives him his power so he returns to our world whenever he can."

I slapped my forehead lightly with my hand. "You're

telling me that Sitri's presence on Earth is part of a long-running contest between superhuman beings?"

Aishe sucked air through her teeth. "Something like that."

"If so, how come demons aren't everywhere we look?" I asked.

"There are rules. Divine Being does not allow demons to run wild over humanity. They can't just show up. They must be summoned. They're not all-powerful. I've always thought they exist to test humanity. To make it stronger and more resistant, almost the way a child develops antibodies through sickness. Perhaps the amount of pain you feel in this world is a measure of your potential greatness. I hope so, child, because otherwise I would worry about you."

I stretched out my legs and glanced at her, confused.

"Of course, I worry." She put a bony hand on my shoulder. "You're so sensitive to other people's pain. I worry that the world asks so much of you and gives so little in return."

I felt my face flame.

Aishe vanished. I started to move again through space and time until I skidded to a stop in my living room.

The light seemed abnormally bright. I flopped down on the sofa and wiped sweat from my forehead with the back of my hand.

Tired, smelling funky, but heartened by Aishe's words, I climbed to my feet, limped to the bathroom stripped. Warm water cascaded across me, and I slathered shampoo into my hair. Maybe if I scrubbed hard enough, I could wash away the ugliness of what I'd seen.

"What a waste." Nothing I heard or saw, not even Aishe's explanation, told me how to fight Sitri.

I picked up a bar of Shea butter soap and lathered up and thought about giving up, staying home, cancelling every one of my appointments. Maybe I could move, hide, become a convenience store clerk in some out of the way place. Maybe, I could have a life.

The soap slipped through my fingers, swirled around the drain. If I left it there and let the water pound, it would be a waste. "Just like my gift."

As if Aishe was still in the room, still guiding me, I heard her distinct voice with its Catalan accent. "No matter how hard, your gift asks you to accept its demands. You've seen evil in the heart of an unloved child. If you spurn your gift, evil wins."

"You're saying I have to fight it?"

She didn't answer.

I picked up the soap. It was way too late to withdraw. I'd turned the corner somewhere. But when? Was it at my initial vision of the girl? Intervened to save Dani? When I turned to Aishe for help? It didn't really matter.

I was committed.

CHAPTER TWENTY-FOUR

Alicia

I dried myself off. I put on a fresh set of clothes and combed my hair, glowering at my reflection. "This is all way above your pay grade," I said to the woman in the mirror. When I was young, I had imagined myself driving along a road paved with the blessings of the universe and my own good intentions, thinking I was safe.

Now I knew the enemy.

"I'm not safe." But the road doesn't fork. I can't pull over and get out. That much was clear. But where was Carver?

I checked my phone.

No text.

No email.

No voice mail.

Carver was confident he could solve the case with nothing but *facts*. Well, I knew things he didn't. Evidence that he couldn't access or imagine might exist.

I went into the kitchen and put up a kettle of water. While it heated up, I opened a cabinet, pulled out my hexagonal tea caddy, and spooned the loose tea into an infuser. Then I poured myself a cup of chamomile tea, inhaled the aroma, and decided to regain control. Find out as much as I could about my enemy.

Or enemies.

My fingers flew over the computer keys. I read up on every crime Ramirez committed, plunging into the grisly particulars. I pulled a yellow legal pad from my desk and charted his victims, starting with nine-year-old Mei Leung. The girl had been found murdered in a hotel basement where Ramirez had been living in San Francisco's Tenderloin District on April 10, 1984. She was the first and youngest of Ramirez's victims.

Closing my eyes, I imagined her terror, as her small fingers with their pink nail polish vainly tried to fend him off. Her body appeared to me lying inert and unseeing in a room shrouded in dust, her feet splayed out in dirty shoes illuminated by bars of light streaming through a faded curtain.

The end of her world.

The doorbell rang, and I jolted. I slammed my laptop cover down as if I were hiding something illegal. I laughed. Illegal no, deadly yes, but now I had a client. A new client. And it had totally slipped my mind.

I pasted on a smile. “Tom Hillman?” I put out my hand.

Mr. Hillman had short brown hair and a well-trimmed beard. “Yes. That’s me.” He wiped his hand on his trousers and shook my hand.

“Please come in,” I said, but he glanced around the room, and scratched his neck like a foreigner deciphering his surroundings.

“Really, it will be okay.” A lot of my clients were surprised by my home. Too much TV, and they expected to find me seated in front of a small table, fingers resting on a crystal ball atop a cheap, purple-fringed cloth. Or a dark room with eerily colored light, dealing tarot cards next to a single eagle feather or a grinning skull. The most exciting thing in my home office was a Venetian blind that met with misfortune and now resembled a Japanese fan. Otherwise, there was nothing but white walls, plush carpet, a foot-tall dracaena with green-and-yellow leaves

“I’m not early, am I? He checked his watch. “You have a nice place here.” He spoke abruptly like a man unable to make small talk.

I ushered him to the living room.

He perched on the raised armrest of my sofa like an awkward condor.

I pulled over a chair and sat across from him.

“How did you find out about me?” I asked.

“I’m a record producer.” He put his hands on his knees. “Vanity told me about you.” He’d been looking down at his shoes. Now he looked straight at me. "She said you are the best."

My hand fluttered to my ear. "How kind of her to say so." Compliments unsettled me.

"Vanity told me how you promised she would find lasting love on her African tour. She thought you meant a man." He put his hand over his heart and tapped five or six times to mimic a throbbing heart. "But then she visited the orphanage and met Grace and adopted her. She says it's changed her life." He swallowed. "And she told me you can communicate with the dead." His voice dropped, and I had to lean forward to hear him.

"I must warn you." I settled back in the chair. "Sometimes I can help. But not always."

"I get it. People hear things they'd rather not know."

I nodded. "And sometimes the path is blocked. Maybe the client, or the psychic, isn't ready to find out." I usually can put clients at ease, but my own chest was tight, painfully so. A higher power is stronger than any murderer. "But I will try my best."

A negative force flowed into the room. The air was heavy with it. I felt stiff, as if made of wax and likely to melt away.

Hillman cleared his throat. He opened his mouth, but no words came out. He took a breath and started again. "We all make choices. But hers . . . I don't understand." His voice was ragged. "Six weeks ago, my mother committed suicide." His tone went matter of fact. "I spoke to her doctor. She wasn't sick. I spoke to her accountant. She had no money problems. I want to know why she did it."

"No doubt she coped as well as she could." I squeezed his hand. "And never, ever thought of hurting you this way." I touched my side. The pain had subsided, but it still felt tender. I blinked and Sitri slinked into the room. Light reflected in his amber eyes as his talons reached toward my neck.

I shifted in the chair. Tried to see past him, to distance myself, to close the door that he'd opened in my thoughts.

I took Hillman's hand. Looked into his eyes and then at the lines on his palm. Usually, a new reading is a joyous adventure, but now my mouth moved mechanically. I tried to pay my client the attention he deserved. But I had my own spiritual battles to fight, and I had no energy left over for anyone else.

Hillman waited patiently for me to speak, as if he were the therapist and I were the client.

My throat constricted and I couldn't breathe. I couldn't talk. I coughed, swallowed a choke. "I don't feel well. I wish I could help you."

Tight lipped, he looked away, stood, and nodded once, twice. "I'll see myself out."

I walked to the door with him. "Listen, I'll be on vacation for the next two weeks. But if you want to come back then, I will make time to see you. I'm so sorry you came all this way for nothing. Of course, I won't charge you for the visit."

He opened the door and then turned. “Thanks for your time. I mean that.”

I closed the door, leaned against the hard wood. Hillman had needed more than kind words, and I’d failed him. Carlos needed . . . I couldn’t even think of all the things Carlos needed. Or all the needs of so many people, with Sitri stalking the city.

CHAPTER TWENTY-FIVE

Alicia

I started pacing the living room. Sitri swam through my veins like a bacterium, a dark blue spirochete spreading disease. But to stop him, I needed to understand more, so I opened my laptop, thought a minute, and closed it.

I had no idea what more was, but maybe if I understood his victims, it might give me a clue to why Sitri chose them. And how he chose new ones.

I shut my eyes and prayed for the courage to withstand the horror. I bent down over all my notes on Ramirez. I sat down in front of the laptop, glanced through the articles and pulled those with photos of the victims. The first was Nettie Lang. I focused my attention on her picture until I was at her house.

It was a warm spring night. I stood outside her trailer.

The shadows of the San Gabriel Mountains hovered above a silent landscape.

I crept to the faded-yellow window. Inside, Nettie Lang sat in her wheelchair. She held a small mirror and tweezed two white hairs just above her right lip while the Tonight Show with Johnny Carson *blared from the box set on a low bench.*

Ramirez's pick-up truck wheeled into her driveway and kicked up pebbles.

I turned from Nettie.

Ramirez opened the car door. His shoes crunched the gravel.

Taking her eyes off the tiny mirror, Nettie cackled along with the canned laughter.

Ramirez closed the car door. He wasn't much older than the last time I'd seen him, but something was different. There was something meaner and harder about the way he glared.

I stood and watched. Hoped maybe his new mask would slip. Maybe his heart would beat with human feeling.

He didn't move. Not for the longest time.

I wished I could cross the span of time and space, touch his hand, tell him "Don't do this."

He crept into the kitchen and rifled through the silverware. Pots and pans clattered. In another drawer, he found something he could use. A hammer.

Nettie still didn't look up from her dressing table. She plucked another hair.

On Johnny, Doc Severinsen blew his horn.

Ramirez slipped into her bedroom.

Nettie turned to him, gripping the wheelchair's arms.

Ramirez bludgeoned with her hammer.

I shrank away, emitting a frail, unheard whine.

Nettie's sparse white hair turned red with blood.

Ramirez bound her with an electrical cord, went into the bathroom to pee, and picked up a red lipstick, inspirer of sin.

He smiled, opened her faded flannel nightgown and drew a scarlet pentagram on her flabby, white thigh.

I pulled myself away, returning to my study where I thought of the child whose face had set into an inhuman mask. Who'd taken the life of a frail, old woman so viciously and without remorse. It was horrible to see, impossible to tolerate. But maybe, just maybe, I could protect others from suffering Nettie's fate, or Betsy's. Anything I saw would only strengthen my resolve. I picked up a photo of a young woman.

Carol Smith glanced over her shoulder at a shadowy, hooded silhouette waiting in her kitchen. She reached for the phone to call for help, but the intruder's leather-gloved hands knocked it away.

I cringed, knowing what he would do and what she would feel.

The phone clattered to the floor.

The man grabbed her around the neck.

She thrashed.

He squeezed. "Swear you love Satan."

She opened and closed her mouth like a fish without water.

He threw her onto the bed, leaned over the bedside lamp.

She screamed.

His face, lit from below, expressed hate and anger. Anger that he pushed to his fists, pounded into her body until her screams grew silent and her body limp.

He laughed while raping her. Her glossy eyes stared at the blank wall. Then she quivered, and I think she heard him.

Hours later, when she was in the hospital with doctors and nurses and a cascade of police officers, his laughter was all she heard.

I thought about the laughter. I'd heard something like it years before, on prom night. But I hadn't been as brave as Carol Smith. I hadn't been brutally beaten. I hadn't reported it, and I still bore the scars. How much more she had suffered, and what courage it took for her endure in a predatory world.

But even predators become prey. The final article I held described how Ramirez was captured, but I could see it in my mind. And why Ramirez bothered with me now made sense in a perverted way.

A pregnant Latina waved a newspaper and shouted, "El Matador!" The killer. A small boy, my brother Carlos, clung to the woman's skirt, his tiny hands reached toward her waist.

Wide-eyed, Ramirez gazed at my mother, who would give birth to me six weeks later. His face stared back at him from the front page that Mother is holding. A curious calm settled over him. He stood and waited for people to notice. He heard the shouts of onlookers, and raised his arms with pride, as if glorying in his notoriety.

They recognized him from the newspaper my mother was holding. They converged like a pack of dogs, pulling him down. The crowd let out a hoarse roar and kicked and beat him without mercy.

A tooth flew from his bloodied face.

Mother put her hand over Carlos's eyes. She couldn't know I'd seen it all, though I didn't know what it meant and would only remember one thing.

Ramirez smiling.

I shuddered and put my hands over my eyes. I wasn't even born yet but somehow, he and I were fated to be antagonists. How could I have possibly known? Mami wouldn't speak about it. She was always secretive. She never told me about her life before coming to L.A. When I asked, she shook her head and said, "I want to forget." She never mentioned my father, except to say that he was no good and he drank away his earnings. But why not speak about *this*? Ramirez was in jail. We weren't in danger. And she was a heroine. It didn't make sense.

For Ramirez, the past was an all-consuming sickness. He had fed on violence, on pain, and on the suffering of his victims, even his own suffering. *If there was a hell*, I thought, *he would be set apart*. But what about me? His all too frail and breakable foe, the woman he targeted because my mother had found him out, or simply because I'd been there in her womb, an innocent, unknowing witness.

It wasn't fair. But life, when viewed narrowly, never is.

CHAPTER TWENTY-SIX

Carver

I didn't understand it myself. I'd been trying to ditch Alicia, but I'd decided to pick her up in time for the lineup. I didn't trust her, but figured she'd earned at least that much by pointing us toward Rojas.

On the way to her house, I passed a building of recently converted lofts near Spring Street. Busses wheezed and moaned, stopping to let people board. Across the street was a dingy, corner grocery; around the corner, a falafel stand, three bars. Cigarette smoke, car exhaust, and muffled sounds of rap wafted through my open windows. Two girls with long brown hair and matching leather miniskirts emerged from half-open doors with tuxedo-clad poodles.

Life in an ever-changing city.

Traces of an older Los Angeles appeared in the form of brick tenements. In the old days, the only thing holding them upright was the mortar between the bricks. But the force of an earthquake can grind mortar into sand. They say in the Long Beach earthquake of 1933, bricks shot across the street like cannonballs. It wasn't until the early 1980s that the powers that be decided either to retrofit or demolish brick buildings.

I swerved to avoid a gangly man in a blue suit lying face down on the street. I pulled over and hit the brake; the car screeched to a halt, and I was out and pulling him to the sidewalk and fumbling for my phone.

"This is Detective Sergeant Carver," I shouted at the 911 operator. "There's a man on Glendale Boulevard near Echo Lake Park with that new sickness going around. He needs to get to a hospital ASAP." I gently let him down on the sidewalk near the curb.

His breath came in short, quick pants. His eyelashes fluttered. I waited with him until an ambulance arrived.

With the paramedics taking over, I returned to my car and sat down. My fingers dug into the steering wheel, and I could feel my blood pressure rising. The air was so humid I felt as if I were breathing underwater. My throat closed. I was choking, as though I had tried to swallow something too large for my gullet. Blood pulsed in my neck. I couldn't breathe. I couldn't fucking breathe. I prayed I wasn't infected with whatever disease the man carried.

One of the paramedics came to the car. "Sir, how are you feeling?"

"I'm fine." I waved him away. I started the car. They were loading the man into an ambulance as I drove out.

It took a while to calm down. Twenty-five minutes, in fact. I passed the Intelligencia Coffeebar. An industrial-chic, red building on Sunset Boulevard, it's well known for the quality of its coffee in L.A., and I was sorely tempted to stop in. But I was already running late.

Alicia's house was set high on a ridge off the reservoir path, with a great view of the lake. It was homey on the outside, with a nice canopy of trees and a gate that looked like it might lead to a small, secluded garden in back of the house. I climbed a steep flight of stairs and stood at the front door; hand poised to sound the brass doorknocker.

Alicia opened the door. She wore an expression I couldn't read.

CHAPTER TWENTY-SEVEN

Alicia

"Sorry I'm late. Got sidetracked on the way." Then, Carver really looked at me. His mouth tightened. "What's wrong?"

My voice shook more than I wanted. My legs shook more than I needed. "Just give me a minute." I tried to collect my thoughts, unsure how to explain what I was feeling when I hardly knew myself. "I was tied to Ramirez even before my birth. In utero when my mother pointed Ramirez out, so he could be captured. My lips trembled. "It happened a long time ago. It's over." I took his arm. "We should get going." I picked up my handbag and prepared to leave.

He grabbed onto the door. "Wait a minute. She never told you, right?" He looked at me, gray with fatigue. "So how'd you find out?"

"The usual way."

"In a vision." Carver's shoulders seemed to slump.

I started to explain further, but he talked over me. "You mentioned a disease that was going to spread, and you were right. I saw one of its victims on my way over here. I had to call an ambulance."

"How awful. Do you think they'll be able to save him?"

"I'm not sure they know what they're dealing with. And it's spreading."

Poor Carver. He wasn't ready to deal, either. I pictured him as set in concrete. A man who'd built an inward bulwark against the supernatural. "I know you don't want to hear this, but it's all connected."

He roused himself enough to shake his head.

"You look tired," I said.

"It's the damn case. I can't get a read on it." Carver grabbed the doorknob. His fingers were strong but delicate-looking, the fingers of an artist. But he was a homicide detective. No doubt those fingers had closed over the wrists of felons, handcuffed those wrists together, and pushed their heads into squad cars.

"I don't believe in demons," Detective Carver glanced at the gray clouds spreading the sky. "But criminals can be devious. Maybe Rojas wanted to get to me. How better to do than through my daughter."

"Don't focus so much on Rojas. He was just bait to catch Betsy Lamb."

"Rojas is more than bait." Carver's brow wrinkled. "He's

not just a kid in Dani's class. He's smart. Cunning even. He plans his moves out in advance, like a chess player."

What kind of man was Carver? Cerebral. Tried to bottle up his feelings. Did he think of people like pieces in a cosmic chess game? If so, he'd be a knight, a warrior whose path was always honorable but never as direct as he would wish.

I followed him out and closed the door. "Don't forget Sitri. He's behind all of it."

"Sometimes you seem so . . . sensible." A dry cough came out, and Carver gripped the railing. "But then you talk about demons murdering people in the same tone you use when you asked why I was tired."

"Thanks for the compliment," I smoothed my hair back from my face. "I guess." Guess he could have come up with a better way to insult me. If he had, I would have told him off, but just then I sensed that Sitri was in the car with us.

He loomed closer and closer until his skin touched mine, melded with mine, and almost *became* mine. Just as suddenly, he was gone.

"What now?" He looked watchful, 'cop-watchful'. Like he was waiting for me to incriminate myself.

"Sitri's always around me. Like a shadow that grows larger and more frightening the closer it gets. I'm not safe anywhere."

Carver grimaced. "God, why can't I have a normal conversation with you?"

I laughed a full-blown laugh, like the child I hadn't

wanted to be, but though he thought I was completely nuts—been there many times before—he still sat beside me. He didn't stop the car, let me out, and speed away

I wasn't alone.

"It's not really as strange as you think," I said. "Nearly all cultures believe people can be afflicted by otherworldly spirits. Did you know about two-thirds of Americans agree that angels and demons play an active role in human lives?"

He shrugged. "Most people are superstitious. That doesn't mean they're right."

"No, it doesn't. But based on my experience, the line between the spiritual and the physical is very fluid. A doctor friend sends me her clients when they don't respond to ordinary medical treatment. But when they learn to accept a spiritual view of the world, they achieve better physical and mental health."

Carver's lips curved slightly as he swung the car onto Highway 101.

I kept my voice measured like my favorite female college professor. "It's been demonstrated in clinical studies both here and in the U.K."

"Interesting, but I'm not sure it helps me with the case." I sensed a slight shifting in the skepticism that held him back. With a little more time, maybe I could convince him that I was on his side.

I glanced at Carver. I wanted him to believe that what I felt, saw, witnessed would help him. I wanted him to stop thinking about me as a crazy woman playing at being a psychic. "It must be hard."

He looked at me with that cop-question look.

"So many innocent victims. So much responsibility."

"Bring justice for the dead, closure for the living." His shrug was anything but light. "That's what I'm paid to do. But yeah, it can be tough." He checked the rearview mirror before changing lanes. "You also seem committed to this case."

There's a look a man gives when he's fishing for something. Carver wore that look, and I wanted to wipe it off his face. I wanted him to believe that I was as earnest in what I did as he was, and I was not a fraud.

"My brother is an addict on Skid Row. Last time I saw him he coughed up blood. I begged him to go to the hospital."

Carver raised his head. "You think you can save him if the case is solved."

My eyes stung with tears. Carver's face blurred.

"Carlos, right?" His voice was gentle, almost a caress. "You don't think that you want to help your brother so much that you've imagined these visitations?" I heard a hint of superiority riding shotgun.

I recoiled, itching for a fight. Carefully, I put my hands on the dashboard, as if afraid too much movement would let my anger rip free. "I don't ask you if *you* know what you're doing." I kept my voice low. "You're a professional, right?"

He nodded.

"Well, I'm a professional too, and I know what I'm doing." I stared at him, letting my anger seep through so he'd pay attention. "I've given you the name Rojas. I've given you a connection with a murderer and the means he uses to act from beyond the grave. You don't want to believe me? Fine, don't." I was nothing to him. If it weren't for the lieutenant, he wouldn't be bothering with me.

As we approached downtown, the traffic became heavier. Anger leaked out of me, leaving me only a wish to get through to him. I softened my tone. "In your work over the years, you must surely have had some very strange cases."

"I have." He pressed the brake, slowing us further. "But no matter how strange, you don't solve them by chance. It's the result of small things coming together. A logical pattern emerges. This particular case is tough, but the longer I hang in, the greater the chance I'll break it."

"Life's not like that for me."

"Like what?" He still sounded like a cop interrogating me, but I also got the feeling that he really wanted to know what made me into a woman who believed in demons.

"I was coloring a picture of a flying fish."

He took his eyes off the road just for a second. They were deep and light and dark and all kinds of in between.

"I couldn't stay in the lines. Then I heard a *zzzt* sound and felt electricity flowing. A hand stretched out to me."

The car in front of us remained stopped. Carver didn't

take his eyes off it, but as if reaching out across the great divide, he pressed my wrist. "What was it?"

"Not what. Who?" I gazed at him, willing him to believe. "Aishe, my mentor in the spirit realm."

He gave me a sardonic smile.

I pulled away my hand. "Aishe taught me to see the future and guided me toward a deeper understanding."

Carver kept one hand on the wheel. He waved the other as if to say go on.

"She taught me this life was only our classroom. The next life is our real home."

There was some roadwork ahead. Carver casually switched lanes, but I knew he was cop attentive and tuned into my every word.

"Once I asked Aishe how divine justice worked here on Earth. She just laughed and said, 'We're all fingers of the same hand.'"

"Connected." He tapped his fingers on the steering one after another. "Maybe so."

"Definitely." I paused for emphasis. "It was Aishe's hand that guided Dani's when she did that drawing."

"What do you expect me to say? I've spent my adult life years seeing the shit people do to one another. I'm not about to start believing anyone out there cares what happens here." Carver shifted gears suddenly. "This happened when you were a child, right? Did you tell your mother?"

"Uh-huh." I fiddled with my purse. "She prayed for the

visions to stop. Then she gave me advice. '*Hija*, say nothing to nobody about you-know-what.'"

"She felt shame." He nodded as if to confirm his own thought. "Supposed you were crazy."

"So, she went to the highest authority she knew, Father Guillermo. He told her I was a very imaginative child, but that I'd outgrow these fantasies. Of course, he was wrong." Words suddenly tasted like ashes. "So here I am. Alicia Flores, Spiritualist. The daughter of a woman who thought until the day she died that her daughter was a freak."

"You're pretty damn unusual, but even I—a virtual stranger—can tell you're no freak."

I turned red. "Carver isn't a particularly Jewish name." I said.

He shook his head gave a little laugh. "Dad's last name was Karnofsky. He changed it when they married. At first we lived in Compton."

"Wasn't it . . ."

"Dangerous?" He scratched his neck. "Not so much at first. But then, yeah, so we moved to the West Los Angeles. I remember a fourth-grade history lesson. Caravans of men and women roped to each other. My ancestors. The other kids in the class were all white."

"I get it." My voice quieted. "Being different. If you're Latina, they say stuff like, 'Oh wow, you speak so well,' or 'They will really like you.' *They* being Anglos. Maybe we were more alike than either of us believed. "What made you become a detective?"

"It goes back to Compton. I was playing catch with my best friend. We were seven. One of my throws went over Petey's head." Carver's body tensed. "When he ran to get it, he was shot by a guy leaning out the window of a black Trams-Am." His gaze drifted away from me, as if back to the past. "Bullets sprayed the house. Petey fell. The car drove away, tires squealing.

"I raced home. Burrowed into my mother's arms. Told her what happened, I couldn't catch my breath, and she didn't understand until suddenly, horribly, she did."

I gripped his wrist, trying to convey what words couldn't.

"My best friend died that day, and I was left with the guilt." The line of his jaw looked less rigid. "If I hadn't thrown the ball so high, maybe Petey would still be alive."

"It wasn't your fault."

"I know that now. Anyhow, after the shooting, we moved to a safe suburb with a good school. Trouble is, dad thought of a good school the way white parents with white kids think of a good school, based on test scores and real estate values."

"What about your mom?"

"She let him talk her into it. She was scared for me. But when your kid gets called a nigger, you don't get to call it a good school, even if Stanford accepts him."

"After college you entered the Police Academy?"

"Not hardly," he chuckled. "Dad expected me to go to

law school. I did, but I was always a bit of a rebel. I quit my job with a law firm. Became a beat cop. Five years later, I took the detective exam."

Hope bloomed in me like a spring flower. "You can change your path. You can do things differently. Think differently. About the case, I mean."

"You're a civilian." Carver's voice was gruff. "You don't know anything about our work."

If I were a cat, I would've arched my back, clawed, hissed. "You know, you're absolutely right." Humans have other weapons, irony and mockery. "I don't know what justice means to a demon." I leaned as far back as the car seat allowed. "Or how you'd build a case against one." I crossed my arms. "And find a jury of his peers."

Carver's jaw locked down so tight, I could see the muscles working. I hadn't won him over. Yet. I would. I had to. He was the lead detective. If I could get through to Carver, I could find the human tool Sitri used to commit his crimes. Maybe weaken him enough to save Carlos, even prevent the epidemic he'd unleashed.

Bring peace to Betsy Lamb's spirit.

CHAPTER TWENTY-EIGHT

Carver

At the precinct, I led Alicia into the observation booth. "We watch from here."

Behind us, Simpson riffled through some papers, and on the other side of glass, a string of men soldiered along the wall. Arms at their sides, they stared straight ahead as if they'd done this a thousand times, and likely, they had.

Volunteers, parolees, and even police officers, we put lineups together from what we had. We dressed the suspects as the witnesses remembered. These five men wore identical black wife-beater T-shirts and jeans, just as Pauline had described. Rojas stood at one end.

I leaned against the wall, observed the men, all carrying a day's worth of stubble. All with olive complexions. I flicked my glance to the next room. where Pauline sat in the single folding chair. The air conditioner in my room hummed.

Pauline sat behind a one-way mirror looking at the men. Standing over her and conducting the lineup was Detective Bill Mitchell. He was not involved in the case, hence no bias

"I don't know which of these men is the suspect," Detective Mitchell said. "Or if the suspect is in the lineup at all. So, don't look to me for any cues. Just look at them and tell us if you can make an unequivocal identification."

Pauline sat back. She took her time, staring at each man, squinting a little, as if to hone in the slightest detail. Finally, her glance seemed to settle on the fourth man from the right.

Pauline looked at Mitchell. She pointed. "He looks a lot like him. But—"

"But what?"

"The young man I saw had dead eyes," she said. "No light seemed to shine from them. He noticed me when they were talking. He looked *through* me. As if I weren't even a person." She shivered in the chair. "No, this man is too normal. I'm sorry."

"Don't be." Mitchell grinned. "We'd have been pretty upset if number four had been your man. He's a rookie cop."

"Of course, he looks normal," Alicia hissed at me. "Because he was possessed before."

Instead of answering Alicia, I stared at Pauline, our plump, sad-faced witness—an actress, used to making things up and making them convincing. It worried me. Hell, lineups always worried me. Eyewitness testimony sways juries, but even the most confident eyewitness can make mistakes. In this case, Pauline didn't have much time to observe what was happening, let alone remember details. She didn't see a crime, just observed a conversation between a young woman she hardly knew and an unknown young man. Why *should* she remember it accurately?

Pauline turned toward the man at the end. Rojas. "That's him. Those eyes." She shook her head. "Why I didn't see it immediately . . ." Her voice trailed off. She looked at Mitchell. "It doesn't matter that I didn't know it was him immediately, does it?"

Looking at Simpson, I thought people who decide things too quickly are usually wrong.

Back in the other room, Mitchell reassured Pauline and thanked her for her cooperation. The men in the lineup other than Rojas were dismissed. Mitchell led Dani's classmate into an interview room and left. I told Alicia she could sit in if she promised not to say anything, and she agreed.

We stepped in and sat down opposite Rojas. He sat back and stared at us. "Do I need a lawyer?"

"I don't know. Do you?" I slid Betsy's picture across the stainless-steel table. "You were seen talking to this girl." I waited for a reaction, a smirk, anything.

The boy didn't even blink.

"The two of you went back to her hotel and had sex."

"Sex isn't against the law."

"So, you admit you were with her."

"Yeah, so?"

With an open palm, I struck the table. "It is with a minor."

"She said she was eighteen." He had a half-smile. "I'm not a bartender, yo. I didn't card her. And she was real cute, if you know what I mean." His hands shaped an hourglass. "Flawless skin." He seemed to have trouble keeping a straight face. "A little like your daughter's, but white."

My knuckles gripped the chair hard enough to drain blood.

"She didn't have much experience," he said. "But she caught on real fast." He sat back in the chair and stretched his legs onto the table. "All kidding aside, detective. I had no reason to hurt her. I wanted to fuck her, and I did. End of story."

I picked up the case file and threw it on the desk. "All kidding aside, don't give me your bullshit."

Rojas turned to Alicia. "You know, he's got it in for me. You saw him slam me into a wall when he found me with his daughter." Rojas tried to look innocent, but he couldn't hide a smirk.

I sat back like a chess player that's seen his opponent make an interesting move. Interesting, but not worrying. "You admit you had sex with the victim in the hotel where she was killed." I smiled, rolling out the words slowly for effect. "Maybe she wanted more than a few quickies. A commitment."

If the kid felt remorse, empathy, any fucking thing, it

didn't show on his face or in his appearance. No sit forward. No twist of anxiety.

"You kill her?" I got right in his face, shouting. Alicia moved to stop me, a second too late. "You were there when she drowned."

He should've jumped out of his chair and shouted he was innocent. But he didn't say a word.

"We have your DNA. It matches DNA on her sheets. Tell us what happened, starting from your meeting."

When I lied about the DNA, Alicia glared at me.

"I told you it wasn't me that killed her," Rojas's voice remained even. "Maybe it was that fat fuck who hangs around in the little room off the lobby." Rojas scratched the back of his neck. "She said he was always looking at her, and it creeped her out."

"Interesting. You notice him watching?"

Rojas shrugged. "Not really."

"Okay. Let's get back to you and Betsy. How did you meet her?"

Rojas licked the sides of his mouth. He flicked a glance at Alicia. "Can I have some water, cop-lady?"

"Just call me Alicia," she said, getting up and going to the water cooler. She returned with a brimming glass and set it down in front of him a little too emphatically.

"You've been brought up on drug charges. I don't care about that. This is a homicide investigation."

"Okay." Rojas's eye roll couldn't have been more clichéd

if he tried. "I sell drugs to students at CalArts and a couple other schools. I met the girl there. We talked for a while."

I sat back, stretched my legs. Now we were getting somewhere.

"I could tell she was interested in me. We went back to her hotel. I offered her some E but said she didn't need it." He shook his head. "Stupid of her. It makes sex amazing. But she was right. The girl was horny as hell."

I gripped the table, thinking of Dani.

Alicia put her hand on my forearm and my breathing slowed. "Okay, you fucked her. What happened next?"

"Nothing, man." He took a sip of water. Held the glass up to the overhead light as if examining it for spots. "The next day, I left. Around five pm, I got a business to run."

"No one saw you leave?" I asked. "Did anyone see you later? Someone who can verify your story?"

Rojas put his hands in his pockets. "Yeah, a guy I sell cocaine to at UCLA. Tim Johnson. If you press hard enough, he'll break."

"Okay, we'll check. Alicia, come with me. Rojas, you stay here. I'd advise you to stay put. There's a guard posted outside the door."

I went out of the room, followed by Alicia and bent over a desk to call Johnson. He confirmed he'd met Rojas outside of his dorm. When I got off the phone, Lieutenant Simpson tapped me on the shoulder. "What about Rojas?'

"Gotta cut him loose."

"No, you don't." Simpson growled.

"He's got an alibi. And the timeline doesn't hold up. He was doing a drug deal at UCLA when she was killed."

Simpson frowned. Shaking his head, he started to walk to his office. Then he stopped, turned, beckoned me to follow him. After he closed the door, he stood next to me, practically toe to toe.

"What's this about you roughing up Rojas?"

I flinched. "I found him alone in the house with my daughter." I paused for a moment to regain my composure. "He was modeling for her. She hadn't said anything to me or to my ex, so I told him to get lost. I wasn't gentle about it, but it was a dad thing, not a cop thing, and he didn't get hurt."

"The Flores woman will corroborate?"

I felt a stab of panic. Murmured something indefinite.

He beckoned to Alicia, who'd followed us, stopping just outside Simpson's office to give us some privacy. "Is Rojas telling the truth when he says Detective Carver used excessive force on him?"

Alicia shook her head.

"You saw nothing." Simpson's expression turned sour. "You didn't see him push the boy?"

"Well, there were some heated words, but that's all."

After a moment of excruciating silence, Simpson said, "You're a lucky son of a bitch, Carver. It's his word against yours *and* hers." His voice rose. "I think you're hiding something, and that she's covering for you."

"I'm not. Hell, you saw the kid. Did it look as if I'd worked him over?" I wasn't sure what to feel, resentment at Simpson for doubting me or gratitude to Alicia for protecting me.

"Excuse me," Alicia said.

Simpson watched her leave his office and walk to the women's rest room. His face had a puzzled frown. "Are you fucking her?"

I just looked at him. What had I done to him? Maybe he felt being black was a crime. Prejudice ran deep in the force.

"No, I'm not fucking her."

Simpson leaned against a wall. "What does she know about Rojas?"

"She's . . ." I made air quotes, "psychic. She knew he'd be at my ex's house."

"Did it occur to you that she might be in on it with Rojas?"

My fists curled and uncurled "Of course. Eight successful years in homicide should me give a little credibility."

Simpson either didn't hear me or pretended he hadn't. He sat back down at his desk and picked up some papers. He waved me away.

I returned to my desk and waited for Alicia to return. I put precinct politics out of my mind. When Alicia came back, she thanked me for letting her sit in on the lineup.

"Now you know Rojas was a diversion, a way to

misdirect you. Sitri's using another person to commit his crimes. He doesn't need Rojas anymore."

She picked up her pocketbook. "I'll grab an Uber," she said. "You've got a lot to process."

Three hours later word came to the precinct that Rojas had driven his car off the side of Angeles Crest Highway.

He was dead.

CHAPTER TWENTY-NINE

Carver

The following day the incident report was uploaded onto the office intranet. While all around others talked and joked, I sat my desk and started leafing through the pages. Rojas was a prick who could've hurt my daughter, but he wasn't a murderer—at least not Betsy's murderer. It felt right to at least know how he died. Alicia read over my shoulder. I'd called to let her know about Rojas. Neither of us believed his death was a coincidence.

The Crescenta Valley Sheriff's Station received a call at 5:56 pm indicating a vehicle had driven off the side of the highway near mile marker 27, near La Cañada Flintridge, A fire crew responded but was unable to reach the Ford Mustang at its resting point some five hundred feet down a steep canyon. Montrose Search and Rescue responded to the scene and were able to access and examine the vehicle.

A driver who witnessed the crash said the car accelerated out of the turnout and continued to pick up speed as it moved downhill before careening off the side.

"Nice of Rojas to close the case for us." Simpson perched on the edge of my desk and nodded hello to Alicia.

My coffee mug was nearly as empty as my case. I leaned back in my chair. "That's entirely too convenient, don't you think?" I added the *you fucking, lazy SOB* in my head and slurped up the dregs of stale brew. "He didn't act guilty or suicidal. And why should he? He didn't do it. Not unless he could be in two places at the same time."

"You never see the big picture, do you?" Simpson folded his arms. "The mayor's chief of staff told me the girl's mother forwarded an opinion piece." He laid a printout on top of the accident report. "She's thinking of sending it to *The Los Angeles Times*. She's even prepared to pay them to run it as an advertisement if necessary."

"Crap." A self-indulgent article wasn't what I needed. I picked it up.

On a hot August day, one week ago, I learned my eighteen-year-old daughter, Elizabeth Lamb, was discovered floating face up in a water tank of a Skid Row hotel.

Why she stayed there, and who could have killed her, remains unknown.

All I know is that she never returned to her home in Illinois alive. I was racked with guilt because I had let her travel to California to visit her best friend attending college in Santa Cruz. If I had gone with her, she would never have stayed in such a place. Today, she would still be alive.

I have asked myself how I might turn Elizabeth's tragedy into an act of devotion to her memory.

Last year, ninety percent of homicide victims in L.A. were black or Hispanic youth from low-income neighborhoods. I am, therefore, filing a lawsuit against the L.A. Police Department for discriminatory and negligent disregard of crimes that take place in poor neighborhoods. Further, I believe that every victim deserves his or her own day in court, no matter how long ago the crime was committed. Hence, I am requesting that all unsolved murder cases that contain forensic evidence that has not been sent to a crime lab for analysis be sent immediately.

To the families and friends of homicide victims push with all your heart for their cases to be reopened. Get your loved ones' names in the paper to prod—even shame—the authorities. Only when you raise your voices will you be heard.

I handed it back to Simpson. "Apparently, Ms. Lamb has the same lineage as the Great White Shark, but instead of fish, she eats and spits out cops and politicians."

Diggs winked at me. His desk was next to mine, and he'd heard our conversation.

Simpson didn't look amused. "We got to get a clearance

on this." His voice was clipped.

"I get it." I made my voice soft and soothing. "This case is high priority, but let's look at this rationally. She sent the story to the mayor's office. I don't think she's ready to file."

Simpson tilted his head, considering. "She just wants to make sure her daughter's case gets the attention it deserves."

"And take a look at this," I pointed to a note in the incident report. "When they examined the wreck, they found a nicked metal line. Enough fluid could've leaked out to empty the master cylinder so the car wouldn't brake."

"You mean it might not have been an accident? "Alicia said, looking smug. She was convinced that Rojas was another of Sitri's victims.

"Tricky to orchestrate sudden failure after normal operation." I slapped the desk with my palm. "You'd have to cut a brake hose to a precise depth where it would hold pressure under moderate braking, but rupture with vigorous braking. It's damn hard but it can be done. But you'd have to know where your victim would be headed."

"What was that Rojas said about you slamming him into a wall?" Simpson said. "Maybe you cut the line yourself."

"Give it a rest, Loo. You talked to Ms. Flores here. The kid was just messing with you. And I'd hardly would have pointed out the possibility it wasn't an accident."

Simpson grunted. He turned back to his office. "Just close the case before the mother goes to the newspapers. Our asses are on the line. Yours especially."

CHAPTER THIRTY

Carver

"Time to get wasted." Diggs picked up his windbreaker. "My treat." He looked at Alicia. "You too."

From the other side of my desk, Alicia smiled. "All right." She opened her purse, checked to make sure she had her wallet, and added, "I'm in."

I offered to drive. "You don't got enough cash to pay for all the beers I'm going to need." I pulled my badge from the desk drawer. Shiny and brass and meaning something. But my lack of progress on the Lamb case made me feel incompetent. Like a fraud.

With the case gone cold and Diggs offering a drink, which I so needed, the three of us stepped into Off the Track Bar near Smuggler's Cove. The deep, plaintive sound of a foghorn sounded in the distance. Even from the outside, the bar pulsed with energy. The place was a dive, but it was always crowded with hardworking men and the scent of salt and rotting fish.

Inside smelled of burnt meat and used grease. "Bad Moon Rising" blared on an old-time jukebox that had actual forty-fives and a bass turned so loud shouting was the only way to communicate. We passed the bartender, a thirty-something woman, sat down at a rickety table, and ordered a bunch of Buds. Diggs cracked jokes about coked-up drug dealers, but I just slumped against the chair.

Five Buds in, Diggs slammed his beer on the rickety table. "So, Carver, what do you think?"

His words slurred over the question, and Alicia didn't look to be in any better shape after two. Her glasses had slid down her nose.

I pushed them back into place.

She gave me a vague, boozy smile. "He thinks he's messed up. He let Rojas loose, and now the kid's a goner."

"That's supposed to make me feel better. The little shit didn't do it." I put down my glass. "And I think, once we're done drinking and bullshitting, I'll get some sleep. The fucking case will still be there in the morning, but my head will be clearer." I glanced away. Across from us sat two Vietnamese fishermen eating mackerel. "Let's talk about something else."

Diggs downed the rest of his beer. His ring glinted in the smoky light. It was big, and ugly, a typical class ring that kids used to be so proud to wear. His had a huge CPS engraved in the gold.

"You were a Catholic school kid?" I shook my head. If you were Catholic, lived in Texas, and your parents had cash, you went to Cistercian Prep School and usually onto Notre Dame. Typically, you didn't end up policing gangs. Then he came to L.A., and his first job was policing gangs. *That* was a mystery.

Diggs smirked. "*Ex favilla nos resurgemus.*" His voice rumbled over the syllables, his pronunciation far better than mine. I'd taken a year of Latin for SAT prep and hated every minute of it.

Alicia poked him in the ribs with her elbow. "Pray tell us poor heathens, what does that mean?"

"From the ashes we will rise."

Alicia wobbled a little in her chair. "Who will rise? Rojas?" Or . . . ," she pointed at me.

Diggs smiled at her. "Who knows?"

"You two seem awfully chummy," I said, feeling oddly discomforted. "You actually getting any work done, Diggs?"

"Someone is." His sonorous voice rose. "I talked to the Cordero girl's teacher. Turns out Maria started acting out in class about the middle of the year. Especially targeting a little boy named Jose. Said his thingy was as tiny as an eraser." Diggs tilted his glass from side to side and watched the beer slosh back and forth. "Remember her stepfather's name?"

"You think he abused her? Did it to shut her up?" Dads who hurt kids were the worst. *Did I ever do anything that hurt my daughter? Nothing like that, of course; but did I ever silence her unwittingly, make it hard for her to trust me?*

"Yeah. And we found the knife. With her blood and his prints." Diggs emptied his glass of beer and slamming it down on the table, "You'll never guess where."

I sat back; legs crossed. "OK. Where?"

"At the bottom of a drawer in the Guatemalan restaurant he cooked at."

Alicia's eyes widened. "You mean he prepared food with the knife he used to kill his daughter?"

"That's so fucking cold," I said.

"No, it's stranger than that," Diggs said. "He didn't remember putting it there. When we found it, he was floored."

"How's that possible?" I wondered.

"I told you," Alicia said. She turned to Diggs. "The two cases are connected. Sitri possessed the killers. They're not responsible."

Diggs just signaled for another round.

I held up my hand. "I'm done. Remember, I'm the driver." I turned to Alicia. "Let's keep it light. No more supernatural talk."

Alicia's eyes blazed. "Don't do this. Not to me, not to yourself. If you avoid the truth, you'll keep drifting around the edges. Never catch the killer or stop Sitri."

I looked at her and saw something that, however

misplaced, was courage. She had her beliefs, and nothing would shift her from them.

But I didn't want to hear about demons. So, Diggs and I sat around swapping stories about the various brain-dead, drug-infested denizens of our trashy cul-de-sac in the shallow end of the city's gene pool and the questionable means we had of setting things right.

"Hey, Carve. You want to feel better, write letters to people you hate, like Simpson or your ex's husband, and burn them." Diggs tried to keep a straight face.

"Did that, but now I don't know what to do with the letters," I said.

Diggs played an imaginary drum set. "Ba-da-bam!"

We couldn't stay all night. The other tables were already emptying out. Plates still laden with half-eaten food hadn't been collected, including the scraps of mackerel from the next table. The bartender wiped down the bar. She saw me watching her and winked. I shifted in my chair, embarrassed that Alicia might've noticed.

Diggs dropped his AMEX card, paid the bill, and we staggered out.

CHAPTER THIRTY-ONE

Carver

I drove Diggs back to the precinct and stopped in one of my apartment's guest parking spaces.

"One for the road?" I asked, and Alicia surprised me by agreeing.

As we approached my apartment, her hand brushed against mine. I stopped. Her eyes were heavy-lidded. Her lips parted. I kissed her lightly, and the moment propelled us through my front door. We passed a sink full of dirty dishes and onto my small, hard bed. She touched my cheek. My skin had toughened with the years, but she didn't seem to care. Like two teenagers we groped, fumbled, went for a long kiss.

She broke the kiss, pulling away. "You'll need to be patient." Damn, the huskiness of her voice made me want to do everything but take my time. "Haven't done this in a while." Another long kiss, and she tensed up and disengaged herself from my arms.

"Be patient. I haven't done this in a long time," she said.

"Me either."

"I'm practically a virgin."

My grip tightened on her back. "Practically isn't." I pulled her closer, but when she struggled, I made my touch gentler. "What happened?" And, of course, something happened. She was a beautiful, intelligent woman in her late twenties. "Tell me."

"I haven't been with anyone. In high school." She dropped her chin. "I was raped by my date at prom." Her voice felt so far away, if I didn't have my hands on her, I wouldn't believe she was real.

I settled her in the crook of my arm. "I'm sorry." I had no intention of being the one to bring all those memories back to life, but she touched my chest and ran her fingers across my belly.

I tensed up, but my prick went limp.

"But don't let that stop you." She ran her fingers along the waistband of my boxers. "I've always wondered what sex would be like if you actually wanted it. Somehow, with all that's going on . . ." She lowered her voice, slurring slightly, "I'm not scared anymore."

"This is not right. You've had too much to drink. Any other time, I swear—"

"Don't swear. I'm tired of talking to dead people. Tired

of feeling half dead." She lowered my boxers. "I'm no saint."

"Okay. If you're sure."

She nodded.

"We'll take things nice and easy. If you want to stop at any point, we'll stop."

My caution proved needless. I caressed her hair, her forehead, felt my way over her eyelids, and fluttered over her cheekbones. The curve of her lips captivated me. I tried to move slowly. She looked at my penis as if she'd never seen one up close before. She caressed it with her hands and lips, spread her legs, and rubbed it between her thighs.

Afterward, Alicia put her head on my shoulder. "I didn't know it was possible to feel this close to someone."

"Thank you for trusting me." It was all I could think to say.

She covered herself in my white robe and walked to the kitchen for a glass of water.

I saw her through the open bedroom door. She was looking at the white appliances and beige walls. I sat in the rumpled bed sheets.

"You're not one for color, are you?" she said, her voice warm and amused.

"That's what you think." I took her arm and led her over to the spare bedroom. Alicia jaw dropped open. On each wall was a painting: an accurate two-dimensional rendition of a green rhinoceros; a rainbow-colored unicorn made from scraps of crepe paper; a dingy gray wall covered with jagged black cracks; pink and yellow fish in a blue-green sea.

"First time I've seen you at a loss for words," I said.

"What *can* I say but *wow*. It's incredible."

"You know my daughter's an artist. I think I mentioned she's got in a gallery show that's coming up. Every time she visits, the room changes. For a while, she did nothing but paper-mâché animals."

Alicia smiled, as if picturing a miniature zoo.

"This room's her sanctuary. And mine, too. When I see too much suffering, I come here to recover. It calms me down . . . I'm curious. Do you feel it, too?"

"I'm not entirely sure what I'm feeling." She put her hands over her chest. "I've never been in a room like this. So much fun, and yet so very audacious! It would certainly come as a relief after a harrowing day." Alicia gave me a sideways glance, her forefinger rubbed against pearly white teeth. "It's beautiful, but we're not done yet."

After breakfast, Alicia put down her mug of strong, sweet coffee, walked over to the chessboard, and idly picked up a black knight,

My hands balled up. "Put that back."

Her shoulders seemed to tighten. "Why so angry?"

"I shouldn't have snapped at you. But this is a famous match from 1927. Alekhine defeating Capablanca for the World Championship. Every move happened for a reason.

It's not something you just change."

"You play all the pieces, black and white both. You don't need a partner?"

"It's not like that." I moved to her side and gave her kiss. "I've been alone for a long time."

CHAPTER THIRTY-TWO

Carver

I dropped Alicia at her house, gave her a quick kiss, and told her to take the day off. Then I got the hell out of there.

Stupid, stupid, stupid. Even though it was consensual—hell she made the first move—I should never have slept with her. She was fragile. She was a colleague. Not the smartest move on my part. But she was damn beautiful and smart.

I couldn't help it

Ortiz would be coming to the precinct in less than two hours. There was nothing like putting guys in an interrogation room with a dusty 100-watt bulb glaring down on them to loosen their tongues. Just as expected Ortiz, in a suit and tie, fidgeted in the straight-backed chair. His lawyer sat rigid.

"We're prepared to answer all your questions," Lawyer dude, a whippet-thin youngster with long hair, jumped right in. "But this is a homicide investigation, not a drug case. My client wants immunity for any statements regarding the use or sale of illegal drugs."

"Take it up with the DA's office." I flipped to a fresh page of my notepad and clicked the top of a city-issued pen.

"That it? That's all you've got?" The lawyer turned to Ortiz." And you want my client here to cooperate?" He closed his file and put his palm down on it. "Then we have nothing to say."

"And your client will remain in custody."

"No, man," Ortiz whined. "I gotta get out. I'll tell him what I know."

The lawyer signaled reluctant agreement, and Ortiz went on. "A year ago, a member of the Bloods paid me a thousand dollars to lend him a key to the roof. From time to time, they'd smuggle something down wrapped in a tarp. The ones that didn't make it through I guess." Ortiz's glance went to the door.

"So you saw . . ." I immediately thought of an acronym I'd heard in the morgue: A-D-A-S-T-W—arrived dead and stayed that way . . . "bodies?"

It could have been paranoia on his part. In any case, he'd never thought to mention it to anyone. Whatever went on up there was probably as illegal as hell.

"Don't know for sure." Ortiz loosened his tie. "Figured it was better that way."

I nodded. Gangs don't look kindly on squealers. "Who paid you?"

"A guy called Snake." He twisted uncomfortably and scratched the stubble along the line of his jaw with a hand that shook. Don't know his real name."

"Where can I find him?"

"He came to me. And I didn't ask questions."

I jotted down a note. I'd ask Diggs. As an experienced cop who'd previously served with the area gang unit, he'd know Snake's whereabouts.

"Do you think the girl was killed by a gang member?" I asked.

"Maybe." His face paled. "Don't know." He bit the nail on his forefinger and then took a quick, deep breath.

The room must've been ninety degrees. I could smell his sweat. The stink of his fear. He put his hands out as if to say I know nothing. And further, if I did, I'd be too scared to say.

He gripped the arms of the chair and looked ready to bolt from the room. I sympathized. I wouldn't have minded being out on the street. It was probably at least ten degrees cooler there. But I had a case to close.

"Well, you've answered one question. We know there's another key out there. And you still have to explain the other nine thousand dollars sitting in your account."

"That's where the drugs come in." Ortiz pulled a coin out of his pocket. "Decker found out what I'd done and blackmailed me." He fingered it like a worry-stone. "Made me sell drugs."

"And the money you deposited?"

"We split the profits." Ortiz sat forward and pulled at his shirt. It must've been sticking to his back. "That's the money I made."

"But then you stopped." I kept my voice low. "What happened?" I leaned into the table so close I could see his white whiskers and smell booze on his breath. I thought there might've even been a slight scent of pee.

Ortiz shrank back. "Got a visit from Snake." The urine scent grew stronger. "So I quit."

I couldn't find fault with his decision. Ortiz was playing a dangerous game, beyond his ability to control, and he was smart enough to know it.

"What about Decker? Did he quit?"

"I never asked."

"You weren't curious?" I stuck the knife in. "Didn't give a shit about a poor, dead girl." I twisted just enough to make him squirm. "Guess you don't have a kid of your own." I rammed the point home because I'd read his file. I knew he had three daughters, and one was just the same age as Betsy Lamb. "Guess you never thought it could've been Rafaela in that water tank."

His face twitched like he was holding back tears. "Why you say that?" He clasped his hands. "Of course, I care."

It didn't feel like an interrogation room anymore. More like a tiny, infernal hot box. The gray walls seemed to lean in. I had a new lead and should've felt hopeful, but my brain lurched around without hope. There was no proof anything happened up on the roof of the old hotel, just suppositions. Nothing definitive connected Betsy Lamb to a gang yet.

"My client's cooperated fully. If you don't have any more questions, we'll be going," the lawyer said, rolling his pen between the palms of his hands.

"All right, you can go." I nodded to Ortiz's smug, smooth-faced lawyer as they left. I thought of getting a warrant to search Ortiz's apartment but decided to track down Snake instead. Diggs would know how to find him. At least, I hoped so.

CHAPTER THIRTY-THREE

Carver

Within two hours, Diggs had tracked down Snake at a bar called Leather and Lace. A sign on the door announced that it was *Show Us Your Ink and Get a Drink Night.*

When Diggs and I stepped inside, it could've been midnight or 10:30 in the morning. That's how gloomy the place was, with a grimy wood floor covered with sawdust and puddles of spilled beer. All around men with three-dot tattoos or swastikas clutched women with rose tattoos on their shoulders or legs.

Diggs lifted his arm. Raised two fingers and shook them back and forth toward the corner of the room where a tall, lean, and well-muscled man with greasy hair and a Fu Manchu mustache stretched out, boots on a battered table. A tattoo with the letters *obbyq* stretched up his left forearm. I looked at Diggs.

"Don't deal with gangs, do you? It's a 13/13 cipher. You replace each letter by its partner thirteen characters further along the alphabet. The tat shows he's a member of the Bloods."

Snake narrowed his eyes and clenched his jaw.

Diggs gave a polite nod and walked over. I followed. When we sat down for a friendly chat, Snake threw darts of ill will at us. We sure as hell weren't in Kansas anymore. A topless, middle-aged woman walked past, sporting a skull with a pink bow on each breast. Her blackened nipples served as the skull's eye sockets.

I felt like a school kid, afraid to be where I didn't belong, and anything could happen. My hand moved to the bulge in my jacket where I kept a 9mm.

A tiny blonde, with the word "outlaw" written in script about an inch below her belly button, brought Snake a beer. Diggs smiled up at her, but Snake kept his eyes firmly on him. "Whatever you want. Don't know nothin' about nothin'."

"Did you ever see this girl?" I slid the photo of Betsy across the table. "Maybe she saw something on the roof of the Greene Hotel? Something she shouldn't have seen?"

Snake spat, adding to the mess on the floor.

"Relax. Sergeant Carver's investigating a murder at the hotel. You may have heard about it. The girl drowned in a water tank."

I glanced away. Looked up at the thick wooden beams on the ceiling, wondering if they'd collapse on our heads. I cleared my throat. "We heard the Bloods got a key somehow and used it to initiate new members. That true?"

"That's some burnt-out, banger bullshit." Snake rose.

"All I want to know is how many keys are floating around and who might've used one to kill the girl."

"Fuck you." Snake turned to leave.

"Wait." Diggs held up his hand. "We just want to know if you heard anything."

Snake stopped and sat back down. "Don't trust cops." He pointed at me. "Don't even know you." He pulled a drag of his cigarette and let a smoke ring out. "Ya'll pin this kind of thing on guys like me even though I got nothing to do with it."

The smoke ring floated in the air between us, warped into an oblong, and disappeared and I just sat there. Didn't contradict. Didn't say shit. Sometimes that's just the best way.

"Sure." Snake went from cocky son-of-a-bitch to jittery snitch. "Got a key." He pulled another lung full of cancer. "Bought it for a fair price and keep it safe." Another smoke ring, another warping, another vanishing. "We don't fuck with civilians there."

"You never saw the girl?" I asked. "Never sold her any drugs?"

"Yeah, I saw her." Snake laughed. "She was all yappy and loony, calling an ounce an onion. Like in, 'Where can I get an onion?'" He cracked up. "What the fuck is an onion?" He turned serious, and a note of pride entered his voice. "Tell me what you want, and I'll hook you up. That's my thing." He stuffed his pack of cigarettes back in his pocket. "I don't kill."

"So, did you? Hook her up?" I asked.

"If she got, it was from someone else. Maybe Decker." Snake picked at his front teeth with a dirty fingernail, "That lame-ass fool got a hotel room and claims it to be his hood 'cause he rents a room. He ain't got *shit*."

"Thanks for your help." I dropped my card and a twenty on the table, but before we even stood up, a short, stout black man approached, rubbing his nose. He wore a blue dress shirt with white cuffs and sleeves. He didn't bother to introduce himself. *Bloods and Crips, we're in for it now*, I thought, tensing up.

Diggs whispered. "It's cool. Gesture means no guns." He dropped another fifty on the table and led me out the door.

I got back into the car with a small kernel of rage. Diggs didn't seem to think Snake had anything to do with Betsy's murder, and he knew a hell of a lot more than I did about gangs. I was spinning my wheels and getting nowhere fast. Okay, so Snake confirmed Ortiz's story. He claimed that he hadn't fixed Betsy Lamb up with drugs but that maybe Decker had.

Just as Diggs was about to start the car, I turned to him. "So, how did you know we were safe?"

He turned on the ignition. "Get me some coffee and

doughnuts, and I'll tell you."

"Doughnuts are the last thing you need."

Diggs put the car in reverse and backed out. "Around here, there's an unusual level of cooperation between the Bloods and Crips. Despite turf wars elsewhere in the city, they've brokered a truce." Diggs laughed. "Hell, just last month a Blood bounty hunter and a Crip woman got married in San Julian Park. Both gangs turned out. It was a real lovefest.

Diggs fished out a pack of cigarettes, looked at it with regret, and tossed it in the back seat.

"Why'd you do that?"

"Trying to quit. Women don't like it." I tried to catch his eye.

"Anyone I know?"

"None of your business, boyo. But here's something for you think about. A lot of people on these blocks know each other. They're like family. I know what the crime stats might say, but it's good to talk to people actually breathing and living in an area before drawing any conclusions."

"Oh, you're telling me, a black man, how I should relate to inner-city folks?"

"Don't be so touchy. Besides, you're not black. You're a cop. Cops aren't black or white. Underneath it all, they're blue."

Diggs and I drove back to the station. It was still hot, but a change in the weather was looming. We passed a grizzled, old man carrying a stuffed garbage bag. He waved at Diggs and smiled a toothless grin.

Diggs pulled over.

The old man dropped the bag. "How ya doin', Officer Diggs?" He shuffled to the driver's side of the car and peered in at us.

Even from the passenger seat, the smell of garbage and body odor hit me hard. I had to fight an urge to hold my nose.

"I'm fine. And you, Deuteronomy?"

"Ain't a makin' much progress with the sinners here on the street." He scratched his head. Diggs had the window down, and I hoped the man wasn't shedding lice. "Otherwise, good, real good. I'm done with crack."

I leaned across Diggs. Deuteronomy's pupils were dilated. He picked at imaginary scabs. There was nothing he craved more than a hit.

"Do you have any words of scripture for us?" Diggs leaned toward me and whispered, "It's amazing. He's memorized the whole book of *Deuteronomy*."

Deuteronomy raised two skinny arms in the air and spat in the street. "Your life will hang by a thread before you. You will be terrified by night and day. And you will not trust in the security of your life."

Deuteronomy stumbled off.

The ground trembled. The car shook. A gray wind kicked up, smelling of car exhaust and human blood. It swirled off the stained streets toward distant towers of steel and glass. A turbulent uncertainty wafted me back to thoughts about the case, then of Dani's picture. But what did it all amount to? Two scared girls, one alive, one dead; a drugged-out preacher; a slight tremor. Just another day in the City of Angels.

"This is no earthquake," Diggs said facetiously. "It's a warning. The end of the world is nigh."

"You'd take the word of a crackie? Tomorrow night is Dani's exhibition. You'll be there, right?"

"*Ars longa vita brevis,* bro. Wouldn't miss it."

CHAPTER THIRTY-FOUR

Carver

I'd invited Alicia to the opening of the local young artists' exhibition at Parkhurst Gallery in the San Pedro Art District to see Dani's work. I expected a white, ultramodern building, but it turned out to be a comfortable house of wood and stone, with Dutch-style wood roofs, full of sharp angles, a blue door, and a quaint, hand-painted, wooden sign reminding me of Solvang, the Danish-themed town on the way to San Obispo.

The gallery wasn't the least bit pretentious, and its owner, hearing who I was, welcomed me effusively. The room was softly lit, with a laid-back ambiance. There were seascapes and lighthouses since we were near the port, but also southwestern art, urban landscapes, animation and abstract paintings.

Dani, my budding artist, was with my ex-wife. As

expected, Dani was the hit of her show. I had to steer Alicia, who seemed oddly distracted, through a crowd of admirers to approach them.

Dani had crossed her feet at the ankles, looking nervous. She stood by a sign that said "Smell the Roses" next to one of her recent paintings, a red flower, with delicate, traces of orange and yellow, that looked like a liquid poured in slow motion into a Celadon vase.

Dani shook Alicia's hand and looked at me with a questioning glance. I had not dated much since the divorce.

Alicia smiled at Dani. "That's so lovely," she told her. "I wish I could paint like that."

Eve's eyes narrowed. She seemed ill at ease. Alicia was a decade younger than my ex, and nothing like her—dark, round, and soft, not blonde, buffed, or manicured.

I gave Eve a quick kiss on her cheek and introduced the women.

Eve cleared her throat. "How did you two meet?"

Trapped between Alicia and Eve, I groped for the right words. "On a case. She gave me some information. Unfortunately, it didn't pan out."

Alicia brushed strands of hair away from her unlined face. "That's *his* story, and he's sticking with it." Her eyes looked stormy.

I'd blown it.

"Sorry, that didn't come out right. I've never been good at small talk. Let me put it another way. We discussed the case. She's a very good listener."

Eve nodded, still looking at Alicia. Probably sizing her up by her ensemble. I looked around for Eve's husband, the only other person in the gallery beside Diggs that I was sure to recognize.

Freddy, a short, balding man with a mild face that belied his reputation as one of L.A.'s most ferocious litigators, was holding forth on some arcane point of law, with a rich, old, white guy in a navy-blue suit and crimson tie. I bailed on the women and sauntered over to say hello.

I passed a small bar. Free drinks always drew a crowd, and the cute bartender looked as if she was in for a rough night. Tourists in shorts and sunglasses guzzled mixed drinks. A tall, model-thin woman, in bright red lipstick, wearing a slinky outfit and towering heels, sipped champagne while a young man in a turtleneck watched her hungrily.

Bet *he* didn't come to look at art.

I moved toward Freddy and the money. Just then, I looked back, curious to see if Alicia, Eve, and Dani were still chatting. Millie and Jimmy approached them. It was nice to see my old friends kept their promise to see Dani's prize-winning painting. Millie rushed over to Dani, brushing aside what must have been a basketball player judging from his height. She stretched out her meaty arms and gave Dani a big hug, while Eve looked on nonplussed.

Jimmy followed his wife, a little breathless. He pantomimed a look of amazement and spoke in voice that carried over to me. "You've been discovered, Dani! Can I get an autograph?" He thrust a catalogue toward her.

She smiled and then made a serious, professional-looking face and signed her name with a flourish Then she doodled a quick, remarkably accurate picture of Jimmy, who stared at it for a moment and opened his lips in huge grin.

"Am I *that* handsome?" he asked, but his face looked gray.

"Oh, hush." His wife poked him in the ribs.

Jimmy grimaced. Though the room was air-conditioned, he was sweating so much he might have been back at Rascal's, grilling meat over white-hot coals. Suddenly, he swayed and collapsed.

Millie leaned over him and screamed. "Oh God, Jimmy! Please. Someone, get a doctor!"

Everyone looked around, but no one answered. A woman rummaged in her purse. She found a pill and ran toward to Millie. "Can he chew this? Aspirin helps."

Someone else knelt at Jimmy's side. "I can't find a pulse. Call 911!"

Millie drew shallow, uneven breaths and trembled. Blood thrummed in my ears. Everything sped up. "Everyone clear the way. Give him room to breathe." I grabbed the aspirin, thrust it into Jimmy's mouth, and punched in the numbers.

A fresh thought forced its way to the surface. *This is what a heart attack looks like. I've never seen anyone die a natural death.*

Alicia bent over Jimmy, shunting me aside. Her hands hovered, palms down, just over his sternum. Her eyes closed, as if she was listening for sounds of breathing. I thought she would clasp her fingers together and administer CPR. Instead, she murmured unfamiliar and mystifying sounds.

The air around her no longer felt like empty space. It was alive, volatile, thrumming with energy. I saw in her expectant gaze a beautiful and terrible intensity.

My adrenalin pumped up. I tried my best to focus, but all I could do was endure the moment. To understand would be to risk insanity.

I thought I knew her. This woman I've slept with.

Jimmy's eyes opened, and he took a deep breath. The color returned to his cheeks. An unfathomable silence filled the room. Jimmy glanced up and noticed people taking pictures with their cell phones.

"Wh . . . what happened?"

Millie closed her eyes. Her mouth moved as if in silent prayer before she answered. "Don't move. I'm pretty sure you had a heart attack. And this young lady," she pointed to Alicia, "saved your life."

Alicia still knelt by Jimmy's side. He craned his neck to look at her. "Thank you, miss." His voice was a low rumble.

"What exactly did you do? And how . . ."

She raised her eyes, now black, sibylline, and so calm I could not hold their glance.

"I don't know," she said. "But as soon as he walked into

the gallery, I sensed I'd have to do something."

I didn't know what to say. I was grateful. Jimmy was a good man. But that didn't make it any easier for me to accept what happened. I could do little but scan her face for clues that might tell me what she'd done and how she'd done it.

Show me how to make this normal. I begged her with my eyes.

Her answering look said, *Choose. How will you live?*

I had no answer for her. I was Osip Bernstein confronted by the black queen.

"Think what you must," she said, frustration in her voice. "Maybe it was the aspirin. Or diabetes and his blood sugar level was too low."

"He had no pulse!" My voice grew louder.

People had put away their cell phones and stopped talking. They listened avidly, as if drunk on a surplus of excitement. They had seen a man brought back from the brink. They would never take anything for granted again.

I wanted them all to get lost.

"Maybe his pulse was too faint to pick up," she said. Then her voice grew regal. "I know you're scared. You don't dare believe. Even when the evidence is staring you right in the face. Betsy Lamb's death and Maria Cordero's death are related. The killers are also victims."

I could hide nothing. It must have shown on my face: *One of us must be crazy.* I stood in front of her, undisguised, desperate, apologetic, and skeptical, letting her read every ounce of fear in my eyes.

Alicia and Millie helped Jimmy to his feet. Feet stepped over wooden planks as the crowd thinned out, but an excited buzz still swept through the room. People clustered in tight little circles, some looking at paintings but most murmuring, most likely about what they'd seen.

There were barriers we couldn't cross. Certainly, I couldn't. Since I met Alicia, it seemed that time after time I threw myself against something I couldn't see.

If Alicia *was* mad, she wasn't a fake.

Eve had disappeared. Dani said she'd gone to look for Freddy. I saw them head to the bar for a drink. My throat was dry. God, I could use a glass of water. It was hot with the press of bodies and the smell of violets and wine.

I needed to cool off.

I felt something I didn't want to feel. Fear as heavy as the solid, bronze hamsa on the front door of her house when I visited her. I didn't want to press it down. I didn't want her to open the door. And I damn well didn't want to see what was on the other side.

I didn't have the strength to argue any more. Alicia didn't seem angry, only uncertain. Would I try to save what we shared, or would I resist, and hold onto the truths I'd always lived by? I watched disappointment pass over her features.

"You're not ready," she said.

CHAPTER THIRTY-FIVE

Alicia

Back in my kitchen, I held a mug of hot tea with a hand that trembled. I'd lied to Carver. Jimmy, his friend, had been dead, and I'd brought him back to life. I wasn't sure how I'd done it. Only knew that I'd never done anything like it before. My stomach felt twisted up inside, as if fingers squeezed me tighter and tighter until I felt I might double over.

I should have felt pride. Instead, I felt terror. The more powerful I grew, the weirder I became. When she was alive, my mother had called me a *bruja.* I scoffed, but I always wondered. Not anymore. She was right, and as a result, I had added burdens. Possibly, I would be strong enough to take on Sitri; if not yet then soon. I didn't need to hit gongs, shake rain sticks, or put up hamsas. I didn't have to rely on Aishe. I was on a tightrope now without a net, and it scared me. Carver, too. I'd seen it in the look on Carver's face. Heard it in his silence.

Before, we'd danced around each other, dueling with words. We'd been colleagues, then lovers. I'd started to fall for this proud, stubborn, smart man. Led him on, and I'd shut him down.

We were done. At least, that part of us was. The case remained. Two lost lambs—Betsy and Maria—cried out for justice. Pestilence roamed unchecked through the city. Carlos was infected by it. And Carver's daughter was still in danger, perhaps not from Rojas anymore, but from something infinitely worse—Sitri. Stopping him was my burden. But if I could help Carver find the human culprit, Sirte's tool, it might slow Sitri's assault on our loved ones. At least I hoped so.

The phone rang, and I picked up.

"Hello?"

No words. An odd blend of chirp and growl. It was Sitri, no doubt about it, calling to keep me scared and off-balance.

And it worked. My mouth felt dry, so I poured myself a glass of water. It seemed entirely too quiet. I stumbled up the stairs to my bedroom, slid on my cotton nightgown worn with age, and slipped between my clean sheets. Even as my eyes grew heavy, I couldn't shake the feeling that danger lurked like a great white just beyond the reef. I imagined myself slowly walking into the ocean. The water curled gently over my toes and rose to my calves, my thighs, my waist, and as it rose, my smile broadened until it stretched as far as it could. No signs of sharks.

The next thing I knew, cold, wet fur pressed up against my face. Nemesis yowling. Awake, I stretched, and the mattress sloshed beneath my hips. Flashes of lightning came through the window and lit the room, but I couldn't make sense of the images that came unbidden and couldn't be unseen.

The room spun. The walls rippled, swelled up, leaked water, rivulets, and torrents of it.

Water, dark gray noxious and sickly sweet swirled around me. The water surged, spread to the door, gushed out. The bed bobbed up and down.

I gagged.

Nemesis dug her claws into me. I screamed, clung to her tightly, scooted to the end of the bed, and dipped my right foot into the water.

Ice cold, it soaked my toes, my ankles, the edge of my gown. I slipped off the bed and slogged toward my door. Nemesis stopped scratching and burrowed into me, and I grabbed the doorknob, twisted, pulled.

The door wouldn't budge.

The water swirled, rising to my waist. Horror and disbelief clawed my throat. Sitri was trying to drown me. But this couldn't be the way I'd die! *What ifs* raced through my mind like tiny, uncontrolled electric pulses. A rush of fear sent chills and fever coursing through me. Sitri, the water demon, was everywhere. Haunting me. Attacking me. Trying to make my house a watery grave. He demonstrated his power over nature with a disease that made its victims cough up blood and the torrential, inexplicable rainstorm. He was growing stronger all the time.

My dresser floated past with my cell phone. I grabbed the phone and punched in 911. I forced my way to the window. Outside, sheets of rain poured down, but I pushed open the window, leaned over, dropped Nemesis out and jumped.

Pain ripped through my knees, my palms, and my twisted ankle. Mud soaked into every part of my bruised, hopefully not broken body.

A couple of feet away, Nemesis mewed. I picked her up and put her to my cheek for comfort. Stiff-legged, I stumbled over to my neighbor's house. I knocked on the door and called out to Dolores. She must've heard me shouting. Minutes passed, then I heard her approaching footsteps. Dolores opened the door with her bony hand but kept the chain securely in place.

She gasped when she saw me, "Oh honey, what happened?" She unchained the door immediately and pulled me inside. "You've got to get out of those wet things." Without saying another word, she ran to her bathroom and returned with a fluffy orange towel. "Dry off. I'll find something for you to wear. And poor Nemesis!"

Dolores handed me a dress four sizes too large and three inches too short. It was still warm from the dryer. I was unable to stop shaking. I put it on. I closed my eyes, grateful to be alive, but so tired.

She talked to me, but I didn't catch what she was telling me, her voice a wisp of sound. Finally, she just gestured for me to follow her into the kitchen. Slowly, slowly barely able to move my body, as if walking through wet cement, I stumbled after her. Dolores switched on the light, and I flashed back to the lightning at the window, the room lit up. Nemesis was at my face and shit, oh shit, the water was rising faster and faster.

Dolores put out a bowl of water for Nemesis. She patted a kitchen chair. "Sit right down and tell me about it."

I leaned my elbows on the table. Put my head in my hands and heaved a sigh. "I don't know where to begin. You know the story of Noah's ark. That's what it was like, but without the ark. And in my house."

Dolores rested her hand on my shoulder. "It's not just you, honey."

Her words seemed to evaporate.

"It's all over the news. There's been major flooding all through L.A., Orange, and Ventura. They're worried about mudslides in parts of Orange County and Riverdale, especially after the recent wildfires."

"But your house is OK?"

"Uh-huh. No power down or anything. Just a lot of wind and rain." She grabbed an umbrella and went outside.

When she returned, her eyes were wide. "There are no

words. You can't go back there, what with the water and the broken glass and live electric wires." She looked around at the clutter in her house. "I don't have much room here, but you can stay with me if you have nowhere else to go."

"Don't worry." I pushed myself out of the chair. "I have a friend in Brentwood." Phyllis.

"You're not going anywhere. It's the middle of the night. You need to rest. Why, you can barely stand. But first, I need to take care of those abrasions. You don't want them to get infected."

I nodded, letting her lead me to the bathroom. She sat me down on the lid of the toilet seat, cleaned the cuts and put on Neosporin and gauze. While she worked, she wondered aloud. "Should I call the police or the fire department?"

I thought of Carver. "Police."

"I'll take care of that. You sleep." Dolores took one last look at her work; satisfied, she went to her bedroom and pulled out an extra sheet and pillow. She pointed to the sofa. "You'll have to sleep there. She looked away, turned red. "I have a bad back." She put down the sheet and covered the pillow. "You can call your friend tomorrow."

I thought about calling Carver. I'd been right all along. I decided to take pictures of what was left of my house with a cell phone. Maybe then he'd believe me. I yawned. But not now. Later. Tomorrow.

CHAPTER THIRTY-SIX

Alicia

In the morning, my cotton nightgown stuck to my back. I sniffed my armpits. Definitely needed a shower. But most of all, I needed to wash away the terror. I was becoming someone I couldn't recognize; a woman that was frightened and without hope. It wasn't the way I'd chosen to be in the world.

I'd always believed myself to be part of the timeless web of unconditional love. Sitri sought to tear that web to shreds. He was here to sow fear and reap death. Each time he appeared, he'd been the aggressor. I'd shrunk back, a timid mouse. But I didn't have to cower. He wasn't all-powerful.

I showered, managed to choke down a piece of dry toast, and called Phyllis. I told her to expect me sometime in the mid-afternoon. I sent Carver the pictures and called him.

"You saw them, right? How could that have happened

when the other houses around me were untouched? It had to be Sitri."

He was silent, but at least he didn't dismiss my fears or make any snide comments. I wondered what he was thinking. I put down a half-empty mug of coffee, started pacing back and forth in Dolores's kitchen.

"Speak to me, John. What do you think?"

"I think something strange is happening. Something very strange. I don't know why you've been singled out. Maybe you're right. Maybe it ties in with the Lamb case. Or maybe the murder and the distruction of your house are unrelated events."

"But you know I'm not crazy."

"I never thought you were."

"Never?"

"Never." His voice held certainty.

My eyes shut briefly. I took a deep breath, a little drunk with thankfulness. "I asked my friend, Phyllis, if I could stay with her, and she agreed. If you need me for any reason, I should be there by late afternoon. I'll text you the address."

Cradling Nemesis, I walked up the stone walkway toward Phyllis's house. Phyllis opened the door even before Nemesis and I got halfway up to her house. She rushed over and gave me a light hug.

When Nemesis hissed at her, she stepped back and

surveyed me. "I'm so sorry this had to happen. But you seem to be coping well."

"That's nice of you to say. We both know it's not true."

Phyllis let out a sigh. "Okay. Your eyes have a dazed look in them. You're pale, terrified within an inch of your life. Does that make you feel any better?"

"Actually, it does." Even now, she'd been able to coax a smile out of me. Nemesis was less impressed. He opened his mouth and yawned in her face. Phyllis laughed. "Poor Nemesis. I'll bet you had a tough time. Alicia, why don't you put her down and follow me into the kitchen. Have you had anything to eat?"

I tried halfheartedly to wave her off, but Phyllis walked over to the oven, pulled out a still-warm strawberry rhubarb pie and cut us generous slices. She poured two strong cups of tea and brought them over to a small, white table with four chairs. I stared at the pie. My stomach felt like a tiny, damaged rodent, unwilling and unable to feel hunger.

Nemesis lay at my feet.

"It must've been terrifying," Phyllis said. "Thank God you both escaped."

"I don't want to talk about it."

There was a knock at the door. Phyllis opened it, and Carver stood there. "I happened to be in the vicinity and thought I'd see how you were holding up."

I introduced Phyllis, who offered him some pie. He seemed to think about it, then said, "I appreciate the offer, but I've got to get back to work."

He looked at me. Probably noticed my eyes were red but pretended not to. "All things considered; you seem all right. Remember, I told you we'd keep an eye out on your brother? Well, a bag lady told one of the beat cops Carlos was taken to Good Samaritan Hospital."

I hugged him. "You're a godsend. I've been so worried."

"Glad to be of use."

Carver was persistent, consistent, and determined. As I saw him out, I couldn't help feeling happy that he'd entered my life, whatever the future would bring.

"I noticed the way that detective looked at you. He's *very* interested."

I tried to keep myself from sounding annoyed. "I know."

"And good-looking."

"I know." This time I did snap at her. "For heaven's sake, Phyllis, my home's been destroyed, why are you talking about my love life?"

"So . . . you're not interested." Phyllis let loose a derisive laugh.

I crossed my arms. "It's not that simple." I laughed ruefully. "How many men can accept what I am?" I rubbed my eyes. "Must we have this conversation right now? After all that's happened?"

I pled exhaustion. Since the deluge in my house, I felt bone-tired through and through, so I went into the guest bedroom to rest. My head sank into the soft pillow, but my senses remained hyper alert.

It was time to bring the struggle to Sitri, to find the portal he'd used to enter our world and send him back to wherever demons came from.

CHAPTER THIRTY-SEVEN

Carver

I sat in a car, sipping lukewarm coffee from a Styrofoam cup, watching Phyllis's house. Alicia walked out the front door. She had dark circles under her eyes.

As she waved and walked over, I rolled down the window. She leaned over the car door.

"You weren't here all night, were you?"

"No. Like I said, people owe me. I told them we were working together on a case, that you got threatening calls, and your house was gutted."

"Well, thanks. I know you're worried about me."

"Damn right, I am. Someone's after you." I couldn't find the right words to tell her how I felt. Fear for her was a razor held to my neck, a shadow on my heart, pushing me to a dark place.

My phone rang. "Diggs? You've got what?" I pumped my

fist. "I'll be there ASAP." I turned back to Alicia. "There's been a break in the case. Want to come?"

"That's great." But her eyes clouded over. "I've got to go to my brother."

"Sure."

Diggs waited for me in an interview room across from a tall man wearing a black T-shirt with a long, gold chain—Snake.

I stepped into the room, "Fuck, it's warm in here." I put my hand on Snake's shoulder. "Can I get you a can of Coke?"

Snake smiled. "Only coke I use is powder."

"Here's what Snake brought us," Diggs held a glittering, beautifully shaped earring. Tiny emeralds spelled out the letter B.

"Nice. Where'd you get it?" I took the perfect, little piece and dangled it in front of Snake's beady eyes.

"Could've belonged to the dead girl." Snake leaned back in his chair. "Might get me a free pass on that drug distribution shit. Diggs, you know I didn't shoot that Logan Heights Calle dumbass. Why didn't he stay in San Diego where he belonged?"

"You find it on the roof?" I asked.

Snake's chin rose. "Yeah."

"Before or after we secured the scene?"

"After."

"And how do you think we missed it?"

I could almost hear the sound of Snake's brain lurching about as he tried to figure out what to tell us. "Fuck if I know."

"How come there's only one?"

Snake shrugged.

"Where's the other?" I asked.

"Murderer has it."

"Thinking of anyone in particular?"

"Yeah." Snake's mouth puckered. "The fat cop, Decker."

"He's not a cop," I said, "Not anymore." There are still too many police in the force like Decker. Assholes who think the badge and gun give them the right to treat people like dirt, especially people of color.

"Tell *him* that. Fucker thinks he's untouchable. Thinks he owns the place. Thinks he owns us"

"Meaning?"

"He's greedy." Snake rubbed his right thumb against the adjacent fingers. "Changed the roof's lock. Said we'd have to pay double. We told him to fuck himself. Showed him the earring. He said he didn't know who it belonged to. Riffin jockstrap couldn't get a mud duck to quack."

Diggs looked at my confused face. "A mud duck's an ugly female." He turned back to Snake, jerked his thumb at me. "Needs an interpreter." His body shifted, so he faced me. "Mud is for the make-up caked on. Duck because she's no swan. You can figure out quack for yourself, right?" He winked.

Snake ignored the byplay. He stared thoughtfully at the spaces between his fingers. Maybe he was wondering if he'd implicated Decker enough. "Soon as he heard police," Snake said, "Decker got spooked. Tried not to show, but he was definitely spooked. Said you'd never believe a gang member." He fingered a heavy gold chain. "Figure *we*'d done her. He'd been a cop himself, he said. Knew how they thought. Lotta crank shit." Snake folded his arms. "So here we are. Now what you gonna do?"

"If it turns out this belonged to Betsy Lamb, we're going to look for that other earring," I said.

"You do that." Snake leaned back nonchalantly." You'll see I'm right. Your job's done. Decker still has it or he pawned it."

"He'd never be that stupid," I said.

"Why'd it be stupid? He knows we have the other one. Asshole thinks he's scared us. And the stone's valuable. Even just one."

"So why are you bringing it to us?"

"Figure Decker's one of yours. Cop, ex-cop. Same shit. You should take care of your own. Besides the fucker's calling us out."

Diggs and I looked at each other. Snake's message was clear. Decker was on thin ice.

Snake left a few minutes later.

Diggs stood, stretched. "I need coffee. Want some?"

"No thanks. Listen, you're the gang expert," I added.

"Why did they bother to send Snake to us? They could've just offed Decker."

Diggs was on his way out of the room. He stopped, put his hand on the doorknob. "Snake's an interesting guy." He turned to me. "He's on the margin of lots of violent crimes, but he doesn't usually get involved. Sure, he wants Decker gone. The hotel's part of his turf. Decker's hurting his business. If he can finger Decker for the crime, he gets business and regains use of the roof. If he's really lucky, he wins some points with us. Maybe we'll go easy on that case he mentioned."

"That'd be a cold day in Hell," I said.

"Hope is the dream of every waking man." He smiled crookedly. "Pliny the Elder."

"Got to hand it to you. You can crank out a saying for every occasion."

"We use what we've got. Remember that night we played chess? I felt like an idiot for a week."

Diggs headed out to get his coffee. Snake's arrival still didn't make a lot of sense. Snake and Diggs joked together. They seemed a little too comfortable with each other.

Diggs returned.

"You know Snake. Do you trust him?" I asked.

Diggs chugged his coffee. He sat at the edge of the desk in the interrogation room, just to the right of my chair. He pinched the bridge of his nose with thumb and forefinger. "Don't know that I do. But, as far as gang members go, he's straighter than most."

"You trust him more than Decker?" I asked.

"Definitely."

"Even though Decker used to be one of us?"

"I did some checking. Spoke with a priest who works with gang members, helping them straighten out their lives. He introduced me to an old gang member, B-Dog." Diggs's lips were a tight, straight line. "Turns out Decker was better known as a businessman than a cop. He was a dealer back in the day. Used to plant drugs on competitors to get them off the streets."

I banged the desk with my fist. "A bent cop. I knew it."

"So . . . one of his rivals was a member of the Bloods named Victor Oviedo. B-Dog said Decker shot and paralyzed Oviedo, planted a weapon on him, and charged him with an attempt to kill a cop. Oviedo got a life sentence.

"Talk was Decker planted evidence to get convictions."

I stood. "I'm going to check with Betsy Lamb's mother. If the earring belonged to Betsy, I'll look for that other earring, starting with all the pawnshops in the area."

Diggs nodded. "Maybe hope the unsub has more greed than brains."

⸸

I immediately placed a call to Bree Lamb.

"Do you have any news for us?" She sounded tired.

"Maybe. We found an earring. Emeralds in a B shape.

Did your daughter have such an earring?"

"Yes. My mother gave those earrings to me when I was a little older than Betsy is now." Her voice broke. "I haven't worn them in years. Betsy always admired them, so I gave them to her just before she went to Los Angeles."

"In that case, we might catch her killer if we can find the other earring. I can't promise anything, but this could turn out to be helpful."

"Thanks for your call," Bree Lamb said. "I want to see justice done." Her voice softened. "Not that it'll make me feel any better. You know, I was thinking about putting pressure on you to solve the case, but I know you're doing everything you can."

When the call ended, I checked the database to see if the emerald earring turned up anywhere. At about the ten-minute mark, it paid off.

"Bingo," I said.

Diggs looked up from his desk. "You don't mean . . ."

"I do. A cute, little emerald was pawned a few days after the murder. By a woman named Amy Brodsky."

Diggs looked bored. "That name sounds familiar."

"Yes. The former Mrs. Decker. I'd heard she was a real live wire, with a loud voice and red hair out of a bottle. I guess they still talk to each other."

"Why'd she help him?" Diggs asked.

"No idea. But I'll have a talk with the lady."

CHAPTER THIRTY-EIGHT

Carver

Amy Brodsky lived in Fontana, a city in San Bernadino County. Once Fontana had been a small agricultural town, but it had mushroomed in recent decades with an influx of industry. Now, new money pushed the smaller single-family homes to the periphery of town.

Amy's home had peeling paint and a wonky roof. Her porch sagged under my weight. The warped door echoed under my knock.

A middle-aged woman with a still-attractive face peered out the cracked glass.

Alicia stood beside me as I flashed my badge. "Detective Carver."

She swung the door open. "What can I do for you?"

"Can we come in?"

She led me into a living room that had seen decades pass

without any real attempt by residents to update its décor. An old-fashioned floral sofa, a rickety La-Z- Boy, a flat screen held pride of place.

"Why are you here?" she asked. She sank into the La-Z Boy. "If it's about my ex, I hardly see him anymore."

I pulled the earring photo out of my pocket. "Does this look familiar?"

She glanced at it "Got one just like it last week."

"Why'd he give it you? And why only one?"

"Sam was a little short of money this month" A cut-glass bowl of mints lay on a battered but serviceable coffee table. She reached up and popped one in her mouth, chewed it. "He told me I could take it as part of my alimony payment. Maybe make it into a ring. I told him I'd rather have the cash. But he said this was the best he could do."

"Did you ask him how he'd gotten it?"

"He said it was from the hotel. It'd been sitting in the lost and found for more than a year, and he figured the owner either didn't know where she'd lost it or just didn't care."

"Has he given you other gifts before?"

"Not for years." Amy looked down. "He stole it, right? I should have known. Guess I'm not too smart." She had the defeated expression of a woman so used to being put down that she did it before anyone else could.

I put my hand gently on her wrist. "You wanted to trust him. He was your husband once."

"You don't ask questions when you're having trouble

making ends meet."

"Is that why you pawned it?" Alicia asked.

She nodded and furrowed her brow. "You came all the way out here because I pawned an earring?"

"It's related to a case," I said.

Amy Brodsky's breath caught. "Am I in trouble for pawning stolen property?"

"No, ma'am. But I do have some questions for your ex-husband."

On the way back, I called Decker to ask that he come in for further questioning, and damn if he wasn't already waiting when I got to the station. Waiting with his fat-ass lawyer.

Before I even got settled in the interview room, Bob Graves leaned into Decker. "Remember, you can leave any time." He gave me the chipmunk cheek I'm-watching-you nod. "You're not under arrest."

"I appreciate your client's cooperation," I said.

Graves rubbed his thighs just above his knees, as if eager to get the meeting underway.

I took out a notepad. "I just have a few simple questions."

Decker angled his chair to the side. He crossed his legs, sat like a still life.

"Tell me, why did you change the lock to the stairs leading up to the roof?"

Graves indicated to Decker that it was safe to answer.

Decker leaned over the table. "After the girl was murdered, the owners wanted to make sure it couldn't happen again."

"Of course," I said. "You found the murdered girl's earring there?" I casually threw in. Would Decker admit to palming it? Finger the Bloods for the crime?

Graves put his hand on Decker's forearm. "Just the one was on the ground."

"How did you get up there, Decker?" My voice ran with thickness. "According to Sahai, you didn't have a key."

"If you're going to accuse my client of a crime, why don't you just come out with it?" The attorney stood up. "Otherwise, we're leaving."

Decker blinked. He had a sly smile on his face as he rose to follow his attorney. "Don't mind, Carver. He's fishing and don't got shit for probable cause."

"Don't you want to know about the DNA sample found on your client's carpet?" I said.

Graves stopped, just for a moment, a second, a breath of air long enough for Decker to whisper.

They continued to the door. On the way out, Decker handed me a piece of paper and whispered something I never expected.

"What, now?" I asked.

Decker smirked.

Diggs watched them walk down the hallway to the

elevator. As soon as they left, he came into the room. "Why didn't he just throw the earing out? It makes no sense. But if he was peddling drugs and offered them to the girl in exchange for sex, she could've been disgusted. Maybe she threatened to get him fired."

"Ifs and maybes don't add up to much." I gathered up my notes and stood.

"Decker's the only one who could've doctored the tapes in the elevator." He rubbed his nose. "And he's the only suspect who would've known how to clean up the crime scene so thoroughly."

I looked at him "But we don't have proof he did any of this."

"What about the DNA sample you mentioned?"

"There is no DNA sample. I just said that to rattle his cage. It didn't work. Bottom line, there's one solid piece of evidence. It's not enough, especially given this." I held up copies of two ticket stubs from Dodger Stadium for the evening in question. "And he's provided the phone number of his date to confirm his presence."

"And he didn't give it to you before?"

"The lady in question is married. He didn't want to get either of them in trouble."

Diggs put a consoling hand on my shoulder. "Against the lucky even the gods are powerless," Diggs said.

I frowned at him. "It's not luck, and I'm no god. The cocksucker's smarter than I thought. He held back a critical piece of information." I looked away, silent, thinking.

"He deliberately slowed the investigation."

CHAPTER THIRTY-NINE

Carver

"Shut the door and sit down." Simpson's desk was buried in a sea of paperwork. "I'm getting heat from upstairs about the Lamb case." He filed some papers, didn't even bother to look at me. "We need to show results, and you don't seem up to the job. I'm thinking that maybe someone else should take over the case."

"You don't change the primary detective in the middle of an investigation. That's simply not done." Most of the time all I felt about Simpson was a mild contempt, but now a kernel of anger rose. "No one knows the case like I do. I've spent hours on it and have working relationships with the suspects."

"You should've brought the Gang Unit in on this. They've got eyes and ears on the street. They've got CIs on the street. They can use gang rivalries to pry evidence loose."

I shrugged it off. "It'd be good to pin this on them. Trouble is, we don't have shit up there. No video. No gang graffiti. No fingerprints, blood, or DNA evidence. The place was scrubbed clean. It's not like them."

"So what about Decker?"

Simpson, you lazy bastard. "It's in my report. He's got an alibi." The rage had built over the past week, and I couldn't tamp it down. I stood and got right in his face. "And what's this bullshit about not being up to the job? In case you've forgotten it, I've closed more cases in the last five years than anyone in the unit."

Simpson swallowed hard. He took a deep breath and glared. "Talk to me like that, you dig a hole you might never climb out of."

"Maybe not. But you don't get to shit on my reputation."

"Command staff doesn't give a shit about your reputation."

The conflict that had been percolating between us had come to a full boil. Simpson didn't want me around. He'd bypass me any way he could. There was only one thing I could do. Solve the case. Make like a cat with a canary locked in its jaw and drop it at Simpson's feet.

"Give me another week before you do anything, Loo."

He nodded curtly. I walked out, the glass door rattling behind me.

I sat down at my desk, feeling defeated. My only lead was Alicia spouting stuff about demons. And after the art show, I didn't know what to think. It was pure hell, if you believed in that sort of thing. I thumbed absently through the case file, searching for an elusive nugget of fact that I could hold onto. But then I noticed something I'd missed.

"Hey, Diggs, look at this." I shoved the file onto his desk and pointed to the article I'd found stuffed in the back of the folder. *Local Kid Makes It Big*. "When Sahai was seventeen, he received a free ride to Stanford as a physics major." I flipped the article over and showed him a report filed by the Santa Clara County Sheriff's Department. "After charges of drunk and disorderly conduct, he left school two months later. Thanks to the Buckley Amendment, we'll never know if he dropped out, got kicked out, or just ran away from everything,"

Diggs grinned. "Over eighteen, right? So, he couldn't get it expunged."

"Sure. And listen to this. In the last ten years, two cases at the Greene Hotel were misfiled. Never solved. One involved a Pakistani girl, the other a male Stanford grad. Who do we know at the Greene who has roots in South Asia and Stanford?"

Diggs gave me a thumbs-up. "Sahai. Baby!"

Feeling pleased with myself, I relaxed and loosened my tie. "Maybe Sahai never did get his head right again. Maybe I should pay him a little visit after I pick up Dani. I might just catch up with him in the evening, when things have quieted down a bit at the old hotel."

"Sure. But how did those files get lost?"

"Misplaced. Just a lazy clerk, I guess."

CHAPTER FORTY

Carver

I drove from Van Nuys to Sherman Way to the LA Museum of Figurative Art. Turned right on Balboa and left on Saticoy Street, parking in front of the museum. I waited for about ten minutes, and Dani came out of the double doors, talking animatedly with a tall, slender boy. For a brief moment, I thought it was Rojas; but no, it couldn't be. Rojas was dead. His wallet and ID were found with the charred body.

The boy that looked so much like Rojas had a loose-limbed walk, as if he listened to some internal music. He wore a black, wife beater shirt and jeans.

Dani came up to the car on the passenger's side, took off her backpack, and slid it onto the back seat before climbing in.

I caught my breath. "That boy over there, the one

walking away. He looks like Rojas. Who is he?"

"It's Rob, of course. I know he seemed kind of weird at the house, but he's got a great sense of humor."

I felt as if my head was about to explode. Of course, it was Rob. In the hunch of the boy's shoulders, the dark, slick-backed swath of hair on his head, the slight lilt in his walk. The bastard was unmistakable.

I stared straight ahead, not trusting myself to look at her. "Rojas is dead. I read the accident report."

"Well, that's Rob." She shrugged, annoyed but laughing a little. "I guess someone made a mistake."

"Damn right someone did. Whatever you do, I don't want you talking to him. And certainly not using him for a model or modeling for him. That boy's dangerous."

The warning made her stiffen. She crossed her arms. Her lips tightened and thinned. "I'm old enough to decide who I can see."

"Maybe so. But you're also old enough to have consequences if you make a wrong choice." I nodded in the direction Rojas had gone. "A boyfriend who sells drugs can land you in prison as an accessory. Be smart, not stubborn."

Dani looked pained. "Is that true? You aren't just telling me this, so I'll stay away from him?"

"No. Of course not."

Her brow cleared. She'd made up her mind. "If you want me to stay away from him, that's what I'll do."

"Good." I nodded, but I didn't tell her what really worried

me. The fact that he was hanging around her troubled me deeply. Would Rojas leave Dani alone, or would he go after her? He had a grudge against me. The best way to strike back would be through Dani. Maybe he'd kidnap her. Get her hooked on drugs.

Or maybe he had other plans. Something even worse

His continued existence raised another question. Who was the person in Rojas's car, and why was he driving it? I thought about Rojas. Such a clever bastard. He'd set us up perfectly. But then he'd decided to stick around. He kept taking classes with Dani, so I could find him. But how could he have guessed that I would pick Dani up today? It had been a spur of the moment decision on my part. He couldn't have known *unless he could read my mind.* Could Alicia possibly be right about a demon? Really, I thought, disgusted with myself. Get a grip. There are no such things as demons. But there are genuinely bad people. And there are people who hear voices, crazy people who aren't responsible for their actions. Yet how to explain that Rojas, or someone who had the ability to look just like him, was stalking my daughter?

I felt as if I were being forced to enlarge my experience of the possible, to go beyond the world my daily horizon made available to me. And I didn't like it. Not one bit.

That night Eve rang me.

"I just wanted to give you a quick call to say how nice of you to pick Dani up today. She really appreciated it. She usually has to take the bus both ways. I've been too busy at work to drive her myself."

"I'm glad you called. I've been thinking of speaking to you about Dani's commute. I think it might not be such a good idea for her to travel alone. If she can't go with a friend, maybe you can hire a car service."

"What do you mean? It's a perfectly safe route." Her voice had an edge now.

"Yeah, I know. But there's this kid in her class. Roberto Rojas."

"She told me about him. She also told me you went crazy when you found him posing in the house. You scared her."

"Damn it, Eve. I know a hell of a lot more about criminals than you do. This kid is bad news. Please do your best to make sure she has nothing to do with him. I know we don't agree about much, but we both love Dani."

Eve sighed. "Okay, Carver. And I'll make it clear. No strange boys come to the house again. Period."

After the call, I didn't feel any better. Rojas, if it was really him, always seemed to be a step ahead of me.

My shoulders tightened. I'd have to keep a careful watch over Dani.

CHAPTER FORTY-ONE

Alicia

Above the large glass doors of the gray hospital the sign read "Emergency Room" in white letters. The doors slid open.

I stalled, stopped, couldn't move. Torn between rushing to my brother's side and not seeing him at rock bottom, I stepped out of the way. Leaned against the wall. I was so tired. Tired of worrying and sleepless nights. Scared to death of whatever I needed to do next.

I pulled my phone from my pocket and sent Phyllis a quick won't be home message.

Predictably, no more than I hit send, my phone vibrated.

I sighed.

"What do you mean you won't be home?" Phyllis said. The edge in her voice was somewhere between anger and worry. "When should I expect you?"

A sweaty palm held my phone. "Tomorrow, I hope."

Phyllis went silent and I knew any anger she felt turned to worry. "I'll let you know if my plans change," I said in a voice that I hoped sounded relaxed and confident.

"Watch out for yourself." She hung up the phone before I could say I will or won't or . . . I put my hand against the wall. *Aishe, please see me through this safely.*

My jaw ached. I'd been clamping down on it. A sign of how nervous I felt. I did a full-body stretch and took deep breaths in and out, in and out. I stretched my arms overhead, and leaned forward slowly, opening and closing my mouth.

I passed into the waiting room, and the warm, intense smell of disinfectant and blood stirred my stomach. Nurses and EMTs wheeled still more hospital beds, pushing past without a single, wasted effort. Shouts for blood, for plasma, but most of all, for more helping hands echoed around and over the cries. I grabbed the sleeve of a distracted nurse and asked for my brother.

"If you can find him, you can see him, "she said and rushed away.

Wall to wall, beds filled every spot as if it were a wartime triage and not a hospital waiting room in the middle of L.A. Overhead the lights glared on pale, delirious faces.

I wandered down the narrow walkways looking for Carlos, skirting a handful of doctors working steadily.

At the back wall, I reached out to touch the shoulder of a youngish-looking doctor with short, dirty blond hair. He stared at a wall with a glazed expression. "Are you okay?"

He jerked away, blinked, hurried over when a nurse called, "Something's blocking his airway."

"Coming," he said. His voice was deep and muffled. His energy level was flat, and I was afraid he might collapse.

Full-blare screaming, an ambulance jerked to a stop out front. Two tired-looking paramedics wheeled in a skinny Latina with a round, pregnant belly. A plump child, perhaps five-years-old, held her hand. Tears silently fell from the little girl's eyes. And from mine too, for her.

It wasn't until I found my way into the hall and down to the far end behind a curtain that I found Carlos lying in a gray hospital bed. Against a gray wall to his left a gray line of monitors charted his vital signs. I could scarcely see him through my tears.

"I'm here." His face was skeletal, his body so still that if it weren't for the slight rise and fall of his chest, and the steady beep of his monitor, he might already have passed away. "You're going to be fine."

He opened his eyes and squinted at me as if trying to sharpen the image. He worked his mouth and tried to speak but found no words.

I twisted my hands together. He looked terribly lonely and small. "Hola, sis." His voice was gruff, rough, and sounded hardly used. His smile seemed to have been used even less.

"I'm so sorry." My words ran over themselves. Sorry for letting him drift away, for not being there for him. "I'm so stupid!"

"You? Stupid?" He turned to face me. "I wish I had my life together like you do." I closed my eyes. Stifled a sob. "Maybe I wouldn't be here now if I did," he said.

"If anything happens to you, I—" Tears strangled me. I took his hand and kissed it.

"Did you . . ." He struggled to take in air. "Find out about the Lamb girl?"

"Yes, and it isn't important, not now." I stroked his arm.

Carlos put his fingers over mine and tried to smile. "Tell me."

I took a deep breath. "An evil man named Ramirez brought a demon into our world." I bit my lip to keep from trembling. "The demon killed her. I think, maybe, the demon made you sick, too."

"Yeah?" Carlos struggled to sit up, to speak. "I never told you about the Night Stalker, but I saw him when I was little." He put his hand to his brow and rubbed gingerly. "It was a spring day. The warm air smelled of blossoms. Mami held my hand." His hand fell back to his side, and he took a wheezing breath. "Suddenly Mami screamed. People came running. She tried to cover my eyes. But I wriggled away and saw. Later, Mami scrubbed me hard to wash away the blood . . . and the memories."

My eyes widened, but I clamped my mouth shut to hear more.

Carlos shuddered. "The water scalded me." He coughed

and couldn't stop and spit blood.

The monitors by Carlos's bed beeped distress.

I rushed to the young doctor, again. He was standing against the wall, again doing nothing. I grabbed his arm. "I need you." It took hardly any effort to drag him back to my brother's side. "Do something for him."

"Miss." He looked at me and looked back to where he had been standing, blinked, and looked at my brother. His shoulders sagged as if the responsibility was too great to bear. "Do what?" His voice shook. "We don't know what to do. And more of them come every minute!"

I wanted to be angry at him. I wanted to shout, "You're a doctor. You're supposed to help people." But I couldn't. I knew how he felt. I'd had a vision of an endangered girl and the presence of a demon in our city, but instead of fighting back, I'd sheltered myself in books and visions.

No more.

I'd guessed where the portals might be. If I was right, he'd be there.

Waiting for me.

CHAPTER FORTY-TWO

Alicia

Outside the hospital, the sky was gray, and the screams still echoed. I imagined Carlos still coughed. But I didn't stop or hail a taxi. I walked. I had no idea how far the Greene Hotel was from here, but I would make it. I would be on the roof by midnight.

I walked through downtown Los Angeles for hours. The skyscrapers' glass windows rose toward the clouds.

I passed abandoned buildings. Stores shuttered for the night. Tan apartment buildings. A spacious church.

Aching feet forced me to take a seat inside.

Above, the ceiling vaulted. Christ sat with his apostles and raised his hand in a benediction. If he could hear me, what could I tell him? What could he do?

The priest behind the pulpit glanced up, adjusted his wire-rim glasses, and put down the thin stack of papers.

A finger to my lips told him I wasn't there to disturb him.

"Sit as long as you want." His voice was as soft as a woman's. When I didn't respond, he went back to his reading.

I slipped off my shoes and winced. A blister had formed on my right heel, but I didn't have time to consider my own pain. Too many others were in peril. I straightened up in the pew and started to intone a prayer. "Blessed goddess of the light/Grant me courage on this night." I prayed and prayed. Not to the Christ, not to the Jesus in the stained glass window. I didn't call out to the apostles but to the Divine Spirit. "Hold me in your loving care tonight." No bowed head and intertwined fingers, I sent my prayer to my center.

A tiny beam of sunlight suffused the stained glass images and added vitality, color, and warmth. I slouched back against the pew and felt the stirring of awe. But then, as sudden as an explosion on a sea-cliff, *the figures on the rosette shrieked and groaned.*

I gasped.

Apostles melted into splashes of color and unexpected shapes that faded into a cave that led down and into the earth.

The ground smelled blacker than night, but I stumbled on. Hours seemed to pass.

My calves ached. I sweated, aware of an unhurried silence descending. There was no wind. The night air was warm. It was hard to breathe. I had to be to there at the stroke of midnight. Tomorrow my brother could be dead.

Tomorrow I could be dead.

I looked at my watch. Its illuminated face shone stupidly back at me.

An aperture opened. A hand emerged from it.

I peered through, but inside was a grainy fog.

Sitri glided through the gap, naked and beautiful, except for one thing. He wore the ulcerated face of Ramirez.

"Scare me all you want." I crossed my arms and held them close to my chest to keep them from trembling. "I'm not going anywhere. Not until I know."

"Until you know what?" His lips were pale worms on a skull half-denuded of flesh.

"Why you killed the girl and infected my brother."

"Killing and birthing are the same." Laughter exploded from Sitri's foul, sulfur-laden mouth. "I am the father of all the people I killed, since it was I who opened the door for them to another world."

"Why Betsy?"

"A lamb."

"That's it? Her name? Nothing more?"

Sitri preened as if admiring himself in a mirror "At first, she fought to stay alive, but in the end she yielded completely. Just an ordinary girl responding as ordinary girls must."

I summoned my courage, raised my hands, and spread my fingers in Sitri's direction. I waited for energy from the goddess to flow from me, to banish him. I expected Sitri to struggle like a beast in chains, explode like a time bomb, or blow away like a hut in an arctic gale. I expected to see him sucked through the portal, back to hell

He lunged at me. I screamed and shrank away from him.

Silence.

In the rosette, Jesus and his disciples sat around the table, restored to their places.

The blood pounded in my ears. It gave way to the ticking of my watch. The priest, pen in hand, made notes.

I left the pew, moved to the front of the church, and lit a candle in remembrance of my mother, recalling the pleasure she took in simple chores—cleaning the house, removing tarnish from silverware. What a sense of accomplishment she received from a job well done. I wanted to feel that way. A challenging task had been given to me. I hadn't asked for it, but I must perform it, claim my power, and remove an unholy thing. Do something profoundly right.

The votive candles flickered with an eerie orange light.

On the roof of the Greene Hotel, a water tank cracked. Through its crumbling gap, my mother appeared in a faded blue and pink muumuu she wore when I was a little child. What was she doing here? But was it really her? Always before, her pursed lips and furrowed brow signaled anger or hurt. Her lowered lids distrust or fear.

Not now.

"How long have I waited for you to find me." Her hair

haloed her face. Her fingertips butterflied against my arm, wrapped my wrist Soft. Gentle. A mother's touch. "Go." She pointed at a narrow dirt path to the right.

"I love you," I whispered and groped my way, listening to a distant spring foaming over water and rocks.

"You know its name." Her voice echoed after me. *"Hope."*

Outside was warm and quiet. Along the sidewalk and tucked in a doorway homeless people talked in hush whispers that felt like you'll-be-okays.

At the corner, a man sat on a pile of cardboard and scratched at the flesh beneath the elastic waist of filthy jeans. His round Buddha-belly poking out from under his stained, green T-shirt was startlingly white. He was looking at me and laughed knowingly.

CHAPTER FORTY-THREE

Carver

I still hadn't received a text or call from Dani. When I tried to leave message, her mailbox was full, so I called the house. Eve answered. After a few minutes of small talk, I asked to speak to Dani.

"She's not here. She's meeting a boy."

"Does he have a name?"

"I imagine he does. She didn't mention it."

"You didn't *ask*?»

"No. Unlike *you*, I trust her. "

"I told you I don't like the ideas of her being out alone while Rojas is out there."

"She said he was killed in a car crash." Eve's voice rose in annoyance. "You told her yourself."

What the fuck! Dani promised me she'd stay away from him. Why did she change her mind?

I tried to calm down, but Eve could probably hear in the fear in my voice. "Do you know where he's meeting her?"

"Some hotel with a color name. Black or blue or something, I forget."

I hung up without saying goodbye.

CHAPTER FORTY-FOUR

Alicia

Just before midnight, I arrived at the Greene. Its front desk was unattended. I glided past and into the elevator. The sliding doors closed behind me. The noise of the air conditioner seemed abnormally loud. I thought of Betsy Lamb, trapped and terrified, and licked my dry lips.

"I've been here before," I said to no one in particular or to the elevator itself.

I'd brought a flashlight. I turned it in my hands as if fascinated by it. How it illuminated just so much of the world and no more. I got out of the elevator at the top floor. I passed doorway after doorway, but no staircase. At the end of a corridor, I turned right, and my pulse quickened. There it was. The staircase. I was about ten feet away when a shadow appeared—Sahai. But how could this be? He approached quickly, his shadow growing bigger against the wall until it met the ceiling.

My heart thumped, but he merely smiled at me and said in a disarming voice, "Here, let me open that for you." He unlocked the door. As he stepped away, I was shocked to see that he was little more than a starved frame in a nightshirt, eyes cast down, a slack, unknowing expression on his face.

On the roof, the sky was clear. The only color in sight was a pink reflection of the hotel's neon sign. I leaned forward, tense. Sitri would be here, if anywhere.

A ladder rested against one of the cisterns, where Betsy had been discovered. Surely, Sitri would be here. I gripped the ladder and felt her presence, as solid as her recumbent body when Sitri slung her over his shoulder and lifted her into the water tank. I relived her final moments:

Betsy woke up, naked, her ribs rising and falling as she breathed and tried to escape. Her torso rested on Sitri's massive shoulders and back. All the questions and answers knitted themselves together. She screamed and kicked, her face gray with fear, until her strength left her, and she fell back against him.

Then there was only the pulse of the night. The splash of the body.

Every sound seemed amplified. An inhuman hand gripped the stairs. A soft footfall and a snout in the air sniffed its prey. Sitri came into view. First his spotted head, triangular ears, and bulbous nose. Then his huge wings unfurled. Instead of feathers, they were covered in deadly leaves of nightshade. His wings were so heavy that Sitri stooped like an old man, awkward and deliberate, as if unused to the Earth's gravitational pull.

His burnt-orange irises scanned the roof dolefully.

A long fingernail—or was it a talon?—clicked against the aluminum railing. He climbed steadily. He came for me.

Click. Click. Click.

All the bones in my body turned to water. My knees gave way and I crouched behind one of the cisterns. I didn't breathe. He'd sense it. He'd sense my eyes dilating, the tiny hairs rising on my arms, my heart beating fast, my blood vessels widening.

In the darkness, I heard the scurrying of rats, but I didn't dare turn on the flashlight.

My right hand was splayed out on the cement floor.

Sitri dipped his head and moved toward me.

"Come out, come out, wherever you are." I could imagine his hot breath on my skin. As if he had all the time in the world, Sitri raised me gently and enveloped me in leathery wings that smell of sewage, filling me with nausea. He opened his mouth, tongued my neck, and his papillae bore into me. Tiny, fibrous hooks. They would flay me alive if I let them.

"How should I dispose of you?" he asked. "I could throw you off the roof. Most assuredly the fall from here would kill you. But it lacks intimacy. You deserve better. I've brought this cord, but I'm really not sure that's how I want to do this."

He lifted me to my feet and shoved me against the cistern. He slipped the cord around my neck, tightening it and raised it above his head, forcing me to stand on tiptoes.

"Is it too tight? Can you breathe?"

The cord cut into my throat. I couldn't speak.

Sitri laughed. "I'll take that as a 'yes.' Fortunately for you, this won't take long." He lowers the hand holding the rope slightly. "But it will do awful things to your face. You'll turn red as a tomato. Your eyes will bulge. And your tongue will pop out of your mouth. I'm sure you wouldn't want your detective friend to see you like that."

I shut my eyes to try to block Sitri out.

"Water is my favorite milieu. And the cistern worked nicely before, didn't it? I think perhaps you ought to go for a swim. Don't worry. I'll let Carver know quickly. You won't get waterlogged. Mustn't have that!"

I could smell Sitri's pelt. His predator's scent. I gulped down air to stub out a sudden urge to throw up. I could make out every speck of dirt on the cement floor. With every fiber of my being, I prayed for love to make me a willing sacrifice, pure and holy, and capable of affirming that good would ultimately triumph.

It was now or never.

I ducked under his wing. Before he could react, I ran to the other side of the cistern. I clenched my fist hard, summoning angels of vengeance. My knuckles whitened, ready to lunge forward and smack his hideous brown snout.

He caught and snapped my incoming wrist. Pain knifed through me. I fell backward onto the cement with him on top of me. In the pitch dark, his taloned hand slid into my pants, not to draw blood, but to warn me not to resist.

I stopped thrashing.

My thoughts focused in. I became a cleared-out forest, stripped of doubt. A force jolted me. Luminous lines of energy pulsed through me, from forearm to fingertips, a sea of energy that I had never experienced. When I extend my hand, bolts of energy arced out and shot up. I threw up my arms and shaded my eyes from the light that flooded the rooftop, Divine energy shot out, piercing Sitri's leathery wing and nailing him to the railing of the roof. Electricity lapped like fire up his arms. His chest heaved in pain. Burned-out eyes fixed on me. His claws, petrified scabs, stony and virtually useless, flailed wildly, still trying to kill. He bared his incisors and snapped at me. I was beyond his reach, though, and he knew it.

Breathing all ragged, I listened to the beating of my heart. Sitri struggled to tear himself free of the unexpected and irresistible power I'd unleashed without further injuring his wing. He pulled desperately, this way and that. But the spell, or whatever I sent from my body, held him fast. At once, he started shivering as if the effort to remain half-human, half-leopard has worn him out.

All around Sitri, the railing dissolved. Whatever held it together was gone, its solid mass abruptly compromised. An aperture opened in the night air. A fetid seam clouded in mist swallowed him.

My gag reflex takes over, and I vomit. Stunned, bewildered, I can't deal with all the questions that remain. Where did Sitri go? Is he really gone? Is the danger over, or can he return whenever he wants? Will he come back for me? How did I banish him? Can I do it again if I have to?

I feel an overwhelming sense of exhaustion.

My last conscious thought comes from Proverbs, "When you lie down, you shall no longer be afraid. Yes, you shall lie down, and your sleep will be sweet."

CHAPTER FORTY-FIVE

Carver

I rushed to the hotel in a cold sweat, my usually crisp, white shirt clammy against my flesh.

It was a silent night. The moon was still and perfect. Ready to unleash a tidal wave of lunacy or mayhem.

Full, all too perfect.

Images of Dani assailed me. Dani floating lifeless in the water tank in Betsy's stead; Rojas, cursing her out; grabbing her by the hair; picking her up as if she were some inanimate piece of furniture and hurling onto a stained mattress. I had to do anything possible to avoid seeing and hearing it all. I sought to hide these images, as if in a closet with the shades drawn. Instead, I turned my mind to other people who died at the Greene. Pigeon Paula, the old lady who fed the pigeons. She had been discovered face down in a bed, her hands tied loosely behind her back, a tiny regiment of bedbugs bivouacked in her sparse gray hair.

John Heywood, the detective on the case, noticed them when he brushed the dead woman's face with long cotton swabs to collect traces of DNA. Later, a detailed forensic examination was conducted. Just before Heywood left the morgue, the pathologist had warned him. "It's amazing. There's not a trace of evidence. I think he's done this before."

Pansy Woo was a young bride, who panicked when her husband walked off into an overcast and windy night. She had not been well for a long time before he'd met her. No doubt she believed he'd stave off the problems and boredom that had led her to adolescent cutting and extensive therapeutic intervention. Didn't her husband know this? According to the police report, she called out to him, but he didn't reply. Did he fan away the air in front of his face dismissively? He denied it. But something had happened. Something inside of her had clicked shut. His apparent betrayal, and her pain at that moment, when she decided to jump out of a window, was something I could hardly begin to understand.

I ignored the homeless people that line the street. None of us do enough for others. We're too lax, too apathetic. Besides, I couldn't stop to help them, even if I wanted to.

I had to save Dani.

When I entered the hotel, it was after 11:00 p.m. A doll-like woman, dyed hair reddish-purple as a bruise, stood behind the desk. She eyed me thoughtfully, taking in the cut of my suit and the bulge under the jacket. I showed her my badge and asked to speak with Sahai.

I needed his key to the rooftop.

The lobby was hot and airless, stale air stirred about by electric fans. Sahai poked his head out of the office. Dark circles sunk beneath his eyes. He seemed tense and amped up. Even, his movements were quick and jerky.

"You look tired," I said.

Sahai almost stumbled over the carpet. Pale and sweaty, he cleared his throat and tried to smile. "I'm exhausted," he admitted. "I've been having strange dreams. Like I was there, and she was looking at me."

"Why didn't you mention it before?"

"It was just a dream. I didn't think it mattered. It's become more and more frequent." He straightened up his shoulders and faced me. The light in his eyes shut off. Something dark and weighty moved under his ribs, near his heart. I reached out, touching his shoulder. A bolt of static electricity made the hair on my arms rise. He bent his face up at me and cackled. "Don't worry. I won't hurt you."

"What?"

A small, amused smile twitches his mouth. His normally high-pitched voice deepens and grows self-assured and commanding. "Excuse me, detective. I have to go upstairs to check the water pressure in the tanks. When I return, I'll be happy to answer your questions."

I shot him a look. "That's not the way it works." His eyes were black pools. Nothing moved in them.

He winked, raised his eyebrows, and silently glided to the elevator. I was struck speechless. The woman with bruised-colored hair at the reception desk murmured into a telephone. It was the only sound I heard, except for an imagined pulse of night and the lapping of the water in the rooftop tanks.

Why would he go there at this hour? I didn't know, but I had my suspicions. Dani could be up there, another unwitting victim, so I waited a few minutes and then followed him.

A wind blows up on the roof. My heart stops. A lost soul was crouching behind one of the water tanks. Not Dani, though.

Could it be Alicia? *What is she doing there?*

Sahai's knuckles rang hollow against the other tank.

"Oh, Detective Carver. Following me? You can't. Not really. It isn't in your nature."

In the bleak night air, your eyes can play tricks. Sahai appeared nude from the waist up. His veins were as blue as water, and his torso, silver in the moonlight, was muscular and oddly delicate. But his nose was wide and squat, his cheeks puffy, his ears rounded.

It was not a human face.

Quieter than a cat, he seemed to float rather than walk. He looked peeved. I'd interrupted his search for Alicia. "You should drift on away," he says. "For your own sake. There are the steps." He casually points. Telling me I was not a threat, as if I was nothing to him.

Ignoring me entirely, he took a deep breath and caught the scent of his prey. "Alicia, I thought I'd lost you." Then he sings in a deep bass voice, "I get my kicks/Along the River Styx." He coughs. "You've come so far. It's time to show yourself."

Alicia sprang up. She was a mess of sweat and fear, tripping and stumbling toward him with her hands raised.

Sahai's face looked normal again, so I crept forward. I waited for the right moment to jump him, using the butt of my gun hard on the side of his head. He wobbled but righted himself, snarling viciously. An arm lashed out and caught me on the jaw, driving me back with unexpected force. I stumbled and almost fell from the roof. I caught myself at the last second and reeled away from the edge with unsteady feet. Panic was like breathing a lungful of water, struggling out for a pocket of air and then hauling your body through. Fear and anger propelled me. I saw red. I rose and struck him again, once, twice, maybe more with a stunning speed and ferocity. He collapsed. His head hit the cement, blood pooling around his scalp.

Not far away, Alicia stood perfectly still, looking dazed and disheveled. She moved toward me like an apparition.

I leaned forward from the force of the pain swelling my jaw.

"Alicia? What are you doing here?" I held back an

impulse to hug her. "And why did he want to attack you?"

"Did you see?"

"See what?"

"Him. What I did."

I felt confused. "You hid behind the water tank, right?"

"Yes, I suppose so. If that's what you saw." Her lips curled up gently, not quite into a smile. Her eyes, though, sparkled mischievously. "Did you come to rescue me?"

I held up my hand because of embarrassment or to silence her while I considered what her words implied and what I was feeling. "I don't really know why I came up. A hunch. Now let's go inside," I said curtly, angry at her for putting herself in danger.

"What about him?" Alicia gestured to Sahai. She bent down beside him, her elbows at her side. Sahai lay motionless on the pavement. Blood oozed from his lacerations.

"I'll call. Get him looked over at the hospital. I don't have enough to book him. But you think he killed the Lamb girl. That's why you're here."

"Uh-huh." She nodded sadly. "When Sitri possessed him."

"Will *you* press charges?"

She thought for a moment. "He didn't actually do anything to me."

The sky brightened ever so slightly. She pointed at a pink star. "Look. Mercury! The most elusive of the planets known in the ancient world, and here it is! On a Wednesday, no less." She laughs. "Did you know Wednesday translates as 'water day' in Chinese and Japanese? And Sitri's a water demon."

Someone had just tried to kill her, and she was laughing. Trauma could take many different forms.

I didn't see any pink stars. And I sure as hell didn't give a damn what day it was.

A frightened voice came from the stairwell, interrupting my thoughts. "Dad! Why did you attack Rob?"

"It's not him. Come up and see for yourself."

"I can't," she said, her voice trembling. The cement steps were wet. "I'm sorry," she cried. "I was scared. My legs started shaking then my whole body shook and, and it just happened. I didn't mean it to!"

Alicia went to her and gently patted her hair. "Of course not," she said. "It's all right. You're safe now."

They went downstairs together. I followed, oddly hollowed out. My task fulfilled, my work done, I thought only of my daughter in front of me, shielded by Alicia, who led her to a ladies' room to freshen up.

No doubt, Dani threw away the sodden underpants. On the way home, I asked why she'd come to the hotel, but she couldn't, or wouldn't, answer my questions. I was sure she didn't want to say anything that would harm Rojas, but I wasn't worried. Alicia said Dani was safe.

I thought she just might be right.

CHAPTER FORTY-SIX

Carver

"You're damn lucky," the doctor said. "The jaw may hurt for a few days, but it's not broken. And you don't show any of the symptoms of a severe concussion."

"So I'm free to go?"

He waved me away.

I went up to the fifth floor where Sahai rested, an IV attached to his arm. I hoped to get evidence linking him with the Lamb girl, maybe even a confession that could be used in court. But Sahai resolutely maintained he hadn't been on the roof, although he admitted that he did not remember anything from the day before, including how or why he ended up in the hospital.

I left the room and went to consult with his doctor, a busty blonde with blue streaks in her hair.

"Blows to the head, if sufficiently hard, can cause

amnesia, and Mr. Sahai's MRI did show swelling around the temporal lobe."

"Okay. So, he's probably telling the truth. How long will his memory remain impaired?"

"It's hard to say. In most cases, amnesia is temporary, lasting from a few seconds to a few hours. However, the duration can be longer. And you did hit him more than once."

CHAPTER FORTY-SEVEN

Carver

Sahai sat in his office, dwarfed, as always, by the old-fashioned wooden desk.

"You still don't remember what happened? Wouldn't you like to know?" I said.

Sahai lightly touched the bandage that covered the right side of his head. "Of course. But how?"

"Would you consider undergoing hypnosis? It's helped us in cases like this . . . when the case is at a dead end and there's nothing to lose."

Sahai settled himself more firmly in the chair, a skeptical look on his face.

I cleared my throat. "This is a true story. Happened when I was still a rookie. A school bus was hijacked with twenty-six children and the driver aboard. The victims were inside a buried van. The driver, Ed Ray, and several of the bigger children began piling mattresses to see if they could reach a small trapdoor in the roof. They succeeded and dug through a mound of dirt and escaped. Under hypnosis, Ray recalled the full license number of the kidnapper's van. The case received a helluva lot of publicity. Maybe you heard about it? It was here in California. In Chowchilla."

"No. Can't say I have." Sahai's knuckles whitened on the desk chair's arms. "I'm willing to help you, but what if I remember and it's really traumatic?"

I walked over to Sahai, rested my hand on his shoulder. "Police officers can't be present, and the law disallows any recall of crime details revealed solely through hypnosis. It goes without saying that you can't be hypnotized without informed consent." I stepped away from his desk, giving him space to decide.

"If I agree, who will hypnotize me?"

"I'd use a very capable woman named Alicia Flores. I can't think of a single incident where a person she hypnotized was adversely affected." That was true, since I hadn't heard anything one way or the other.

"I'm sure my family would disapprove. They'd tell me it might be appropriate for a television crime show but not for the police in real life. They'd beg me to think it over. Maybe even consult a lawyer." Sahai moved his hands to his lap, fingers intertwined, palms up. "But if hypnosis can help me remember anything, anything that'll stop my nightmares, I'm all for it."

I blinked. Nightmares? He'd never mentioned them before. "That's why hypnosis is used in an investigation. To shine a light on dark places."

CHAPTER FORTY-EIGHT

Carver

I called Alicia and told her I'd stop by Phyllis' house as soon as possible. I sat down on a sofa, shooing her cat. When I told Alicia what I had in mind, her face darkened.

"Everything I do is in the name of love," she said. "How can you ask me to betray someone, like some sort of spy?"

I took a deep breath, hoping to say the right thing. "You've told me more than once that you want to do your part. Here's your chance. I want us to be on the same team." I kept talking without pause. She was sorting white from color laundry. I hoped she was paying attention. "And don't worry, unless I get hard evidence—the kind I can bring to the DA—nothing he says will harm him. Probably it'll make him feel better to get whatever it is off his chest." Something I may have said, or maybe something she was thinking about while I talked and talked, overcame her misgivings, and she agreed to meet me at Sahai's office.

The next day, Alicia arrived at the Greene with a carryall of equipment. While Sahai sat behind his desk, she set up, and performed a final sound check.

I watched her center the camera. "I'll be in the lobby. When you finish up, we'll see what we've learned." I dreaded the wait. Wondered if Sahai would attack her. Wondered what would become of my career if he didn't, and Simpson learned I'd attacked Sahai.

The clock in the lobby ticked. A half hour passed.

Alicia came out of his office and around the front desk. She looked utterly drained. "I haven't brought Sahai out of the trance. You need to see the video first. And tell me what to do."

I followed her back into Sahai's office. He sat there doing nothing, staring blankly ahead.

Alicia started the tape.

"Tell me about the girl."

"I saw her in the elevator." Sahai's voice dropped a full octave. He sounded rougher, more aggressive. "She was alert and confident, like the girls at Stanford with their daddies' trust funds and the big bronze goons they dated. Those girls!" The corner of his lip tightened and rose in a look of contempt. "They looked past me in class. Their boyfriends beat me up in bars when I chatted them up and tried to show them that I was the kind of person they might want, a person who would treat them with respect."

Sahai leaned toward the camera until he was face to face with Alicia, their eyes were less than a foot apart. "The girl in the elevator was the same. She came into the hotel with that Latino lover of hers." His voice rose. "She didn't notice me. Not until later. When I asked her to spit in a small cup."

"Why did you ask her that?" Alicia said.

"The voice told me."

"The voice?"

"The one that comes to me in those quiet moments. He said if I killed her, if I drank her saliva, I would be immortal."

Alicia shot me a quick look that said see, I told you. I just shook my head. No, it couldn't be. Or could it? My stomach knotted.

Alicia turned back to Sahai. "And you wanted that?"

"I . . ." he paused, mouth open, as if he were trying to speak but something blocked him. The moment passed. "No. I never thought about it really. But it sounds like a good idea." He furrowed his brow. "Doesn't it?"

She leaned forward. "What happened next with the girl?"

"After I spoke to her, she moved to the elevator buttons." His right hand mimicked her pressing them. "But the doors didn't close. She stared at me as if she thought I was someone else. 'Let's go back to my room. Do it again.' Then she blinked. Shook her head. She stepped back, punched a button, any button, like all she wanted to do was get away from me."

Sahai shrugged, smiled, but it didn't reach his eyes. "She

wasn't getting away. He leaned back in the chair and put his hands behind his head, a satisfied smirk on his face. "I pulled rubber gloves out of my back pocket. Pushed her out of camera view. She screamed and punched and kicked out at me, but I didn't feel any of it." His hands came around his neck and toward his chest. He drew them together. "I just kept squeezing. After, I lifted her, put her over my shoulder. She seemed amazingly light. I opened the door to the roof. The air was cool. I carried her up the stairs and threw her into the cistern. I returned to my room, tossed down my clothes, and went to sleep."

Got him. I felt a rush of pleasure.

"I slept wonderfully well that night." Sahai's face fell. "It was the last time. Since then, I've had a different dream." His shoulders tensed. "Of hands squeezing my throat. Choking the life out of me. I wake up before dawn, thrashing to escape." Sahai's words trailed off. He continued to sit, eyes open, a blank expression on his face.

Soulless. Like a puppet.

The video ended. Alicia looked tired and depressed. "He'll want to hear if he's helped. I could lie. Say he hadn't given us anything useful." She sighed and looked down at her black loafers.

"You could. But I'm sorry. There's the recording. I've heard it." I gave a quick glance back at Sahai. "I'll search for the clothes. To make an arrest, I'll need hard evidence."

CHAPTER FORTY-NINE

Carver

Alicia brought Sahai out of the trance, brought a chair next to his, and took his hand.

"Nothing you've said here can be used in court. But if what you said was true, you murdered the girl." She took slow, deep breaths, as if she were trying to calm Sahai—or herself, perhaps. "No one wants to hurt you."

Sahai's gaze rested on her. When she played the video, his expression shaded from doubt to fear to guilt and disgust. He put his hand to his throat, as if he couldn't bear to breathe any more.

His eyes filled with tears. "Please, just hold me." He looked at her as if asking for permission, and when she neither gave nor withheld it, he leaned into her and rested his head on her shoulder. She didn't touch him but didn't push him away. She sat still, as if waiting to see what he'd do or say next. She looked outside and back again, as if she watched the sun filter through her curtains, patterning the red carpet.

"It's true." His eyes seemed drawn to hers. "I tried locking the door to my past, but memory crept in through the window. Seeing the tape, I can feel it flowing through my entire body, the hatred. But why? I didn't think . . ." his voice trailed off; his hands made vague, helpless circles in the air. "Something came over me. I can't explain it. It's like I was possessed."

Sahai stood up. He looked resolved, as if he'd found an inner reserve of strength. "I don't care if this is admissible or not. I have to be punished. Please, I want to speak to someone in the District Attorney's Office."

Leaning against the door, I mused on the irony of it all. I'd walked to the hotel through the slum day after day, looking for clues, in vain. Now I had the killer pleading for a chance to go to prison.

Alicia saw my expression. "This looks like a case of DID, Dissociative Identity Disease. My friend Phyllis told me about it. The presence of two or more distinctive identities." Sahai snorted and glanced away. Alicia turned to him. "You didn't know you'd killed someone. That's not the kind of thing you'd ordinarily forget." She looked at him. "Is it?"

Sahai's lips drew a grim line. He didn't answer. Didn't *have* an answer.

Alicia clasped her hands nervously. She looked at me.

"What happens to people who commit crimes in a dissociated state?"

"I didn't train as a lawyer for nothing. People have used DID as a defense, but it's rarely been successful. Although a patient may have distinct personalities that control his or her behavior, this condition does not preclude criminal responsibility."

Sahai nodded vehemently. "Of course not. A man's always responsible for his actions."

"Sometimes the law makes no sense to me," I told him. "Say the prosecution and defense agree about the presence of DID when you committed the crime, the court still has to make sense of the situation in terms of existing laws."

Sahai's face scrunched up like a kid given a math problem in school that didn't make sense, so I went on. "The court only asks whether you were mentally competent when the crime was committed and during the trial or the plea process. That means if you were aware of what you were doing at the time. In your right mind . . ."

I tried to make my voice kind, but I don't think I managed. Alicia gave me a sharp look. "During the trial and plea process. I mean, if you're capable of helping your defense."

Sahai stared, maybe at a string of lights across a dark, cold sea; maybe at an old-fashioned noose or a modern electric chair. Listless, he rubbed the stubble along his jaw. Could he be remembering something?

"I stashed her clothes. They still should be there. If there are traces of the girl's DNA, you should have enough evidence to convict me. It's better that way." He blinked, looked at me, even found a hint of a smile. "My family would rather consider me a murderer than a madman. Madness in the family would make it very hard for my little sister to find a suitable husband. A prospective groom's family would be afraid our bloodline is tainted."

Together, we went upstairs. I didn't need a warrant since Sahai agreed to the search. His apartment was beyond Spartan, as though he'd taken a vow of poverty. There were few personal effects in the bedroom, except for a colorful, Indian bedspread and loose change in a silver bowl with some kind of insignia. The only other trace that an actual person lived in the room was a formal-looking photograph of Sahai's family on the dresser: a frail-looking father, a plump smiling mother, and a lean and prosperous-looking brother.

Sahai opened the closet, rummaged through the clothes and pulled out a plastic bag with a shirt, slacks, and gloves and a girl's dress and her underwear. He held it up with his thumb and forefinger.

"The proof was right where you said it would be." I moved closer and put out my hand. The poor bastard stood there, almost in tears. "It's a hell of a situation. The video shows you didn't even know you'd done it." My voice softened. "I'll have to meet with the DA, though."

"You have the proof. And I take full responsibility." He crossed his arms. "I don't deserve special treatment."

"Of course not. But there are laws. We have to follow them. First, you'll have to come with me. I'm arresting you," I said. "You have the right to remain silent. Anything you say can and will be used against you in a court of law. You have the right to an attorney. If you cannot afford an attorney, one will be provided for you. Do you understand the rights I just read to you?"

"Yes, I understand," he said, nodding.

"With these rights in mind, do you wish to speak to me?"

When I asked Sahai about the hotel's cold cases, he leaned forward and grabbed my shoulder frantically. "*I don't know*. If I killed her and didn't know it, I could have killed them, too."

He went into the bathroom to wash up. Coming out, his hand massaged his neck, as if he imagined a noose tightening on it. He was dazed and disheveled as a couple of uniforms took him to booking.

I returned to the precinct. Pressed the icepack the EMTs had given me on my jaw. They swore it wasn't broken, but it hurt like a motherfucker and the shouted questions from the reporters and camera crews didn't help much.

As a precaution, I stopped in Simpson's office. "Be sure to put him on suicide watch."

Simpson was busy writing. He put down his pen, glanced at me. "Your evidence. Is it conclusive?"

"That depends on the jury, doesn't it?"

He looked up at me as if I'd just crawled out of a sewer. "Go to the DA's office. Talk to Lacey. This has to be bulletproof."

CHAPTER FIFTY

Carver

The Los Angeles County District Attorney's Office is the largest local agency in the country. Its jurisdiction stretches from Antelope Valley to Long Beach, from Pomona to Malibu. On average, it prosecutes over 63,000 felony charges a year. Its main courthouse, the Clara Shortridge Foltz Criminal Justice Center is a twenty-one-story building located in Downtown Los Angeles between Broadway and Spring Street.

I headed to the downtown courthouse to discuss the case with Jordan Lacey, the Chief Deputy District Attorney. After waiting for twenty minutes, I was shown into Lacey's well-appointed office. I took a seat opposite a large, mahogany desk, leaned forward and said, "I know it's your job, not mine, to disclose all evidence, including evidence favorable for the defense, but this case bothers the hell out of me."

Lacey's fingers drummed impatiently on his desk.

"I'm convinced we've found a murderer," I said. "But I'm not sure we can go to trial if we disclose the facts. And if we did go to trial, I'm not sure you'd get a conviction—*or that you ought to.*"

"No disrespect intended. But isn't it *my* job to decide?" Lacey said sardonically. I explained how Sahai had supplied evidence against himself after hearing his confession while under hypnosis.

"The man's not trying to save his own skin. Not at all. He *wants* to be punished for what he's done. But he's under tremendous emotional pressure. He's terrified his family will find out about his illness. He's told me the shame would be too much for him. That anything would be better. Even a murder conviction."

Lacey steepled his fingers under his chin, thought for a moment. "You know that hypnosis isn't a truth serum. People can make things up. How do I know you didn't lead him in the direction you wanted him to go?"

I stared at him. Sure, I was angry; but I wouldn't let him see it. Instead, I said, "It's been corroborated by the evidence. Besides, that's not how I do my job. I'd never work with an expert who'd do such a thing. Listen. Prosecute or not, it's your decision, not mine."

I stood up. "I've sent over the transcript and video of the session, as well as the evidence against him. And I wish you the best of luck."

CHAPTER FIFTY-ONE

Carver

As soon as I left the DA's office, Diggs called. "Sahai's hung himself with his bed sheet."

I saw red. "Why wasn't he watched?"

"Does it matter now?" he asked.

"Yes, it matters! First, there was the missed earing. That was bad enough, but now this? He was on suicide watch, for God's sake. When I find out who's at fault, I'll rip him a new asshole."

"Even the lieutenant?" Diggs asked. "He told the guards not to bother."

"You're kidding, right? Politically correct Simpson?"

"I know. It makes no sense. And guess what? Sahai left two notes, one for his parents written in a foreign language and another one for you."

"Read it to me."

To Detective Carver. My parents have raised a murderer. How can I bear to see their faces when they hear this? But if I'm found unfit to stand trial by reason of insanity, how can I live with myself? This is the only choice I have left.

The other note is for my parents, please make sure they receive it.

"This ties things up," I said, "but it's entirely too neat."

"Maybe for you it is. But who's to say what anyone else is capable of doing? You said it yourself. Sahai was a mess when you brought him in. Look at the bright side. Now you can tell Betsy's parents. They won't have to spend the rest of their lives wondering what happened."

"Yeah. I can tell them their daughter died because she resembled some Stanford coed the murderer knew twenty years ago. That'll console them, I bet."

"Maybe it will."

"I'll make the call," I said. "They deserve to know, of course. At least that I kept my promise. I'd told them I'd follow up until I found the culprit."

My voice trailed off. "I just wish I felt better about it. Sahai may've been crazy, but he wasn't a bad person. And something still bothers me. How could he have dragged the girl to the roof or thrown her into the cistern? She must've weighed close to one hundred and twenty-five pounds. He wasn't much bigger than that himself."

"We'll never know," Diggs said, returning to his desk.

I hung up the phone and took a deep breath, trying to calm down. I wondered why the lieutenant had neglected to follow procedure. It wasn't like him at all. And the misplaced files, was that also negligence or something more ominous? It wasn't quite enough to convince me that demons existed, and that Alicia was right all along, but facts were stubborn things. I didn't know what to think.

Then there was Sahai. I'd misunderstood him. I knew he was desperate, but I didn't realize how determined he was not to be saved. How disgusted he was at the thought that the men and women representing our system of justice would pick and pick at him until his soul was worn away to a nub.

CHAPTER FIFTY-TWO

Carver

The following day, Sahai's parents came to collect his belongings. I walked out to meet them, holding Sahai's note in my right hand.

The plump, happy-looking mother I'd seen in the picture in Sahai's apartment was gone. Her eyes were red; she held a soggy handkerchief to her nose, sniffling. Her cadaverous husband had an arm around her shoulders and wore a stony expression. His eyes were flat with distrust, as if he thought the police might have murdered his son simply to close a vexing, high-profile case.

"Mr. and Mrs. Sahai, I am so sorry for your loss." I felt a surge of anger at Simpson for his carelessness. I'd solved the Lamb case, but at what cost? One more man of color suffering as a result of white negligence.

Mrs. Sahai looked up gratefully through watery eyes. Her

husband stared straight ahead. His expression didn't change.

"I want to see the man in charge of the investigation."

"That'd be me," I said.

"My son was in your custody. How could this happen?" It was an accusation, but I was smart enough to treat it as a question.

"We try as hard as we can to prevent such things from occurring. But it's not always possible. Not when a man really wants to die."

"And why should our son have wanted to die?" Mr. Sahai asked pointedly.

"I don't know. Not really. But he left you a note. He wrote on the envelope that we should give it to his Amma and Appa. I saw your picture in his room."

I handed them the letter. The father opened it and read it. His wife peered over his shoulder. The light died in his eyes, as if the core of his world had collapsed. The woman at his side ached out loud for the child she'd never see again, the child whose final words tore at her.

Sahai's father looked up at me. "It's his handwriting. I should know. I taught him to write Tamil script."

He looked down at the note as he continued, breathing jaggedly. "What can we tell everyone? How can we explain to them when we still don't understand ourselves? They will say we were bad parents. But we weren't bad parents. We raised him in a home of warmth and comfort. Amma fed him his favorite foods. We included him in everything. We worked hard in this country. But we still found time for family outings. We took him to Disneyland and to the Grand Canyon. Everything we did was all for him and his brother and sister, always."

"I'm sure you were fine parents," I murmured. It was a meaningless cliché. I knew they deserved something better, but I had no words that could comfort them.

"Walk down this hallway," I said, pointing to my left. "See that window? It's the mailroom. Your son's possessions will be waiting there."

What must it be like to lose a child? What if it were my Dani? Every parent who ever lived had plans and hopes for their children. And every time some lunatic or bastard killed a child, they stripped away their future and made a void that would never, ever be filled.

CHAPTER FIFTY-THREE

Carver

After Sahai's parents left, I crumpled up Sahai's note, straightened it out, and walked back to my desk. I took out the Betsy Lamb file and put the note in its proper place. Then I sat with my elbows on the desk and rubbed my eyes.

Janice was back at work.

A week before, she'd been in intensive care. Three days ago, her vitals returned to normal levels. Two days ago, she returned home. And so did hundreds of other people, suffering from the unexplained illness. It had been all over the news. Doctors shook their heads. They couldn't explain it and didn't even try.

"It's great to see you. But the Sahai case is so fucked up," I said to Janice. "You know what I'm saying. Does everybody else see how fucked up it is?" Does *anyone* see that? How do normal people see this and *not* get pissed off?"

Janice was buried under a blizzard of papers. All I could see was the top of her curly hair. "Carver, I've got a lot of catching up to do. If you don't let me work, I'll be here all night. Anyway, you should know better. We're *not* normal people. We're cops."

"Yeah."

I grabbed the copy of *The LA Times* that rested on Diggs's desk to see if they'd printed a story that we'd solved the Lamb case. And to look for the things that never managed to find their way into the newspaper accounts. A man on suicide watch had killed himself and Simpson was responsible, not that he would ever admit it.

Just then, he glided up to me, smug, the picture of confidence. "It's on page seventeen. Look, I heard what you told Janice. It's not a perfect world or a perfect result. But it's hell of a lot better than dragging your ass into the office to stare at the same fucking photographs of the crime scene and wondering what you've missed. Congratulations are in order. You've closed the case. You've gotten the brass and the girl's mother off our backs. That ought to be enough for you."

"Yeah, you're right," I muttered, fighting hard for control. Simpson's little speech effectively closed the case, as least far as *he* was concerned. But not for me. There was another Lamb, the Cordero girl. She wasn't rich or white. Her mother had no pull in the mayor's office, so she was nothing more than a statistic on one of his charts. Alicia had claimed the two cases were connected. Sahai had denied it. He'd never heard of her and had nothing to do with her death. The two Lamb cases weren't connected after all. Alicia had been wrong.

CHAPTER FIFTY-FOUR

Alicia

I stepped onto Phyllis's deck to greet the sun as peach and salmon stained the darkness on the eastern horizon. A breeze swept across my cheek, and the dome of the sky lightened until it was pale and luminous. Birds hidden among the foliage chirped a joyful greeting to the day. I thought: *In a mere eight minutes, sunlight has traveled a hundred million miles. Here on Earth, it turns into color and light. Energy filters through plants and animals, indeed all of life.*

I sensed a pure white radiance no longer dimmed by mortality. It was Betsy Lamb, smiling. She was holding the hand of a small, dark-haired girl.

For the first time in many years, I bought a bouquet of roses and drove out to Calvary Cemetery. It's not far from our old home in East Los Angeles, but a world away from the buckling sidewalks and graffiti-plastered walls of the barrio, the smell of overheated engines, hot tortillas, and small, tired-looking men in undershirts leaving work.

Among 1300 acres of serene, rolling hills, I knelt at her grave. "Hello, Mother."

Eight years ago, the door of the hearse slammed behind me, the shovels stabbed the mound of soil, and the wooden box hit the floor of the pit. Each sound struck. But my eyes were dry. From beneath their kerchiefs, the eyes of the old women condemned me.

"What kind of daughter are you," their glances said. "You're supposed to love your mother. You're supposed to think good thoughts about her. Tell her your troubles. Mourn her."

When I was fifteen, I said, "Mami, I want to go to the university. I want to study our people's history and culture, maybe even become a professor someday. I want a life like . . ."

"A wealthy Anglo," Mami said, finishing my sentence like an accusation.

I tried to explain. "The more you cage someone, the more they try to escape."

Mami, I understand better now. How grief crippled you. Watching your son's rapid progress into addiction, I can feel fiercely the damage it did to our family, the loss of love and life it caused, and on top of that, my own strange path. I grieve for the years I spent vainly trying to please you, not recognizing you wanted your son back, not a changeling daughter. I tried to forget you, but that didn't work. So now I come to you with roses. You loved roses, Mami. Now I know that life is too short to hold onto resentment. Parents leave or die, and when they do, sorrow and resentment continue to flow like wine through the veins unless you decant it, remove the poisonous sediment. Mami, you showed me the way that day in the church when you told me which path to take. You believed I could confront Sitri. Reminded me that goodness could triumph.

You taught me so much at that moment. And I am ready to let go of anger and sorrow.

"Oh Mami, you should have seen how the doctors were confounded when the outbreak of disease ended. I couldn't tell them it was because I'd defeated Sitri. But I know the truth. I've done something right, Mami. Something for the entire community. Also, something for Carlos that he can accept. He's promised to go into rehab now. He knows I will support him every step of the way. And I will, Mami, I swear to you."

As I sat down in the grass by her gravesite, the world came into focus. Every green blade was preternaturally clear, revealing its perfection. There was nothing but the wind to ruffle the grasses and disturb the little green pots of flowers on the recent graves.

I will spend these moments quieting down and feeling

the love in my heart go through every organ in my body, and this healing will reach you, no matter where you are, because the language of the heart opens all doors.

How to describe this feeling I have? Casting out a demon requires so much power. Power I would never have guessed at. How strange that such a terrible threat has made this change possible. And your gift to me has been priceless, too. You healed me through your love, and it brought us together.

I feel the energy within growing. As I plant your flowers, the earth glows under my fingertips. I must tamp down a surge of power before it causes the roses to bloom instantly.

I am lit from within.

CHAPTER FIFTY-FIVE

Carver

When I called Alicia, she was at her mother's gravesite. She didn't sound sad, not at all. Instead, her voice seemed sweet, as if she'd found what she'd sought—comfort and peace. I asked her if I could see her that night, and we agreed to meet at a cozy little spot not far from my apartment.

We had been seated and were about to order.

The waiter turned to Alicia, bent over, and eyed her breasts surreptitiously.

She folded her arms under her neck and ordered the pasta special. She turned her head away and mine followed. A white-haired, russet-faced man sat with his service dog. The dog watched as his owner cut a rib eye steak into tiny pieces that barely fit on the tines of his fork, hoping they would drop. The room bubbled with a subdued hush.

"You must be relieved the case is over. No more pressure

from Lieutenant Simpson. And Janice is back at work."

"How did you know?"

Alicia lifted her water glass and took a sip. She didn't meet my eyes. "I read the paper. The epidemic's over. Hospitals are emptying out. People have been cured. Do you still think it's all chance? Or coincidence? The sacrificial lambs, the hotel of killers, the sudden outbreak of disease, my house?"

"Are you still going on about that demon of yours?" I unfolded the heavy cotton napkin and placed it at my lap.

"You were there."

In chess, it's called *zugzwang. I couldn't move if I wanted to. My thighs felt like blocks of ice.* Whatever I did now, whatever I said, would lead me to a place I didn't want to go. I could either be rational or honest, not both.

"Okay, I thought I saw something you might call a demon. When my mind cleared, all I saw was Sahai."

Alicia harpooned me with a glance. "Reason only takes you so far. You saw it all. But your mind refused to accept it."

"So, you're going to tell me what I saw?"

She leaned toward me. "No. I'm going to show you," she whispered the words with an intensity that raised goose bumps on my flesh. She gripped my hand.

I held onto the edge of the table with my free hand. Held on for dear life. I feared what was coming.

A surge of energy and I see a light that wasn't physical.

I'm on the roof inside Alicia. Sahai impassively watches us struggle against Sitri. Sitri turns to him and says, "jump." For that split second, Sitri's attention is elsewhere. We duck down and away. Energy pulses from our shoulders to fingertips and shoots out. It pierced Sitri's wing and nailed him to the railing. His chest heaves. Burned-out eyes fix on us. His claws flail wildly, still trying to kill. He bares his incisors and snaps.

The railing dissolved. The portal opens and a fetid seam clouded in mist swallows him.

An instant later, I found myself back in the restaurant.

"Sitri came through that portal, and I had to send him back. It was the only way to save my brother and your daughter. And Sahai. Now that he was done with Sahai, he'd have him commit suicide like Rojas. You think Rojas had an accident? And you think Diggs just happened to stumble on the knife that killed Maria Cordero?"

I shook it off. "Rojas isn't dead. I saw him again at school with Dani."

"You thought that was Rojas?" Alicia watched me closely. "You're wrong. It was Sitri."

I felt myself caught in deep mire with no place to stand. A person deep in the thick of magic can't see anything beyond it. I watched Alicia for subliminal signs of deceit—eyes breaking right and away or the like. But I saw only truthfulness. Then I glanced at the tables around us, worried that someone might be listening.

People were eating and talking calmly. Nobody looked anxious or stupefied. None of them wanted to shut down their conversation and listen in to talk of demons and death. And none of them believed, as I did, that Alicia's insight was a thing to grapple with, to submit to, to marvel at and honor.

But then again, Alicia could have hypnotized me just now.

The waiter finally came by with our food. It was the first normal thing that happened since he took our order. Alicia stopped speaking and thanked him.

She raised her fork and started eating. "Mm, this is delicious! Try some." She held out her fork for me to taste it.

"Wait! Stop for a minute. Sahai confessed to the crime. He left a note explaining why he killed himself. I don't need Sitri to explain *any* of this."

Alicia put down the fork and wiped her mouth with the napkin. "Unless you accept the demonic, you'll never see the true horror of what happened. Sitri *toyed* with Sahai. Rearranged his mind. Played on his unresolved hurt. Treated him as if he were less than human. That's a terrible, inhuman crime. Maybe even worse than killing him."

I picked up my knife and fork but then put them back down. "If you're right, Sitri's back wherever demons go." I smiled as the logic took root. "So, the good people of Los Angeles don't have to worry about anything but each other."

"You think so?" Her words were quiet but hard. Her

voice managed to impart conflicting emotions: empathy, patience, and despair. "The anger, the hate that brought him here still exists. It's nourished anywhere hate replaces love and anger replaces accord. That what's been happening in Los Angeles—and in the entire country. The portal will open again—here or somewhere else. And you'll need me again, whether you like it or not. When the evil returns, *and it surely will*, I'll be waiting.

I nodded. Cut my steak and pieces and took a bite. While we'd been talking, it'd gotten cold. Not that I minded. Perfection is rare. Belief and understanding are elusive. Ethereal truths all too often disappear in the daily grind of a homicide detective's work. Alicia offered the hope that they might someday connect, even for me.

I was almost ready to listen.

AUTHOR'S NOTE

THE WORLD IS FULL OF MAGIC THINGS, PATIENTLY WAITING FOR OUR SENSES TO GROW SHARPER.

—*W.B. Yeats*

It is easy to overlook the miraculous in our world. We grow accustomed to seeing the world in a certain fixed way. Nothing new seems to happen, as every experience readily repeats experiences we've already had.

But what if the opposite is true? Perhaps magic is everywhere. In the flight of birds. In the people you pass in the street with their hidden thoughts. In the innumerable, unseen cells working ceaselessly to keep all living things alive.

Sure, it's thrilling to be pulled into bizarre landscapes, with amazing heroes, but isn't it even more exciting to discover the world you thought you knew in a different light? That is why I write paranormal fiction. I love weaving the known and the unknown together to create something new and empower experiences that defy everyday understanding.

If you would like to continue our journey together and follow the story of Alicia and Carver, contact me at StephenWechselblatt.com, and consider placing a short review on Amazon or Goodreads.

ACKNOWLEDGEMENTS

I want to thank my superb editor Rhay Christou for cleaning up a hot, smoking draft. She is both wise and kind. I am grateful to the talented, supportive, and sometimes demanding members of the Black Cap Writers past and present, particularly Jennifer Fulford, Leissa Shahrak, Linda Whitaker, Cori Adams, and Alyssa Nedbal. Thanks also to Jeff Schlesinger, James Barrow, and Linda Duider of Barringer Publishing. And finally, to Marlene, who always has my back.

www.ingramcontent.com/pod-product-compliance
Lightning Source LLC
Chambersburg PA
CBHW051136030726
47504CB00004B/903
9781954396159